Maddie stared. Then she blinked. Twice.

At first, she thought her eyes were playing tricks on her. She peered into the darkening day.

There, underneath the black wrought-iron Victorian street lamp, the evening fog drifting along the sidewalk, stood Nate Barzonni. He looked directly at her, and when their eyes locked, he smiled.

Her heart thrummed in her chest and blood pounded at her temples. She felt dizzy.

In the eleven years since Nate had abandoned her, Maddie had not had a single boyfriend. She had dated a few men here and there, but all her energy had gone into her business. She had convinced herself that she was strong and willful, that she owned her own power. She purposefully fanned and fueled the fire of her anger against Nate to mask even the tiniest possibility that she still had any feelings for him. For eleven years, Maddie had told her friends over and over that Nate Barzonni was the devil to her.

There was no way Nate was actually standing outside Bride's Corner. No way. Maddie closed her eyes and opened them again.

Nate was gone.

Dear Reader,

The inspiration for my Shores of Indian Lake series
came right out of my own life when I returned to my
hometown after thirty-five years of living in big cities
like New Orleans, Houston, Los Angeles and Scottsdale,
Arizona.

It has been a revelation to me that the lives of those
in small towns are filled with just as much pathos,
romance, chaos and eternal struggle as people in
glamorous cities.

The Shores of Indian Lake series is filled with endearing,
haunting and oftentimes seemingly eccentric characters
who will steal your heart. *Heart's Desire* is the second
book in the series. In this story, Maddie Strong is faced
with impossible choices with regards to her own career
dreams when her first love, Nate Barzonni, returns to
Indian Lake, in pursuit of his own long-held dream of
being a cardiologist and dedicating his services to those
most in need. Nate finds himself face-to-face with the
one woman he'd left brokenhearted…and very angry.

I would love to hear from you and what kind of story
you would like to read about along the Shores of Indian
Lake. You can write to me at cathlanigan1@gmail.com
or visit my website at www.catherinelanigan.com. I'm on
Facebook, Twitter and LinkedIn, as well.

Catherine

HEARTWARMING

Catherine Lanigan
Heart's Desire

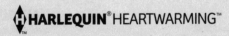

HARLEQUIN® HEARTWARMING™

Recycling programs
for this product may
not exist in your area.

ISBN-13: 978-0-373-36687-3

Heart's Desire

Printed in U.S.A.

www.Harlequin.com

CATHERINE LANIGAN

knew she was born to storytelling at a very young age when she told stories to her younger brothers and sister to entertain them. After years of encouragement from family and high school teachers, Catherine was shocked and brokenhearted when her freshman college creative writing professor told her that she "had no writing talent whatsoever" and that she "would never earn a dime as a writer." He promised her that he would be her crutches and get her through his demanding class with a B grade so as not to destroy her high grade point average too much, *if* Catherine would promise never to write again. Catherine assumed he was the voice of authority and gave in to the bargain.

For fourteen years she did not write until she was encouraged by a television journalist to give her dream a shot. She wrote a six-hundred-page historical romantic spy-thriller set against World War I. The journalist sent the manuscript to his agent who then garnered bids from two publishers. That was nearly forty published novels, nonfiction books and anthologies ago.

Books by Catherine Lanigan

HARLEQUIN HEARTWARMING

40–LOVE SHADOWS

Harlequin MIRA

DANGEROUS LOVE
ELUSIVE LOVE
TENDER MALICE
IN LOVE'S SHADOW
LEGEND MAKERS
CALIFORNIA MOON

SILHOUETTE DESIRE

THE TEXAN
MONTANA BRIDE

This book is dedicated to my granddaughter, Caylin Pieszchala, whom I love with all my heart. It is my fondest wish that you have happiness, love and laughter all of your life, my darling.

Acknowledgments

There are some who would say I live under a lucky star, but I know better. It takes a choir of angels and then some to bring any novel to the readers who patiently wait for authors to pound out a story that will come alive for them and haunt them long after the cover is closed and it collects dust on a shelf.

I have been blessed for decades with exceptionally talented editors and publishing mentors. From my first Harlequin MIRA books that were honed and polished by Dianne Moggy and others on her team to my present editors and master wordsmiths, Victoria Curran and Claire Caldwell. Ladies all, it is my honor to bang our heads together, cut, slice, dice and chop my oftentimes cumbersome manuscripts into the magical romances I intended them to be. I am forever grateful.

CHAPTER ONE

THE FEBRUARY FOG rolled across the frozen flats of Indian Lake and curled long, diaphanous fingers around the pines and maples at the water's edge. Canadian geese flew in V-formations across the slate sky above, honking at no particular inhabitants below. There was no wind to rattle the winter-bare branches of the shrubs and neglected rosebushes around the Pine Tree Lodges of Indian Lake, and few tourists were out and about in the dark predawn hours.

Inside Cupcakes and Coffee Cafe, strings of red Valentine lights and glittering silver beads hugged the ceiling in a mock drape, reflecting happy red light into every cranny. Aromas of sugar, butter and freshly ground coffee beans mingled with the clanging of dozens of baking trays being tossed in and out of ovens.

Maddie Strong shouted instructions to her staff of one, twenty-one-year-old Chloe

Knowland. Three of Maddie's closest friends were also on board to help with her Valentine's Day cupcake orders.

"Next year, I'll know better than to agree to this insane torture," Sarah Jensen said, laughing as she slung back the last smidge of Maddie's special-brew latte. She hoisted two full trays of iced cupcakes onto an empty table marked New Buffalo, then reached for a yellow legal pad to record the details of the order. She counted twenty-four double-chocolate cupcakes with pink peppermint icing, forty-eight vanilla cupcakes with white whipped-cream icing, each topped with a red marzipan heart, and thirty-six red velvet cupcakes with white cooked-flour frosting. Sarah marked off the inventory and looked around for some bakery boxes.

"Torture is a bit strong, don't you think, sweetie?" Maddie retorted, winking at her best friend. She yanked a very full pastry bag from a stainless-steel rack and placed a fine-point pipe on the end and secured it. The bag was filled with her new recipe for vanilla-bean whipped-buttercream filling. She stuck the pipe into the centers of several double-fudge cupcakes, which she had previously cored out, and squeezed the bag.

"It would be fine if I didn't have to get up at 4:00 a.m.!" Sarah shouted above the latest cacophony as Isabelle Hawks dropped a stack of aluminum muffin tins on the floor.

"Sorry," Isabelle said, whisking her dark hair away from her startlingly pretty face. She quickly gathered the muffin tins. "I'm just all thumbs today. Not enough sleep," she said, endorsing Sarah's comment.

"Maddie, you do know we make these sacrifices for you because we love you," Sarah said, flashing a grin at Isabelle.

"It's either that or you're expecting a free cupcake out of the deal," Maddie replied, keeping a critical eye on her work.

"I'll take the free cupcake," Liz Crenshaw said offhandedly as she stuck bottles of her grandfather's new white-grape ice wine into Valentine's baskets that already contained cupcakes and bags of Maddie's blend of Colombian and Middle Eastern coffee beans.

Sarah tapped her cheek with her finger. "In that case, I need at least a half a dozen cupcakes. There's Luke, Annie, Timmy, Mrs. Beabots, me and Beau, of course…"

Maddie froze and shot her best friend a horrified look. "Beau? No way your dog gets one of my gourmet creations!"

"He loves them!" Sarah grinned, keeping her eyes on Maddie's piping bag. "Squirt a little extra cream into Beau's cupcake. He adores that stuff."

In mock horror, Maddie shook the piping bag at Sarah. "That dog has excellent taste. He gets a double blast."

Sarah carefully arranged a grouping of pineapple-and-coconut cupcakes with coconut-cream frosting onto a round tray and marked it for delivery to the Pine Tree Lodges of Indian Lake. She looked quizzically at Isabelle, who had just been promoted to assistant director at the lodges. "Edgar only wants two dozen cupcakes? I would think the lodges would be booked up for months for Valentine's dinner."

"We are," Isabelle answered confidently and in a somewhat smug tone. "Edgar didn't like the idea of opening the lodges just for one night when we're normally closed all winter. But thanks to my online winter ad campaign and the raffle for a free weekend at the lodges, even the cabins are completely booked. Truth is, I took an entire vanful of cupcakes out there last night."

"Yeah," Maddie said, waving her piping bag triumphantly. "We just had to make the coconut cupcakes at the last minute so they stay very fresh. I grated the coconut just an hour ago. Nothing but the best for our Isabelle. Aaaannnd," Maddie said dramatically, piping a huge swirl of peony-pink icing onto an oversize strawberry cupcake. "Edgar Clayton is probably my most loyal customer ever." She finished the cupcake with a flourish, then licked an errant glob of icing off her wrist.

"Having worked for Edgar for seven years," Isabelle said, "I have to say that 'loyal' defines him quite well. He's always been diligent about distributing Maddie's business cards to tourists."

"Word of mouth. My kind of magic." Maddie said, never taking her eyes off the pearlized sugar spray she used to decorate the next order. "That, and unique product ideas," she added.

Sarah finished her inventory and handed the list to Maddie. "Just how many recipes have you patented now?"

"Twenty. And at two grand a pop for legal fees, I haven't been able to go shopping or on vacation for three years. But, it's all been worth it."

Maddie looked just past Sarah. Next to the register was a three-foot-high, perilously thin, black glass vase. Streaming out of the top of the vase were jungle-red anthurium flowers, green palms and white orchids. They were from Alex Perkins, of Chicago's esteemed investment firm Ashton and Marsh. Sarah's uncle, George Regeski, had helped Maddie prepare a business plan for franchising her "made-on-the-spot cupcakes and Italian café" concept last year. George had scoured his network of investment firms and had finally found some interest at Ashton and Marsh. Their initial response was lukewarm, but they were willing to "take a meeting," Uncle George had told Maddie last November.

Since then, Maddie's nerves had been on overload. She had worked ceaselessly since high school graduation for this one opportunity to prove to herself that she was accomplished. This was her blue ribbon; her Oscar.

Because Maddie was the only child of a single mother, Babs Strong, who worked in a bread-manufacturing plant, Maddie hadn't had the money or means to go to college. But no one was more passionate about acquiring a business degree than Maddie.

Maddie had learned accounting and business management by copying the reading lists of the required classes her wealthier friends took in college. She read all the same materials and texts they did. It was her bet that on any given day, she was on an even par with the best of them.

It was Sarah's mother, Ann Marie, who'd seen Maddie's business potential and believed in her café-and-cupcake vision right from its conception. Ann Marie had gone to Austin Carlson McCreary, by far the wealthiest man in town, and asked him to be an "angel investor" in Maddie's café. Austin, twenty-eight years old at the time and a near recluse, agreed to put up a small amount of working capital for Maddie, but only because he respected Ann Marie and her judgment.

Maddie's café was a hit from the day the doors first opened. She worked fourteen hours a day and repaid the twenty-five thousand Austin had loaned her in less than three years. Because Austin never asked for interest or a dividend, Maddie was only too happy to fulfill his one eccentric request. Every Friday at eight in the morning, Maddie was to hand-deliver a box of seven assorted cupcakes to Austin's front door. Maddie never missed a Friday.

After ten years in business, Maddie was about to take her first step toward her ultimate goal. She was working with Alex Perkins on franchising her café. There were hundreds of ifs between this moment and the actuality of a dozen Cupcakes and Coffee Cafés opening across the Midwest. Maddie had always believed in her dream. If she didn't dream it, it would never happen. And she intended to make all her dreams come true.

Maddie stared at the expensive bouquet, which Alex had sent several days ago, and which she'd almost been too busy to notice, though Chloe and her girlfriends certainly had. Gazing at the spectacular flowers, she wondered why Alex would send her such an ostentatious gift. They were only business associates. She was his client, that was all. Wasn't it?

"Are you listening to me, Maddie?" Sarah asked.

"Sorry," Maddie said, wiping her hand on her bright red-and-white-striped apron. "Could you repeat that?"

Sarah's eyebrow cocked inquisitively. "I said that Chicago investment firms certainly treat their clients well. That's some pretty good PR."

"Yeah." Maddie smoothed her short, highlighted blond hair around her ears with her palm. "It makes me nervous," she admitted.

"Why?"

"Is Alex sending me these flowers because he's found an investor and he knows something I don't, or because he can't find anyone for my franchise? Or is it because he likes me more than he's letting on?"

Shrugging her shoulders, Sarah asked, "Either one sounds like a winner to me. Doesn't it to you?"

"Sure. I guess," Maddie said. She whirled to look at the clock over the counter. "I gotta get. So do you," she told Sarah.

"Right. I still have to run home and take Beau out for one last potty break before my big presentation for Charmaine." She picked up two boxes of cupcakes. "I'll put these in your car for you, Maddie. Are you taking them up to New Buffalo right away?"

"It's first on my delivery list," Maddie said. "You guys have been a great help to me today. I can't thank you enough."

"I was just teasing about the torture," Sarah said, going to Maddie and kissing her cheek. "Keys, please."

Maddie dug around in her jeans pocket and pulled out her car keys. "Pop the side doors in back and put the cupcakes on the driver's side. I'll bring out the rest of the order. Good luck with Charmaine."

Isabelle gazed at Sarah with what looked like hero worship in her eyes. "Is it wonderful, Sarah? Your new project?"

"More than wonderful. I can't tell you about it. Not yet, anyway. The owner wants everything kept under wraps until we get a go from the city council. But it's exciting."

Maddie withdrew another bakery box of cupcakes from under the counter and held them out for Sarah. "I put this together last night when Isabelle and I were working. I made Luke's favorite lemon cake with lemon-flavored cooked icing. Dutch chocolate for Annie. Double devil's food for Timmy. Carrot cake and cream-cheese icing for you, and of course, Beau's cream-filled vanilla cupcake."

Sarah smiled broadly. "This is very sweet of you."

"Hey, you're the generous one, giving me your time and energy when I know you probably should have been putting the final touches on your drawings."

Sarah looked at Maddie with genuine gratitude and an air of conviction that Maddie had always admired in her friend, even when they were in high school. For a while last year, after Sarah's mother died, that conviction, the abundant, sparkling hopefulness that Sarah shared with everyone in town, had faded under the storm of grief and loss. To lose one's mother was always difficult, but to lose a person like Ann Marie Jensen, whose kindness was nearly legendary and whose lifelong dedication to the town had left not just a mark, but a swath of beautification, creativity and civic improvement, was almost insurmountable.

But since Sarah's engagement to Luke Bosworth, she had come back to life, and her effervescent spirit was bubbling over with enthusiasm.

"This time my drawings are nearly perfect," Sarah reassured her. "I'm totally confident about this presentation."

Maddie beamed. "That's great to hear, Sarah." This was her friend's first project since her boss, interior designer Charmaine Chalmers, had laid her off a year ago.

"I'm in such a different place than I was last year at this time. When I look back at the work I did then, I don't blame Charmaine for kicking me to the curb. Thank goodness it was only temporary."

Maddie followed Sarah to the door. "You had lost both your parents in a very short period of time. You left Indianapolis and that great architecture job. It was a lot of change. Too much change in a couple short years. Then taking care of your mother before she died. That's heartbreaking and physically exhausting. But you're an inspiration to us all. Like the 'comeback kid,' Sarah. I'm so happy for you."

The two women walked over to Maddie's black Yukon, which served as her delivery van. Maddie had emblazoned both sides of her SUV with her phone number, website, email, Facebook, LinkedIn and Twitter accounts in gold lettering. Sarah put the boxes in the back end of the SUV. "Speaking of mothers," she said. "How is your mom?"

"We don't speak. You know that. She lives her life with her cigarettes and television reruns and I push for my dreams. Two different universes." Maddie shrugged her shoulders flippantly. "Doesn't matter."

"It's just sad, is all," Sarah said.

"Not really. Your mother was more of a real mother to me than Babs, whose biggest regret is that she gave birth to me. Babs will be bitter till the day she dies because my father had already picked out a new girlfriend before she even told him she was pregnant. She blames him and me for the fact that she never finished high school. She should have stuck to cheerleading and she knows it."

Sarah squinted accusingly at Maddie. "The real truth is that your mother has been jealous of you since you were in a training bra."

"Check." Maddie nodded. "She thinks I'm too entrepreneurial, not that she could spell or define it. And the she hates the fact that I'm perfectly happy without a rich husband who would pay her bills so she could sit around and smoke more cigarettes and watch more innocuous television."

"I guess it really is best you don't see her much."

"It took me a long time to face the fact that my mother just doesn't like me. Enlightenment is knowing when to let go. I let go of her a long time ago, Sarah." Maddie hugged Sarah quickly. "Beat it, or you'll be late."

"Deal," Sarah said and rushed off to her car. "Don't forget, we're meeting at four-thirty at Bride's Corner to choose my wedding dress!"

"It's burned into my brain!" Maddie waved as Sarah got into her Envoy and drove off.

Maddie turned her attention to the red sandstone of the clock tower on the county courthouse as the dawn rays struck the beveled-glass windows.

"Valentine's Day," Maddie whispered. "A moneymaker day." She smiled, then felt her smile drop off her face like icing off a cake when it's been sitting in the sun too long. For the first time in over a decade, Maddie remembered that Valentine's Day was a day for love.

She'd received beautiful flowers a few days ago, which was a first for her. Alex had even called her last night to make certain they'd arrived.

"Hey, beautiful. Happy Valentine's Day tomorrow," he'd said, his voice filled with anticipation. He spoke in a sultry baritone she'd never heard during their office meetings. Their conversations had always been about profits, projected earnings and potentials.

"They're just gorgeous," she'd gushed. "So exotic. Especially for this time of year."

"I like unusual and unexpected things. Were you surprised?"

"Very. I couldn't figure out who would be sending me flowers."

"Ah. That's good," he said. "I wanted you to have something special while I was away…" His voice trailed off as if there was something else he was going to say before he thought better of it.

So I don't forget you? Is that what you were going to say, Alex?

"You're going away?"

"To Dubai. For three weeks," he'd said, as if in apology.

"United Arab Emirates," she'd whispered as her mind flitted halfway across the globe. "That's a long way."

"It is. Listen, I scheduled a meeting for us when I get back. We'll need to catch up. And I'm hoping to have an investor for you by then."

Maddie's heart had actually tripped a beat. "Investor?"

"I don't want to get your hopes up quite yet. But I have someone on the line. I'll tell you about it when I get back. You take care, Maddie. I'll try to text you while I'm gone. I hope their cell coverage isn't as bad as the last time I was there."

"You've been to Dubai before?"

"Several times. I'm working on some-thing…." He had a way of leaving valuable information hanging in space like tiny crumbs leading to hidden treasure.

Remembering their phone conversation, Maddie's head was filled with thoughts of Alex. He was like a dream to her. He was tall, blond and wide-shouldered, and had a very strong jaw that looked as if it was chiseled from granite and a dimple in his chin. His blue eyes were the color of cornflowers in summer. His smile revealed sparkling white even teeth, and his full lips completed a face so handsome she finally understood why the Greeks invented a god of male beauty. Alex could have been a dead ringer for Adonis.

The first time she'd met him in his office, she was impressed with his confidence, sincerity and assuredness. He was the kind of man people trusted with their entire life's savings. He was the kind of executive people turned to when their world was crashing down around them. Maddie's first impression was that this man was smart enough, savvy enough, to turn around even the worst-case scenarios.

Now, he'd sent her flowers, and he'd been especially sweet to her on the phone, making her think about things romantic.

It had been a long, long time since Maddie had had time or room in her thoughts for anything other than her passion for her career.

Romance was something she'd discarded when she was seventeen, when Nate Barzonni had asked her to marry him and then left town the next day. He'd never called or written. She'd never received an explanation. He'd simply disappeared.

For over a decade, she'd been heartbroken and very, very angry.

No, Maddie thought. Romance was something that existed only in her past.

CHAPTER TWO

NATE BARZONNI WAS early for his seven o'clock meeting with Dr. Roger Caldwell, chief surgeon and head of the new cardiology wing at Indian Lake Hospital. Nate had been sitting in his car in the foggy cold since six thirty-five, his hands wrapped around a large, double-shot latte from the drive-through window at Book Shop and Java Stop.

As he entered the hospital and took the elevator up to Dr. Caldwell's office, Nate realized he was nervous as a cat about this interview. It wasn't that he didn't think he'd get the job. He knew the position was his for the taking. He was the only applicant who had any experience with the new cold beam laser surgeries that every hospital in the nation wanted. Though catheter ablation surgery, the process of "burning" away misfiring nerves inside the heart to treat arrythmia, had become as common as bypass surgery, the cold beam laser was truly cutting-edge technology. Cold

beam created a clean, open channel to the
heart by drilling several holes from a dying
heart muscle to the left ventricle. Once the
holes healed, they triggered a growth of new
muscle, so oxygenated blood could flow into
the heart, which hadn't been receiving proper
oxygen and nutrients. Finding the surgeons
to perform the procedure was difficult. Nate
was keenly aware that he could have gone to
Los Angeles or San Francisco, and he'd been
offered a position in Scottsdale, but most hospitals wanted him to sign a three-year contract. Indian Lake demanded only a single
year. One year was more to his liking because
Nate wanted to prove himself—fast. With a
year under his belt as a top cardiac surgeon
at the Indian Lake Hospital and working in
their Ablation Department, he could go wherever he wished and he would get the kind of
financial backing he would need. For years,
Nate had dreamed of one day landing a department chief position at a major hospital.
But last year, that all changed.

Nate had spent a year on an Indian reservation in Arizona, ostensibly to whittle his medical school loans down by half. He'd learned
about the government plan that enticed newly-
licensed doctors and dentists from a shipmate

of his in the Navy. Within a few days of treating patients on the reservation, Nate saw a desperate need for doctors with his skill level. He'd never considered himself a humanitarian, but something happened to him during that year that changed his view of life. These people could not afford highly specialized ablation surgery. And there were very few surgeons in his field willing to sacrifice money and possibly fame to help them. Nate realized he could make a real difference in the world.

By the end of his stint at the reservation hospital, Nate had come face to face with his life's passion.

Indian Lake was exactly the place Nate needed to be for the short term. And afterward…he'd ratchet himself up another several notches toward his dream.

"DR. BARZONNI?" A MAN'S voice asked in a clear, clipped tone.

"Yes, sir." Nate snapped to his feet from the uncomfortable metal-and-plastic chair he'd been seated in. Nate presented his hand to the tall, slender man with an angular face. Dr. Roger Caldwell was in his late forties and looked fit, in a long-distance-runner way. He wore black slacks and a long white lab coat over a cheap maroon oxford-cloth shirt and blue-and-red-striped polyester tie. This was the third interview Nate had been on, and at every hospital, every major clinic, the administrator responsible for choosing the hospital uniforms and outlining the dress codes apparently won the job based on their obvious lack of fashion sense and color blindness. "Dr. Caldwell. It's a pleasure to finally meet you, sir."

They began walking down a carpeted hallway.

"You can drop the 'sir.' We aren't all that formal around here." Dr. Caldwell flipped through some papers in a manila folder marked with Nate's name. "And you haven't been in the navy for quite some time."

"Sorry, sir. I mean Doctor. It's my upbringing as much as the navy." Nate smiled.

"I know your parents quite well, so I understand completely."

"They're still old-world Italian, I'm afraid. In fact, they're insisting I live at home with them once I move back to Indian Lake."

"Nothing wrong with that," Dr. Caldwell replied, scratching his temple. "Frankly, I'd like to see a bit more of it myself." He took a couple steps back and then waved his right arm in front of an open door. "Let's step into my office, shall we?"

"Thank you very much, sir. Doctor." Nate laughed good-naturedly.

For as austere and sparse as the waiting area was, Dr. Caldwell's office was quite the opposite. Colorful Persian rugs covered the laminate floors. The furniture was modern and sleek, made of glass, chrome and wood. A butter-yellow leather sofa sat against the back wall with two massive, off-white leather Barcelona chairs flanking it. A squatty black vase of tropical flowers sat in the middle of a kidney-shaped coffee table. The room was lit by dozens of tiny halogen ceiling fixtures, and natural light flowed in from skylights and a very large window that looked out on Main Street where the morning traffic was building to a bustling crescendo. The sun skirted around and through huge snow clouds, which had come to perform their own kind of magic and alter the scene below. Slowly, a very light snow started to fall. From the fifth floor, the view was captivating, and as Nate gazed out across the commercial-building rooftops and toward the housetops of Maple Avenue and Lily Avenue, he realized he was eye level to the many church spires that dotted nearly every block of Indian Lake. From this height, it didn't take much imagination to see the fantasy aspect of the town. As the snowflakes grew in size and number, they fell delicately on the grand shoulders of the Presbyterian church, creating white, lacy epaulettes. Nate had always loved all the churches of his hometown and how they stood for hundreds of years, never swerving, never capitulating or seeming to decay. Unlike many other cities or towns, the people of Indian Lake renovated, renewed and shored up their treasures. They put new foundations on their buildings, installed new roofs on their banks and fixed storefront windows. They adapted and perfected, modernized and improved, but they never destroyed the original structure, the soul of their buildings, which was part of the soul of the town. He'd forgotten how little things like that mattered to him.

"Nice view, isn't it?" Dr. Caldwell asked.

"Spellbinding."

"Interesting you say that. I thought the same thing when I moved here. I came from New Jersey. The unpretty part of New Jersey. I was a class-A nerd in a street-gang-infested world. I couldn't wait to get out of there."

"Is that why you joined the navy as well, sir?"

"It is. Best move I ever made. I fell in love with Chicago the minute I walked off the bus. But once I got married and left the navy, we started looking around for a small town. You know, to raise kids and all. We came here on a winter vacation, actually, and stayed four days. Everyone was so friendly and we loved all the little shops and cafés. My wife and I were hooked. I've always wanted to live in a small town."

"Funny. When I was growing up here, I couldn't wait to leave. See the world. Have an adventure."

Dr. Caldwell laughed and sat in his black leather desk chair. He leaned back in the chair and watched the falling snow. "I had plenty of adventure. Persian Gulf. I was fortunate enough to be part of the launch of the *Sullivan* to the Mediterranean Sea on August 12, 1995. I'll never forget it. This was the second ship, Nate, to be named for the Sullivan family, who'd suffered the greatest loss of any one American family in the Second World War."

"I remember the story well."

Dr. Caldwell smiled to himself. "I was

lucky. I sailed over half my naval career. How about you?"

"Not so much. I spent most of my navy years in and around the Great Lakes. I signed up as a corpsman and worked at the Great Lakes Naval Hospital while I received my training. I didn't mind it so much, though. I used my time wisely. I took advantage of the extracurricular college classes. I took every class that was a requirement for premed. By the time I finished my service, I had three years of credits piled up. I went to Northwestern on the GI Bill and finished up my undergrad. Then I got more loans for medical school and stayed on at Northwestern. I rejoined the navy as a doctor after med school and completed my internship and surgical residency. I finished my cardiology residency at Northwestern as well. As you know, I'm finishing up my year-long contract at an Indian reservation in Arizona, which pays off the bulk of my loans. I'll still have a bit of debt, but it'll be manageable."

"No family?"

"No, sir. I have a single-track mind and I wanted to get myself set up in medicine before I took on that kind of responsibility.

Frankly, taking care of me was just about all I could handle."

"Smart man," Dr. Caldwell replied.

Nate glanced outside at the spires that poked through the frosty cotton quilt that nature was spreading across the town and wondered why the scene tugged at him. Nostalgia, probably. "Thanks."

"These letters of recommendation from Northwestern, from your commanding officers, the other naval doctors you've worked with and the head of the Hopi and Navajo tribes attest to the fact that you're quite a gifted heart surgeon, Dr. Barzonni. Imagine what you could do here with all our new equipment."

"I'm very excited about working with the cold beam laser. I got my initiation at Northwestern when I was doing ablations with Dr. Henry Klein. Do you know him?"

"Haven't had the pleasure."

"He's been my mentor for years," Nate replied, his words laced with respect.

Nate was extremely grateful for the guidance and friendship Dr. Klein had given him. Nate was also aware that the man looked upon him almost as family.

Nate continued. "Dr. Klein is the one who

talked me into doing work on the reservation. Not only was the program government run and would pay a good chunk of my student loans, but he said I needed to get my hands away from the luxuries of big-city methods and equipment. He wanted me to learn how to use my instincts. Listen to my gut when dealing with patients. He wanted me to treat the patient not just the disease. My entire perspective on life changed. Thanks to him and my time on the reservation, I believe I found my calling."

"Interesting. Is that what he did? Work on a reservation?"

"No. He spent five years in Kenya."

Dr. Caldwell whistled. "When was this?"

"It was back in the eighties, when the AIDS epidemic was rampant. Not that it isn't now."

"Sounds like a good man. I'd like to meet him." Dr. Caldwell steepled his fingers, placed his lips against them and considered Nate. "Do you mind my asking why you aren't going back to Chicago and working with Dr. Klein? I'm sure he wants you."

"He does. Desperately, in fact.

"I'll be frank if I may. I have an offer from Dr. Klein. But working in Chicago or at any big-name hospital, where I'm just another rat in the pack, isn't what I want anymore. I want to go back to Arizona and work on the reservations out there. There's an incredible need and I believe I can fill it. But to do that, I need the experience with cold laser beam surgeries."

"And that's why you need me?"

"Yes, sir."

"So, you're going to hold me to that one-year contract."

"That's my intention, yes. Barring anything unforeseen."

Dr. Caldwell leaned forward. "I know your family fairly well. Your mother is still active with the hospital foundation. There are no health issues with either of your parents?"

Nate smiled broadly. "No, no. Mother and Dad are just fine. As are my brothers."

"Well, my team would very much like having you on staff. Now, I'd like to show you our electrophysiology lab. It's quite something. We have fourteen different computer screens on which the team watches an in-progress ablation. We have two new ORs for open-heart and bypass surgeries. We're performing a half-dozen pacemaker and defibrillator implants a day. We would do more, but we're taking on the more difficult hypertrophic cardiomyopathy cases. Those surgeries last about four hours each, as you know."

"I do. Makes for a long day," Nate commented as he rose and followed Dr. Caldwell out to the newly carpeted corridor that led to the surgical area.

"I guess I'd better tell you now, Nate, this hospital pulls from an eight-county area, and it's my goal to really put this cardiac center on the map. I want the best on my team, and so far I've been able to get them. South Bend has the orthopedic business socked. But this hospital has been shooting for awards in the cardiac field for twenty years. In the past six years or so, we've made some real headway. I want to be the best of the best. I sense a competitiveness about you as well. My conjecture is that you have the makings of an exceptional surgeon."

"I'm flattered you consider me that good."

"You aren't yet, but you will be. You're a man of single focus, and that's what I need. This job will be a lot of hard work."

Nate smiled as they approached the elevator and Dr. Caldwell pressed the up button. "I like challenges," Nate said firmly and sincerely. "They make for the sweetest victories."

CHAPTER THREE

MRS. BEABOTS SMOOTHED the skirt of her black silk dress with the red-rosebud print and white starched collar that she loved so much. It was the last dress her husband had bought for her before he died, and therefore, it carried great sentimentality for her. It was important for her to wear something special today. Despite it being Valentine's Day, today was a most remarkable day in her life and that of Sarah's as well. Mrs. Beabots was here at Bride's Corner to give her opinion and advice about this most auspicious of all dresses a woman would ever wear—her wedding gown.

She was honored that Sarah had sought her counsel, but she had also told Sarah she would tell the unvarnished truth. "You look like a strumpet," Mrs. Beabots said evenly. "It's not that I don't like it, it's just not what I pictured you would want."

"Come on. This is a designer dress. It was

featured in two of the fourteen bridal magazines I bought. I thought it was…" Sarah looked at herself in the mirror and frowned. "I thought it was sophisticated and the clean lines made me look a bit taller. Thinner."

"Stay away from Maddie's cupcakes and you won't need to worry about your waistline," Mrs. Beabots said with a smile on her face that nearly dripped honey. She knew exactly how to deliver the truth when the truth was not exactly what was expected. She swept her eyes over the yards of white peau de soie that were tucked and wrapped around Sarah's perfect figure. The dress was strapless, in the mermaid style, which was all the rage, Mrs. Beabots had been told. A bolero jacket covered Sarah's bare shoulders with dozens of lace and silk flowers around the collar and bottom of the jacket. At the lower hips, the tightly wound section ended, and the skirt flared out into a long fantail of peau de soie. It was sophisticated. It was extraordinarily elegant. But it wasn't Sarah.

Maddie sat next to Mrs. Beabots on the faded gold brocade settee that faced the large front window in the store. On either side of the window, angling in toward the room were enormous cheval mirrors.

Sarah looked at Maddie. "What do you think?"

"It's too low-cut for St. Mark's, that's for sure." She tilted her head to the right and then the left. "It's a beautiful gown, but I always thought of you in something wistful and dreamy, with a train of little boys in white satin knee pants behind you."

Sarah turned and observed her backside in the long mirror. "Maybe I'm not the city sophisticate I thought I was."

"I doubt that's how Luke sees you, dear," Mrs. Beabots said flatly. "I know I don't. You're too sweet." Mrs. Beabots shuddered. Being sophisticated was a bitter-tasting idea.

"True," Sarah replied. "I just look too…"

"Poured in," Maddie said, getting up. "The dress is lovely, Sarah, but this mermaid style is so formfitting that no woman but a very confident supermodel would be comfortable in it. You need…" Maddie wandered over to a rack of spring wedding dresses that Audra Billingsly, the owner, had just rolled into the front room.

Audra pressed a clump of errant red hair back with her palm as she bent down to put the brake on the rack. "These just came in, Sarah. None have been ironed, but maybe there's something here that suits you better. I've got several top designers as well as some very affordable gowns. My yummiest is this Carolina Herrara, with embroidered cabbage roses along the tiered second hem. It's frightfully expensive, though."

Sarah shook her head as she looked at the price tag. "It's gorgeous, but out of my league."

"This Claire Pettibone has a knee-high hem in front and falls to a train in back, and look at all the appliquéd spring flowers. Isn't it gorgeous?"

"It is," Sarah agreed, "but it's still not quite right." Sarah sank onto the settee next to Mrs. Beabots. "I had no idea this was going to be so difficult. I can't seem to choose—they're all so beautiful. I like these dresses with the high-low hem, since we're going to be on the beach for the reception. But if I spend more on the dress, I don't think I'll be able to afford flowers. And as much as I envision a church filled with flowers, I'm afraid my budget can't stretch that far."

"Don't worry about flowers now, Sarah," Mrs. Beabots said. "I'll be planting a new rose garden for you this spring and we'll have plenty." She nodded reassuringly.

Sarah gave her a hug. "You are always a step ahead of me, aren't you?"

"I should be. I've been around longer."

Maddie perused the rack of new gowns and took a dress off the rack and held it up to herself. "Sarah, now, *this* is your dress." She turned to Audra. "Who's the designer?"

"You have exquisite taste, Maddie. It's an Oscar de la Renta. Why don't you try it on. It's a six, just your size."

The elegant, A-line, white peau de soie skirt was embroidered with green-and-white lilies of the valley. With the green-and-white strapless bodice, the dress would give the impression that the bride had just walked out of a forest garden.

"That would be fun, Maddie," Sarah urged. "You and I are about the same size and both blonde. Let me see what it looks like on you. Besides, it will take a crowbar to get me out of this gown, and we'd be here till dinnertime if we had to wait on me."

Maddie couldn't tear her eyes from the gown. "I've never seen anything like it. May I?"

"Absolutely. Let's go into room two. I'll help you with the dress." Audra led Maddie toward the fitting rooms.

While Sarah and Mrs. Beabots discussed floral arrangements for the church and possible plans for their spring gardens, Maddie went to the dressing room and let Audra help her into the gown.

Audra supplied a white lace strapless corset and bra, and a straight white nylon half slip. Then Maddie donned a horsehair net underskirt that would allow the A-line of the skirt to bell out. Over that, she pulled on a second underskirt of white silk. Audra handed Maddie a pair of thigh-high, elastic-topped white hose to wear and a pair of white peau de soie pumps with two-inch heels. Finally, Maddie stepped into the gown and Audra zipped up the back and fastened the white satin ribbon that encircled Maddie's waist, tying a bow in back. In the center of the bow she pinned a tiny fabric nosegay of lily of the valley. The entire bodice and skirt were covered in eight-inch leaves in varying shades of green. The flowers were embroidered in white silk, and in the center of each was a crystal bead, so that each time Maddie turned under the chandelier in the dressing room, she sparkled a if dew had just settled on each flower.

"It's absolute magic," Maddie gushed in an

awe-filled whisper as she looked at her reflection in the gilded mirror. "I had no idea…"

"That you were so beautiful?" Audra finished the thought for her.

Maddie was spellbound by her own reflection. She honestly didn't know who that woman with the sparkling green eyes could be. She'd been so used to working in jeans, corduroys, sweatshirts and aprons nearly all her adult life that she'd never once stopped to think of herself as a girl who wore pretty dresses or gowns, or even as a…bride.

And you aren't a bride. This is just pretend. Standing in. Wishful thinking.

Dark shadows filled Maddie's eyes as she continued to look at herself. Was it possible that only today, the flutter of a memory of Nate Barzonni, her first love, a high school romance, had haunted her? Even now, as she recalled his blazing Mediterranean-blue eyes and the intoxicating, addictive kisses they'd shared, her emotions were a storm of anger and pain. Nate had abandoned her eleven years ago, and she still felt the heartbreak.

If she ever saw him again, it would be too soon.

But then, there was the very real fact of Alex's flowers—real and aggressive. He was spinning her dream for her, and though he would be gone for nearly a month, he promised to call and text her often. He'd told her they were close to finding an investor. Alex knew there was nothing more important to her than her business.

"You're beautiful, Maddie," Audra said. "This dress was made for you. The green in the lilies matches the green of your eyes. I can watch your thoughts in your eyes. Did you know that? Your eyes change from light green to dark green along with your mood."

"My mood?"

"Uh-huh. When you first saw yourself in the mirror, you were happy, and your eyes were a sparkling, light spring green. Then they turned darker, as if you were thinking of something disturbing."

"Hmm. Disturbing," Maddie grumbled. Nate was always a disturbance. "You could see that?"

"Yes."

"I didn't know I was so transparent."

Audra hid her smirk by bending down and passing her palms over the skirt to smooth out a few wrinkles. "I see a great deal in my business. Weddings are like funerals. People usually reveal part of themselves at both events, and it isn't always the best side that I see, even though people think of weddings as being a happy time. It's a very stressful time. All big decisions are."

"But it's not my wedding," Maddie said. "So, I'm off the hook."

"I'm thinking that you wish it were your wedding," Audra offered, leveling her brown eyes on Maddie.

"Not hardly," Maddie retorted.

Audra waved away her objection. "I've always found it just as interesting to watch the bridesmaids and maid of honor as to watch the bride. There are so many little dramas going on around us every day. Dozens of innuendos and intrigues, mistakes and missed fortunes. Lives being slowly knit together and others, sometimes sadly and methodically, being torn apart. Most people are oblivious to these little underpinnings of life. But they are what form the structure of our lives and create our finales for us. Me? I pride myself on observations."

"Well, there's nothing to observe here. I have no fiancé. No boyfriend. And to be honest, I have a lot of world to conquer before I get tied down with marriage."

Audra smiled. "Is that right?"

"Absolutely." Maddie looked at herself again. "Still. It's a very pretty dress, isn't it?"

"It was made for you. Just you."

"I think it would look marvelous on Sarah."

Audra chewed her bottom lip thoughtfully and walked around Maddie, studying the dress from all angles. "I have another theory. It's taken me over twenty years in the bridal business to come to the conclusion that there really is one perfect wedding dress for every woman, and when the dress finds her, sometimes it's an omen of changes to come."

"I bet you believe in soul mates, too."

"I wouldn't be in the wedding business if I didn't."

Maddie stared at Audra as if she was nuts. This wasn't the kind of conversation she needed to have, today of all days. She came here to help Sarah pick a dress, and now she was standing here, looking frankly fantabulous—better than she ever knew she could look—and this woman was telling her this dress had "found" her and was mystically going to change her life. Maybe Audra had been hitting the champagne a bit early. Or maybe she was just trying to make an extra sale.

"Well, let's see what Sarah thinks of the gown, shall we?"

Audra took the change of subject as her cue to open the dressing room door. "We should, indeed."

Maddie walked into the main showroom and up to the front window where there was a step-up round riser. She lifted her skirt and heard the swishing of all the underskirts and the peau de soie next to the horsehair net. She stood still and looked at herself in the two cheval mirrors. The gleam of the light from the crystal chandelier overhead pirouetted off the crystals in the dress.

Mrs. Beabots clasped her hands together and brought them to her smiling lips. "You are a vision for my eyes, my dear!"

Sarah was dumbstruck and could barely speak. "It's you, Maddie. The dress is like the angels made it for you."

"I can't deny I feel like Cinderella," Maddie said, admiring herself once again, still not believing her own reflection. Maddie turned back to Sarah. "But I thought it was perfect for *you*."

Mrs. Beabots and Sarah stared at Maddie and allowed her to revel in the moment.

"Let me see the back," Sarah said.

"Oh, I just love the little bow and nose-gay," Maddie said, turning toward the front window.

Maddie stared. Then she blinked. Twice.

At first, she thought her eyes were playing tricks on her. She peered into the darkening day.

There, underneath the black, wrought-iron Victorian street lamp, the evening fog drifting along the sidewalk, stood Nate. He looked directly at her, and when their eyes locked, he smiled.

Her heart thrummed in her chest and she could feel a pounding of hot blood at her temples. She felt dizzy for a moment, but steadied herself by using the mind-over-matter techniques Sarah's uncle George had once taught her.

In the eleven years since Nate had abandoned her, Maddie had not had a single boyfriend. She had dated a few men here and there, but all her energy had gone into her business. She had convinced herself that she was strong and willful, that she owned her own power. She firmly denied and crushed any idea that she might fear being rejected again by a man, especially Nate, and moved on. She purposefully fanned and fueled the fires of her anger against Nate to mask even the tiniest possibility that she still had any feelings for him. Maddie didn't dare think about Nate and love in the same thought. Such musings could lead to her ruin. For eleven years, Maddie had told her friends over and over that Nate Barzonni was the devil to her.

Maddie continued to stare at the vision outside the window.

If it was at all possible, Nate was more handsome than ever, with a man's face and a man's physique under a double-breasted black wool coat. His dark hair was worn shorter than she remembered, but still parted on the right side. He wore a grey, black-and-white-plaid scarf around his neck, and suddenly she realized it was a scarf she'd bought for him their last Christmas together, in his senior year of high school. His hands were shoved into the pockets of the coat, and he did not raise one to wave to her.

He only stared.

She was spellbound.

There was no way Nate was actually standing outside Bride's Corner. No way.

Until today, she hadn't thought about Nate in months. Okay, weeks. After more than a decade, she could now go a full two, sometimes even three, weeks, and never actually think about him, wonder about him, curse him, rail against him and the cruel, heartless fates that had brought them together in the first place. Maddie closed her eyes and opened them again.

Nate was gone.

CHAPTER FOUR

"Did you see him?" Maddie asked Sarah and Mrs. Beabots, raising a shaking arm and pointing out the window.

"See whom, dear?" Mrs. Beabots asked.

"Nate. He was there."

Sarah jumped up from the settee and rushed to the window. "Nate Barzonni was here? In Indian Lake? Right now?" She turned to Maddie.

Maddie felt the color drain from her face. "I swear I saw him," she repeated as her eyes flitted from Sarah's concerned expression to Mrs. Beabot's clear, blue compassion-filled eyes. She wanted desperately for her friends to believe her, but even more important, she wished to high heaven that they'd seen Nate as well. Clearly, they hadn't, or they would be confirming her statement. Instead, their gazes were filled with surprise and censure. She wasn't sure if they just didn't believe her, or if they disapproved of Nate, as well. Hopefully, they would still side with her against the slimy jerk who had abandoned her with no explanation. Maddie couldn't help wondering if they, and her other friends, would think if Nate came back and finally gave his side of the story, whatever that side might be.

Clearly, he was a jerk. A creep to the nth degree. A scum that no one could or should ever trust. What kind of guy tells a girl he'll love her till the end of time and then disappears? Vanishes without a single goodbye? For eleven years?

Now that Maddie thought about it, if Nate was truly back, she would have to face the humiliation all over again. She would have to go through the entire abandonment, the dumping, the heartache all over again because everyone would want to talk about it. Again.

Why couldn't he just stay away?

God, but she felt violently ill.

Maddie placed her shaking hand on her flushed but icy cheek. She felt beads of sweat trickle from her temples. "I don't feel so good," she said, her voice warbling.

Sarah rushed to her side and grabbed her arm. "And you don't look good. You look like you've seen a ghost."

Maddie sat next to Mrs. Beabots on the

settee, barely noticing that she was trembling from head to foot. Suddenly, Sarah's words sunk in.

"That was it! I saw a ghost. That's what it was." She was off the hook. He wasn't back at all. She was just seeing things. She wouldn't have to go through the humiliation and embarrassment in front of the whole town again at all.

Mrs. Beabots harrumphed and pulled her hands together, then pressed them into her lap. "Fine day for ghosts. It's Valentine's Day not Halloween. You'd think they'd know the difference."

Maddie shook her head to clear it. She was stronger than this. She couldn't push the truth under the rug anymore, and she wasn't one to run from a confrontation. The best way to beat a fear was to meet it head-on, vanquish it and be the conqueror. "What's wrong with me?" she said aloud. "Why would I start hallucinating all of a sudden? I mean, what's so special about now?"

"I can think of a few things, dearie," Mrs. Beabots offered.

Maddie and Sarah lifted their heads and looked at their octogenarian friend. "Like what?" they asked in unison.

"This is a very critical time in your life, Maddie. Your best friend is getting married soon and you haven't a prospect in sight. What's more, you've been pushing to expand your business and get this franchising idea off the ground, but it's been a longer process than you'd anticipated...."

"Hey, how do you know that?" Maddie demanded and looked accusingly at Sarah. "Maybe someone has a big mouth."

"I—" Sarah began but Mrs. Beabots interrupted her.

"I have other sources than cross-your-heart Sarah, who would never betray a confidence. I know a lot of things that go on in this town, especially to those whom I love," Mrs. Beabots replied with a haughty tilt to her chin and a twinkle in her eye. "In addition, you're not getting any younger, Maddie Strong, and it's high time you began beating the bushes for a beau instead of sending every prospective groom out your café door with a cynical retort and a very icy shoulder."

Maddie graced her octogenarian friend with a smile. Mrs. Beabots's view of life was charmingly old-fashioned, but Maddie strongly believed she would have plenty of time for love and romance after she had her business secure. Maddie's life was happy and very full with her work and friends.

"I'm too busy for men."

"So you say, but I wasn't the one seeing an apparition of my former sweetheart out that window," Mrs. Beabots concluded with the kind of sharp clip to the end of her comment that warned others that the Oracle had spoken.

Sarah's eyes tracked from Mrs. Beabots back to Maddie, who was clearly confused and still a bit shaken by the vision or ghost or whatever it was she saw. "Maybe it was just all the excitement of these gorgeous gowns and dressing up. Maybe..."

"No, Sarah. My corset is not too tight and the dress is not so elegant that my brain went off track. I saw Nate out there. In the flesh. He's come back. I'd know him anywhere. What I don't know is what he's doing here and why he would choose the very moment I'm standing in the window of Bride's Corner in a wedding gown to stare at me?"

Mrs. Beabots nodded. "Stalking. That's it."

Sarah sighed deeply. "Nate is not stalking Maddie."

"How do you know?" Mrs. Beabots asked. "I watch *CSI Miami* and *Law and Order* and even *Elementary* and *The Mentalist*. Every single one of those detective shows has a murder a month committed by a stalker. It's quite common." She looked from Sarah to Maddie, but neither woman appeared to be following her line of reasoning.

"Nate's been gone for eleven years. Why would he stalk Maddie now?" Sarah asked. "Why not just come into the shop and talk to her?"

"Good point," Mrs. Beabots answered.

Maddie looked at Sarah. "You think I was seeing things?"

"Uh-huh. I do. But don't take my word for it. Just call his mother and ask if he's in town."

"What?" Maddie jumped up and put her hands on her hips. "You know she's never liked me. Always thought I was after the Barzonni millions and that I didn't really love her son. I wouldn't call her if I was facing the devil himself!"

Sarah stood and put her hand on Maddie's arm. "I know, sweetie. I know."

Tears filled Maddie's eyes in an instant. She crumpled into Sarah's arms and let her friend hug her. "I don't understand what's the matter with me."

"You had a shock. That's all. The only reason you would have had such a hallucination would be if you'd been obsessing about Nate lately, and we all know that's not true. It was probably just some look-alike."

Maddie sniffed and straightened to look Sarah in the eyes. "Right. I haven't been thinking about Nate. Well, not so much. I always said that if I saw him on the street I'd ignore him like he was nothing. Just like he's done to me all these years. He told me every day in high school that he loved me. He wanted to run away to Kentucky and get married, but I was the stable one. I was the one who said we should put our careers first. He proposed right there on my doorstep on the Fourth of July. And the next day, he was gone, without a word to anyone! Anyone, Sarah!" Maddie nearly spit she was so angry. "He left me. He was able to forget me. It didn't cause him any pain or heartache. He just took off. He wanted to see the world, he said. Guess he did. All of it! What a jerk."

"I'm glad you remembered that aspect of his character, dearie," Mrs. Beabots said. "He treated you shabbily and you deserve the very best, just like my sweet Sarah."

"I agree," Sarah said. "You know what, this

just isn't the right day to find my dress. Let's go over to my house for a glass of wine to celebrate Valentine's Day."

"I thought you and Luke were going out tonight," Mrs. Beabots said.

"Not a chance. I'm making dinner for all of us at home. I decorated the house with valentines and red lights. I have homemade heart-shaped sugar cookies for Annie and Timmy. But they won't be over until six-thirty. We have time for a girl toast beforehand."

"Done!" Maddie said, and started walking toward the dressing room. "I'll be out in a jiffy," she promised.

Sarah swished into the dressing room next to Maddie's.

Mrs. Beabots smiled at both women, and then turned around to gaze out the front window. The sun had gone down and the street lamps were coming on. Moving closer to the pane, she craned her neck to see a tall man dressed in a double-breasted black wool coat pass under the lamp and then vanish into the dark of nightfall.

Mrs. Beabots sat back on the settee. She knew a ghost when she saw one. She'd been seeing her husband's spirit for years. Ghosts didn't fool her one bit, even though people often did. No, what she saw tonight was a real man.

It was Nate Barzonni.

CHAPTER FIVE

NATE BARZONNI HAD always been a man of single purpose and clear-minded goals. Never once had he thought his mind was incapable of reasoning out the best course of action for the highest possible good. He was a man of honor and conviction. He was a leader, and little swayed him off his chosen course or derailed him from his beliefs. He'd never been drunk, never used drugs, never lied or cheated. His mind was as sharp as a razor and as tight as a trap.

But that day, Nate was sure he'd lost all his senses and the entirety of his reasoning ability when he'd purposefully gone back to that bridal shop to confirm whether what he'd seen was real or a mirage. The shock of seeing Maddie Strong trying on a wedding gown was enough to rip his insides apart. No earthquake under his feet or hurricane at sea had ever unsettled him as much as the sight of her. Even after he'd walked away, when he realized she'd seen him and recognized him, he could barely put one foot in front of the other to get back to his Hummer. Climbing numbly into his vehicle, he tried to catch his ragged breath. His mouth had gone dry. He attempted to rake his hand through his hair and wipe the sweat from his brow, but his hand was shaking too much.

He'd seen beautiful women before, but the moment he saw Maddie in that wedding gown, lights glinting off the flowers in her dress like tiny fairies attending an earth angel, he thought he'd lost his mind and certainly his heart to her all over again.

She's getting married? Nate stared at his hands as they gripped the steering wheel and his knuckles turned white.

For the past eleven years, Nate had pursued all his dreams. After literally leaving Maddie on her doorstep, he'd packed his camping duffel bag and taken the bus to Great Lakes Naval Station to enlist in the navy. He hadn't left a note to his parents for fear they would talk him out of his decision, and to be truthful, he'd known he would have been convinced.

At eighteen, Nate had no fear of the unknown, but he was an absolute coward when it came to confrontation with his mother and father.

His loving mother, Gina, had doted on him and his three brothers all their lives. He loved her dearly and it crushed him to leave like he did, but he knew no other way. His father, Angelo, was possessive of his mother and his sons. He expected them all to carry on with the lucrative family farming business. Though each of the Barzonni boys secretly harbored their own dreams and ambitions, Angelo would not tolerate even a whisper of dissention. Their lives were to be lived Angelo's way and only his way.

Though the navy was a six-year stint, Nate didn't care. He would have signed up for twelve years if that had been a requirement. He wanted to leave Indian Lake behind and get on with his dream of becoming a doctor.

His only regret was leaving Maddie. But to do what he knew he needed to do for himself, he felt he had to cut all his ties to his past. Above all, Nate wanted to find out who Nate was, and to do that, he needed to disappear.

Nate declared in boot camp that he was interested in medicine and being a medic. He didn't travel overseas, as a great deal of his fellow recruits did, but remained near Chicago, where he later went to Northwestern's medical school, completing his internship and residency there as well.

After six weeks in boot camp, Nate buckled under to the need to call his parents and make his explanations. He wanted to be sure he was locked into his commitment to the navy before he told his parents his life plans. Because he'd graduated, he wanted them to attend the Review and be a part of his new life. He was terrified to tell them the truth. They were angry and disappointed...at first.

Nate had planned the reunion well. Being surrounded by the pomp and pageantry of the navy graduates marching in their navy whites for the Review altered his parents' attitude considerably. His mother, Gina, especially, was overcome with love and pride for Nate and hugged him with tear-filled eyes.

From his brothers, Nate had heard the gossip about him and the fact that half the town had sided with Maddie. She'd painted him as the jerk of all time. He knew that if Maddie ever found out where he was, she would come after him, and he would cave to her. They would run away together and he would never realize his dream. She had been so right to refuse his proposal. She'd been wise and forward-thinking.

Nate asked his parents never to reveal his whereabouts to anyone in Indian Lake. No one outside the Barzonni family ever knew where Nate was or what happened to him.

Despite body- and mind-numbing days in boot camp and the years he spent in the Navy and pursuing his career, Nate never forgot Maddie, not for a single day.

Nate looked out the Hummer's windshield to the bridal shop. *Maddie*. They had been so young and naive back then, but she was the only one who knew him inside and out. It was as if she held his heart in her hand and gazed into it like a crystal ball. The great mystery to him was that his heart had spoken back to her.

Nate told Maddie he wanted a career in medicine, but he'd never told anyone about the moment when a cosmic clash had taken place in his life. It had been as if his future had rushed to the present and shown him his path.

Nate was only ten when he spent an entire afternoon huddled in the horse barn with one of his father's prize mares, who was in labor. His father, Angelo, had called for the vet, but the man was late in coming to the farm. Angelo had been anxious and short with the vet. This mare was his most prized horse. He was terrified she would die.

Nate stroked the horse's neck and calmed her with soothing words and whispers, never leaving her side. When the vet finally arrived, he went straight to work. The mare's heart was weak, and though Angelo had been warned not to breed her every year, he had not listened. The strain on her heart was too much. However, the vet was a skilled and knowledgeable man and saved both the mare and the colt.

Nate had decided that day that he wanted to be a doctor. Not a vet or a general practitioner. He wanted to be a cardiac surgeon. His mind was made up.

However, Nate's parents had always insisted their sons devote their careers to the ever-expanding farm and produce business. Nate struggled for years with schemes and scenarios for how he would tell his parents about his own dreams. He believed Gina would understand, but there was no doubt in his mind that she wanted him to live at home.

By the time Nate was in high school, he had observed that his parents weren't affectionate toward each other. They didn't hold hands the way he held Maddie's hand. He never once saw his father put his arm around Gina. And whenever they sat anywhere in public—baseball games, movies, plays—they always placed the boys between them as if trying to keep their distance from each other.

Angelo was domineering and he had high standards when it came to his sons. By the time Nate graduated from high school, he'd allowed his parents to think that a degree in agriculture was just fine with him. He'd been accepted at Purdue and pretended to make all the necessary plans for the fall semester.

He'd been a coward, and it had caused a lot of people a great deal of pain.

Nate took one last look at the bridal shop where Maddie was no doubt making more wedding plans. When Nate first applied for the job at the Indian Lake Hospital, he'd briefly thought about Maddie, but he'd he'd shelved his memories of her a long time ago.

Nate believed that people didn't change their core personalities as they matured. Even at seventeen, Maddie had been compassionate, kind, bright, fun and deeply loving.

There had been times during his stint in the navy and later in med school when he'd remembered all too well what it was like to be with Maddie. To love her. As much as he wanted back then to return to Indian Lake and sweep her off her feet, he couldn't do it. It wouldn't have been true to himself. He'd sacrificed love in order to be the cardiac surgeon he was today.

Nate had saved numerous lives already, and he intended to go on saving more.

In all his planning and goal-setting and returning for his interview with Dr. Caldwell, not once had he considered that he might actually see Maddie. Seeing her in that gown was a shock. He hadn't counted on his immense reaction to her—even from a distance. He hadn't planned for jealousy.

His entire past with her rumbled over him like a tsunami, and he was swept away in it. For the first time in a long time, he felt helpless. He didn't know who the other guy in her life was, but at this moment he couldn't imagine any man having ever loved a girl as much as he'd loved Maddie Strong.

Nate expelled a deep breath as a new realization hit him like a fist to his chest. *I still do.*

CHAPTER SIX

MADDIE PARKED IN a garage off West Lake and South Wacker drives, as she had on her previous trips to Chicago to meet with Alex. She walked down Wacker to the large granite-and-glass office building that housed Ashton and Marsh and checked in with the security guard at the front desk. The guard was a tall, older man with a barrel chest so large, Maddie wondered if he wore a bulletproof vest under his shirt. She noticed he had Mace, a billy club and a pistol attached to his thick leather belt. Maddie should have been used to him by now, but still she found herself swallowing hard as she approached him. She was certainly not in Indian Lake.

"Maddie Strong to see Alex Perkins at Ashton and Marsh."

"I see it here," the man said, running his finger down a list of today's appointments for all the offices in this building. "Sixth floor.

Hey, I remember you! Maddie, isn't it?" He smiled broadly.

"Yes. Thanks for remembering."

"No one would forget you," he said with an appreciative glimmer in his dark eyes.

"See you on the way out," she said, and crossed the black granite floor to the bank of brass elevator doors. She pressed the up button and watched the numbers tracking the elevator's descent.

Almost a dozen people walked out of the elevator when the doors opened. Maddie noticed, once again, that nearly everyone looked to be about her age; men and women handsomely dressed, smiling and chatting with one another about which restaurant in the area was best for lunch.

So very not Indian Lake.

Maddie got in the elevator and hit the button for the sixth floor.

When she stepped off the elevator, she was face-to-face with enormous, heavy glass doors etched with the Ashton and Marsh name and logo.

The reception area was decorated sparely, with modern Asian furniture and a few plants. The reception desk was a curved glass block, lit from the inside and topped with tortoise-shell granite.

"Hi," Maddie said to the new reception-ist, who hadn't looked up from her computer screen when she'd walked in. "I have an appointment with Alex Perkins."

The girl lifted her beautiful face, her scarlet lips covered in enough gloss to refract fluorescent light. "And you are?"

"Maddie Strong."

The receptionist's expression lit up. "You're the cupcake lady!"

"Uh. Yes. I guess so."

"I was so excited to meet you." The girl practically jumped out of her chair to shake Maddie's hand. "I love your concept. Alex, I mean Mr. Perkins, let us taste the cupcakes you sent. They were to die for! I've never had anything so…decadent," she practically squealed.

"I'm glad you liked them."

"I loved them! We all did. Oh, gosh. So sorry. I'll let Alex's assistant know you're here." She tapped her earpiece. "Sean. Miss Strong is here to see Mr. Perkins." She nodded several times, still looking at Maddie as if she'd just seen her first Christmas. "Sean will be right out. Alex is finishing up a call.

It won't be long. Would you like a water or some tea? We have a nice variety. Hot or cold?"

"Water is just fine," Maddie replied as she glanced around for a comfortable chair. She spotted an angular S chair next to a gold pot that held six-foot-high bamboo.

Maddie sat down, and though there was a smattering of financial magazines and newspapers laid out in painfully neat rows on the glass coffee table, she was too nervous to read anything. Not only had Alex implied that a bona fide investor might be in her future, but there was the matter of his ostentatious Valentine's flowers and his text to her last night: Can't wait to see you.

What did that mean, exactly?

The receptionist came back, her high-heeled boots clomping on the wood floor, and handed Maddie a chilled bottle of water. "My name's Mia, by the way. Julie left two weeks ago." Mia leaned close. "Pregnant." With a toss of her hair, she twirled away gleefully, as if she'd just won the lottery.

Just then, a thin man in his early twenties nearly pounced into the reception area from the long hallway leading to the offices. "Miss Strong? Mr. Perkins will see you now." He looked down at her water and briefcase. "Can I take any of that for you?"

"I'm fine," Maddie replied, hoisting her purse strap onto her shoulder and following Sean.

"So nice to see you again," Sean babbled. "You do know we all just adore your cupcakes. Just yummy," he said. "I can't eat too many sweets, you know. Bad for the waistline, and God forbid I'd develop diabetes or something."

They arrived at Alex's enormous corner office with a window that peeked through to a narrow view of the Chicago River. "Thank you, Sean," she said.

"Ciao," Sean chirped and whisked himself away.

Alex rose from his desk. "Maddie! You look terrific." He walked around his desk and took her hand, leading her to a chair opposite his. "Please, sit. Thanks for meeting me at the office. I had some calls to New York and I just couldn't put them off any longer. I've been swamped since I got back."

"Understandable," she said. "This is fine."

"Actually, it's not."

"No?"

"Is Bandera okay with you?"

"Uh," she stammered, not understanding what he was talking about.

"I mean, we could go to a sushi bar if you like. Or Thai? There's a great Thai restaurant…"

Maddie giggled, covering her mouth with her hand. "Bandera is a restaurant."

"Yeah. American food. That okay?"

"Sure. I've never been there."

"Oh. Right. Sure." His expression became serious. "I guess I should tell you right off the bat I found you an angel."

Maddie's eyes widened. "For real? But I haven't even shown you my new concept drawings for the café interiors. My friend, Sarah Jensen, did them for me." Maddie dug into the leather briefcase that Mrs. Beabots had loaned her and pulled out the professionally bound report that she and Sarah had prepared. "I was thinking that because I sell so much cappuccino and espresso, we could do an Italian theme, you know, with yellow-and-white awnings out front, Italian chairs and stools, and of course, brass-and-copper espresso machines as the focal point—"

"We can get to that in a bit," Alex interrupted, glancing at his watch. "I ordered a car to take us to the restaurant. Let's get a jump on things and head out. You bring your drawings and let's see." He picked up several manila folders.

Maddie rose and Alex followed her out of the office. He stopped for a moment at Sean's desk.

"I'm on my cell if Quinton needs me. If that Dubai call comes through, patch them over to my cell. We'll be at Bandera. Hold any other calls."

"Yes, sir," Sean said. He shot a wink at Maddie and gave her two thumbs-up.

They rode the elevator in silence as Alex texted someone. Once out on the street, he pointed to a black Lincoln Town Car parked in a no parking zone.

"This is it," Alex said, rushing to get the door for Maddie.

She climbed in and Alex got into the back-seat with her.

"It's only a few blocks to Bandera, but they kept saying it was going to rain today and I didn't want us to get caught in a downpour."

"Thank you for thinking of that," Maddie replied, realizing she hadn't checked the weather forecast in days. Only the worst snow blizzards kept her customers away. On most rainy days, the café was packed. It was Maddie's theory that people liked to "huddle" on dreary days, looking for energy from others to give them a boost…along with the sugar and caffeine she offered. She hoped Chloe was doing all right with only a few hours' help from Sarah's aunt Emily, who had volunteered to work part of the day so that Maddie could come to this meeting.

Emily explained that George, her husband, was quite excited about the prospect of Alex and his company putting together a franchise for Maddie. Emily also wanted to do her part in giving Maddie a shot at her dream.

They pulled up to the restaurant and Maddie got out. Alex gave the driver some instructions and then followed her into the restaurant. The hostess led them to a booth. Soft lighting emanated from linen-covered chrome cylinders on the walls and tables. Overhead was a dark wood ceiling from which were suspended flat, oval-shaped paper lanterns that reminded Maddie of flying saucers. There was an open kitchen where the patrons could watch the cooks preparing the meals.

The smell of garlic, onion, beef, chicken and shrimp were laced with the smoky, woodsy aroma of the open-pit grill where trout and other seafood were mesquite grilled.

Alex and Maddie sat opposite each other in the booth. After the waiter took their drink and appetizer orders, Alex said, "I didn't mean to rush you out of the office, but I worked till after ten last night, didn't have any supper except for a stale half a bagel someone left in the break room, and I am starving."

"I can understand why," she replied.

"Besides, I had those two calls coming in and they could wind up taking all our lunch hour. And I really didn't want that to happen. So," he said, searching her face with his blue eyes. "Gosh, you look great."

Maddie smiled, tilted her head and then peered at him from the corner of her eye. "You're flattering me a lot, Alex. Is this because I'm about to be rich?"

Alex laughed, then covered his mouth with his napkin. "I hate to burst your bubble, but this is just the beginning of a long trip."

"Rich is a relative term, is it not?" she asked.

"True. But do you know what the best part is?"

"What?"

"We'll be making the journey together. I'll

be there every step of the way. At least for most of them."

"I need a professional to guide me," she said.

"I, er…was hoping for a bit more than that." Alex stared at his silverware, then lifted his head and shot her a purposeful look.

Responding to the intensity in his eyes, she asked, "What do you want, Alex?"

"A date."

"This could be a date," she observed, noting the chic businesswomen and -men in the booths near them.

"This? Nah. This is steak and business. I was thinking more like escargots, truffles and champagne in a really nice joint."

Maddie was surprised, though she shouldn't have been. Alex wasn't just flirting with her, and wasn't just interested in her as a client. He wanted a romance. But did she? The idea instantly filled her with trepidation.

Alex glanced at her hand, which was trembling. "Okay. Forget the escargots. Let's stick to business for the time being."

Maddie exhaled. She couldn't imagine what was wrong with her. Here was a perfectly formed dreamboat—every girl's ideal—and she was refusing his offer. She must have lost her mind. Maddie had to move her hands to her lap and clamp them together to keep from shaking.

What is the matter with me?

Just then, the waiter brought the chips and spinach dip Alex had asked for. Maddie smiled at the waiter. Alex kept his eyes on Maddie, observing her every move.

"Let me see these drawings you have," he said. He took huge gulps of iced tea and wolfed down the first few chips as if he truly hadn't eaten much in days.

Maddie reached into the briefcase and withdrew the bound folder. "Do you often work such long hours? No dinner and all that?"

"Absolutely. Especially when I'm obsessed with hitting my project out of the park. In this case, that would be you," he said, glancing at her seductively.

Maddie only blinked.

He dropped his eyes and wiped his hands on his napkin. He took the folder from Maddie. "It's my bet you're no stranger to long hours."

"A lot of nights it's midnight or later by the time I get home. Business has been picking up."

"Looks like it. Or maybe you just haven't done the necessary hiring," he said critically, but then softened his face with a sincere smile.

"It's hard to find good people," Maddie retorted. She watched him slowly go through the drawings. He stayed silent and didn't look at her. Maddie realized that Alex was truly unnerved by her rejection. Despite the fact that he'd sent her flowers, she hadn't been prepared for a personal discussion about "them" today. She certainly hadn't thought about a relationship, either. Maddie didn't have time for love…or so she'd told herself for the eleven years since Nate Barzonni abandoned her for no reason at all. She invested her energy and emotion into her business.

She wanted to achieve her dream. All of it. For years she'd told her herself that all she needed in life was to reach her goal of franchising her business. Romance was for other women. Maybe she'd find love one day, but Maddie couldn't allow it to get in the way of her success.

"It's a matter of trust, Maddie," Alex said, his stern voice piercing the Kevlar vest of excuses Maddie wore around her heart.

"Trust?"

"The real reason you haven't hired someone to do the night work is because then they would know your recipes. You don't want anyone to steal them because in the recipes lies one of the secrets to your business."

Maddie stopped midmotion as she took a sip of her tea. "That *is* the reason I haven't hired anyone but Chloe, and she just works days. At the counter, selling."

"My point."

"How would you know that?"

"I know business, and I know *your* business—what you're doing and not doing."

Alex polished off the last of the chips, wiped his hands and sat back, putting an arm on the top of the banquette. "From what I can tell, you've always seen your business as a small-town, small-time operation. It makes enough to cover your overhead and pay for you to live. Deep down, you're scared someone will steal your recipes. So, you trademarked them along with your iced-on-the-spot concept, and you don't let anyone have access to the recipes themselves. That's good. But not good enough. Once you franchise, all your 'partners,' we'll call them, will sign nondisclosures. The employees they hire will sign iron-clad nondisclosures as well.

If they leave and steal a recipe, we sue. We can garnishee their wages, put a lien on their house or car."

"You can do that?"

He shrugged his shoulders. "It's done all the time, and has been done for a hundred years, especially in R & D departments in big corporations. You own your idea. No one has come up with this one in quite the way you have. I'm not the only one who thinks so."

"There are others?" She urged him on.

"Quinton Marsh thinks so, and he runs the company. You saw the excitement from my staff. They love your cupcakes."

"So, it's the cupcakes that are different."

"And the way you sell them…made to order. Brilliant."

Maddie noticed that he grew more excited with every breath he took and every word he spoke. He gestured when making a point and his face beamed with enthusiasm. Maddie realized that Alex cared for her business as if it were his own.

"Just remember, Becky Field made chocolate chip cookies," he continued. "Nothing special about that. Except her megamillions."

She smiled back at him. "You flatter me."

His smiled dropped. "I'm not conning you," he said defensively.

"I didn't mean it the way it sounded. It's just that where I live, where I come from, no one has talked to me the way you do. No one has ever given me—"

"Respect?" he interjected.

"Exactly." Sadness filled her as she thought about her mother and all the complaining and harping she'd done over the years as Maddie had struggled to make her little café a success. Babs had hounded her to get a "safe" job in the bread factory, just as Babs had done. Babs told Maddie constantly that no one was going to pay four dollars for a fancy coffee and over three dollars for a cupcake. She ridiculed everything that Maddie said or did.

As Maddie gazed at Alex's handsome, confident face, she realized that her mother had not wanted her own daughter to succeed. Suddenly, realizations about her own past were flying at her like the myriad of stars that pass by a spaceship as it zooms through space. "Yes. Respect. It's been a tremendous amount of hard work."

"And now you're getting your payoff." Alex smiled even more brightly, if that were possible.

He opened one of the manila folders he'd carried with him from the office. "Your investor is named James Stapleton. Ever hear of him?"

"No. Should I have?"

"Probably not. He's been investing in restaurant chains and buying franchises since the sixties. He buys only a few at a time—two to six locations—and then waits to see how they do. If he doesn't make any money, he shuts them down, and he may or may not use the location for a new franchise. He's been moving businesses from the suburbs back into the city since 2000. I think it's because as he's gotten older, the suburbs are too boring for him and he and his wife like city life."

"City life?" Maddie stopped him by reaching forward but not actually touching Alex's hand. It was an unconscious move, motivated by years of standing on the shore of Lake Michigan and staring out to the west to see the skyline of Chicago glittering in the sun. She dreamed of living in the city, of leaving Indian Lake and all her heartbreaks behind. If she had this success, if she had respect, she could dare to live another life. A better life. A happy life.

Alex looked down at Maddie's hand but didn't make a move.

Maddie was dreamy-eyed when she asked, "Do you know what about the city they enjoy?"

"His wife is a theater buff. Goes all the time. She also likes the ballet, and I think she's on a couple foundations around town. She's a busy lady for someone nearly eighty."

"Sounds wonderful." Maddie smiled wistfully. "One of my two best friends will turn eighty-one this summer. She loves the theater. I should bring her with me sometime. We could see a play."

"Or I could take you," Alex said, and before Maddie could retract her hand, he captured it and raised it to his lips, kissing her fingers. "Maddie, I would like very much to show you my Chicago."

Maddie squirmed in her seat. "Alex…"

"Do I make you that nervous, Maddie?" he asked with a chuckle.

"It's not you, Alex. It's just that I've put my heart and soul into my business and until it's a real deal, I'm just not geared to think about anything else. Not plays or escargot, and certainly not champagne."

A slow smile crept across Alex's face.

"Then I'm almost in the clear. How does a hundred thousand sound to you?"

"For what?" she asked.

"For the first two franchises of your cafés. James wants six, but I declined. After this first purchase, if James or any other investor wants to open a Cupcakes and Cappuccino Café, they'll be a hundred thousand a pop. Once the first twenty are sold, our price moves to a quarter million for each opening. I didn't think you would want to go low."

"Go low?"

"You know, ask for just two hundred thousand for the entire franchise and let James open six cafés. It doesn't work that way. At least not for me," Alex explained.

"And they'll need money for the build out and decor. The appliances and the brass-and-copper cappuccino machine."

"James knows that. We'll supply them with drawings, blueprints, scripts for employees, operation procedures, the standard regulations. You would be required to help train the managers and some staff in the beginning until these first cafes are up and running. And there would be the usual consulting. So, the hundred grand goes straight to you until we sell more sites. And believe me, I'll make that happen for you."

"You think so?"

"Absolutely. I can give you your dream, Maddie," Alex replied. There was such earnestness in his eyes, Maddie felt warmth ripple through her body.

Maddie believed Alex was the right man to could sell her franchises. She couldn't help wondering how many of her "dreams" he was scripting himself into.

CHAPTER SEVEN

EASTER SUNDAY WAS one of the three days of the year, the other two being Christmas and the Fourth of July, when just about every business shut its doors and hung out the closed sign in Indian Lake.

Maddie had been one of the first to post her Easter hours. Though she was always closed on Sunday mornings, she closed on Good Friday afternoon and used the time to fill Easter catering orders for hot cross buns, coconut cupcakes, bunny-shaped cakes and her popular lamb-shaped, vanilla-bean, cream-filled cake.

But Easter itself was a day off for Maddie, and she planned to spend it at The Pine Tree Lodges' Easter brunch with Sarah, Luke, his kids, Mrs. Beabots and Olivia.

The Pine Tree Lodges began its tourist season every year at Easter. Because so many holiday visitors came to Indian Lake for the early-spring dogwoods and red buds that blossomed on the property, the lodge was booked to capacity. Another main attraction was the six-hour-long Easter champagne brunch that Edgar Clayton had been serving for four decades. Not only did the out of towners book tables for brunch, but so did the townsfolk.

Maddie knew that Isabelle would be doing double duty all day on Easter. Normally, the bookkeeper and accountant, on Easter she had to serve as head hostess in the dining room.

Isabelle was a talented artist, but she had to work at the lodge to make ends meet, since she couldn't yet support herself with her art alone. This winter again, Isabelle had entered several of her sculptures and three of her oils to various galleries in Arizona, New York and Los Angeles and was rejected by them. She was now faced with the fact that as good as her work was, it just might not be good enough. Maddie constantly told Isabelle not to give up and to keep submitting her work. Because Maddie was teetering on the precipice of success, she encouraged her friend to stay the course, too.

Maddie often dreamed that if she were rich, she would find a way to help her artist friends—Isabelle with her paintings and sculptures and Olivia Melton with her photography. They just needed connections, as she'd found with Alex.

Maddie had gone to the lodge early Easter morning to deliver the hot cross buns and cupcakes that would be served all day. She found Isabelle already at the hostess podium in the dining room.

"Breathtaking," Maddie said as she looked around the main lodge. Each table was set with silverware and pink and yellow alternating napkins in the water glasses. In the center of each table was a nest of Easter grass with a small vase of tulips and white narcissus. Around the base of the flowers were jelly beans, foil-covered chocolate eggs and speckled malted-milk eggs.

Maddie noted the reserved sign for Jensen/Bosworth/Regeski, where she'd be sitting later with all her friends. Maddie felt an inner glow that Sarah always included her in her family outings. It had always been that way with the Jensens. When Sarah's mother, Ann Marie, was alive, Maddie was never left out, no matter what the holiday, birthday or special dinner. Thinking about the past, Maddie realized that she had been like an adopted sister to Sarah. They had spent nearly their entire lives together. No wonder they knew each other so well.

"I brought my Easter dress to change into. Mrs. Beabots will be here with Sarah and Luke soon."

"Sure." Isabelle smiled. "Use the ladies' lounge. I just have a few more tables to set up and we're ready." She reached into a bag of Easter candy and sprinkled a few extra chocolate eggs on Sarah's table for Annie and Timmy.

MADDIE, NOW WEARING her jade green sleeveless sheath dress, was standing at the podium with Isabelle when Sarah, Luke, Annie and Timmy arrived. "Happy Easter!"

"Happy Easter, Isabelle," Sarah replied. She hugged Maddie. Isabelle led them to their table. The lodge was nearly full as they sat down.

Isabelle helped Annie with her napkin. "That's a pretty dress you have on, Annie."

"Thank you, Miss Isabelle. Sa...I mean, the Easter Bunny brought it to me this morning." Annie, who had just turned nine years old and clearly considered herself the "adult" of the two children, winked at her father and Sarah.

"He did?" Isabelle asked dramatically.

Maddie looked at Timmy. "And did you get that new blazer from him, too?"

"No. My dad took me downtown to the Little Men's Shop. I had to try stuff on." He nodded. "But I got an extra-large basket with candy from the Easter Bunny."

Annie glared at her brother. "And what else?"

Timmy's seven-year-old face lit up. "I got a baseball mitt! I didn't even think the Easter Bunny could do that. Bring presents. I mean. But Sarah told me that when we are little kids, we just get candy and chocolate eggs. Then when we get older, sometimes we get stuff we need instead of sweet treats."

Annie nodded. "It's better for our teeth."

"You are so right, Annie. That's a wise Easter Bunny, isn't it?" Maddie said.

"I'll say," Luke said, taking Sarah's hand and squeezing it.

Just then, Olivia, Emily and George walked in together.

Luke stood up. "Uncle George." Luke shook George's hand. "Aunt Emily." He leaned over and kissed the pretty brunette's cheek.

Emily was wearing a pale green silk suit with a single-breasted, collarless jacket. She wore her signature pearl-and-diamond earrings and bracelet, and the pearl necklace Ann Marie had passed on to Emily shortly before her death.

"Oh, you wore Mom's pearls," Sarah said wistfully. "She always wore them on Easter."

"Precisely," Emily said. "I think she would want me to keep the tradition going. Speaking of tradition, would you like to wear them for your wedding? I don't know what kind of dress you're thinking about…"

"Don't ask," Luke said, rolling his eyes and laughing.

Emily's eyes searched Sarah's face. "No luck?"

"It's really hard." Sarah looked glumly at Maddie.

Maddie's mind was suddenly filled with the vision of Nate standing outside the bridal shop on Valentine's Day. She hadn't heard a word about him around town, and she hadn't seen him again. She'd finally come to the conclusion that Sarah was right. She'd seen a ghost. Her mind had played tricks on her that day. Maddie had been in a wedding dress, and Nate had been the only man she'd ever thought about marrying. It made sense. Or not. It didn't matter. Nate was in the past, where he needed to stay.

"What can be so hard about picking out a wedding dress?" George asked. "They're all white."

Sarah sighed. "This is the dress I'll begin my new life in. It's the dress in which Ill be photographed at least a hundred times—"

"And posted on Facebook," Annie chimed in.

Maddie helped Mrs. Beabots with her chair and then sat down. "We still have time, Sarah. The wedding isn't until late June. As long as you find one by the day before, we're good."

"Sage advice." Mrs. Beabots chuckled.

"The champagne is on its way," Luke said. "Or would you rather have a mimosa?" he asked Mrs. Beabots.

"No need to spoil good orange juice. I'll take the champagne straight," she said with an impish smile.

Maddie sat on one side of Mrs. Beabots, and Olivia sat on the other, rounding out the table. "Looks like a great crowd," Maddie said, taking in the bustling lodge. "I hope it's a harbinger of the season to come."

"I have a good feeling about this year," Mrs. Beabots said. "A very good feeling."

"What makes you say that?" Maddie asked.

"I suppose it's because I've seen so many years come and go. You get a gut feeling about them when you're my age." She put her right forefinger to her cheek and thought for a moment. "No, it's more than that. There's a sense about things. An energy that makes everything feel more positive or more negative."

"What makes it do that?" Timmy inquired.

"I think it's me, dearie. Maybe I've just become more sensitive to people—how they think and what they need. I know this is going to be a glorious year for me because you're all going to be living right next door to me. Sarah smiles all the time now that she has Luke and you children. Even Beau is happier. He's cut out all that digging he used to do."

"Beau is not a digger," Sarah retorted. "It was just that one time. When I threw the dead squirrel over the fence. It was my fault."

"Oh, right."

"Well, I wish I thought it was going to be a good year." Maddie said, then noticed everyone was staring at her. "Did I just say that out loud?"

"Yes," Sarah affirmed.

"Sorry."

Mrs. Beabots patted Maddie's knee. "Now,

dear. Don't you worry. Your Alex Perkins is making things happen for you. When do you see him again?"

"Next week. I have a meeting with James Stapleton to finalize the deal."

"Why, that's wonderful!"

"I'm just so nervous about it. What if James changes his mind?"

"He won't," Uncle George said firmly. "I've talked with Alex several times, as you know. He's quite eager to get your deal going. He's even searching for other investors."

"You like Alex, do you, George?" Mrs. Beabots asked.

"I do. Seems mannerly, intelligent, and if I didn't know better, a bit fond of Maddie."

"Fond?" Sarah's eyes grew wide.

Emily looked from Sarah to Maddie then back to George. "How fond? And what else do you know about him, George? Does he come from a good family? Where did he go to school?" She rattled off questions like an Interpol interrogator.

"Maddie?" Sarah's voice grew stern. "What are you not telling me?"

Maddie toyed with one of the long, gold knockoff Chanel chains around her neck. "He might be interested in more than just my business."

"Might?" George laughed. "You ought to know better than me."

"I'm not sure. I certainly haven't encouraged it," Maddie said.

"I believe that," Luke said under his breath. He smiled wanly at Sarah, then picked up his champagne. "Happy Easter, everyone. Good health."

They toasted and fell into convivial chatter, sharing their recent news. Nearly all the adults at the table ordered the lodge's signature eggs Benedict along with smoked lake trout. Annie and Timmy opted for waffles with lots of whipped cream and strawberries. There were cranberry and walnut muffins, Irish butter and fruit compote for the table, as well.

WHILE HER FRIENDS finished their brunch, Isabelle was helping the busboys set up for the second seating. The only other large table reserved that day was in the Garden Room. She placed the pink and yellow napkins in the water glasses and helped with the silverware before going back to the podium.

She checked the last name on the reservations list.

"Barzonni?" Isabelle said in horror as her head whipped up. She glanced across the room at Maddie and then down at the sheet. "There's gotta be some mistake."

She looked back at the reservation. *Barzonni for six.*

Unless someone was bringing a date, that meant the entire family was coming. No way. Nate? Impossible. She had to get Maddie out of there before they showed up.

Just then, the main doors to the lodge opened and the Barzonni family walked in. Anyone in Indian Lake who had ever laid eyes on Rafe, Gabe, Mica or Nate knew it was useless to try to cast a vote for the most handsome. They looked like four Adonises marching shoulder to shoulder toward the podium. Gleaming black hair, piercing blue eyes and faces that appeared chiseled and carved. They were all dressed in dark suits, white shirts and dark ties, probably all overseen by their fashion-conscious mother. They were smiling as if they owned the world.

All except for the youngest.

Nate.

Angelo and Gina Barzonni entered behind the boys. Angelo was in his mid-sixties and stood over six feet tall like all his sons. Though he had a small paunch, and his face was weathered and lined from years of making his fortune in the sun, he was as robust as his offspring.

Gina still had the figure of an Italian movie star from the early sixties, and Isabelle knew she was devoted to long workouts as well as tending her famous rose garden. Gina wore a white designer suit with gold buttons down the single-breasted front. Her expertly colored dark hair was worn mid-shoulder and behind the ears, all the better to display her two-carat diamond ear studs.

"Mr. Barzonni." Isabelle greeted Angelo with a smile. "Happy Easter and welcome to the lodge. We have your table ready, sir. It's in the Garden Room, just as you requested."

"Thank you. My wife loves the Garden Room. She can see the beach better from there, she says."

"Absolutely."

Isabelle purposefully chose a route to the Garden Room that would keep the Barzonnis out of sight of Maddie and her table.

MADDIE HAD JUST RISEN to help Mrs. Beabots with her chair. She froze like an animal being stalked by a mountain lion. She could feel his eyes on her just as clearly as if he'd walked up to her and touched her. She straightened and stiffened.

She held her breath.

Then she turned.

Sarah, who was beginning to stand, took one look at startled Maddie and sat back down, pulling Luke with her. "Kids, sit down."

"What's going on?" Annie asked.

"Shh," Luke replied.

Maddie stared at Nate. She didn't know if she'd turned to ice or fire. She felt afraid and bold all at the same time. She told herself again that Sarah had been right. She was seeing a ghost.

Somehow, she managed to gather the courage to put one foot in front of the other, and with half the town staring at her, she walked across the dining room.

Streams of sunlight came through the huge windows that overlooked the lake as Maddie made her way around the chairs and tables, never taking her eyes off Nate. She didn't hesitate as she pushed through the French doors to the Garden Room and came face-to-face with Nate.

He stared at her, his blue eyes matching her lilting green, fire for fire. He started to smile, but his lips stuck to his teeth.

Maddie balled her right hand into a fist and with every ounce of her strength, she delivered a blow to his midsection.

"Ooomph!" Nate grabbed his middle and doubled over.

"So," Maddie growled. "Not a ghost."

CHAPTER EIGHT

"DID YOU SEE that?" Timmy asked Annie, bug-eyed and lips parted in awe.

Annie nodded silently, not understanding Maddie's actions at all. Annie was confused and dismayed. Her mother and her father had taught both she and Timmy that violent means only begat more violence. Annie went out of her way to be friendly to the kids in her school, though some of them didn't deserve her kindness. She avoided the aggressive and mean kids she'd seen on the playground, but they were older and didn't even notice her. It wasn't that she was afraid to fight anyone. If someone ever tried to hurt Timmy, she knew she could get angry enough to hit them. But she had never actually seen a woman hit a man. Her mother never had, that was for sure. And even though her dad had been in the navy, and fought in Afghanistan and Iraq, he never talked about his experiences. He always told her and Timmy that a person had to have "provocation" and "good cause" to resort to violence.

For Annie to see Sarah's best friend, Maddie, hit a total stranger for no reason at all was totally bizarre.

Annie didn't know what to do. Her first instinct was to seek shelter. She scooted over to her father and grabbed his hand. "Are they going to fight some more?"

"No," Luke answered quickly.

"It's okay, sweetheart," Sarah said uncomfortably.

"But he's a stranger," Annie said to Sarah.

Sarah lifted Annie's chin. "No, sweetie, she knew him a long time ago."

"He must have done something to make her mad," Annie offered.

"I'm guessing he had it coming," Luke said. They watched Maddie storm out of the lodge, her victim still rubbing his stomach.

Luke scrunched his eyes as he scrutinized Nate. "Hey. Wait a minute! I know that guy."

Sarah whirled to face Luke, her blue eyes flashing with surprise and disbelief. "You know Nate Barzonni? How?"

Luke smiled, scratched his head and nodded. "Yeah, I know him. We were in the navy together. We were really close—for a while."

"He ditched you, too? Must be a character flaw," Sarah muttered.

"Hmm. I better see if he needs some help." Luke patted Sarah's shoulder.

Luke rushed off, leaving Sarah dumbfounded. "Did he say they were in the navy together?" she asked the others at the table.

"He most certainly did," Mrs. Beabots confirmed with a smart snap of her head.

"So that's where Nate has been all this time," Aunt Emily said. "I always knew we'd figure out the answer to that mystery someday."

"Mystery is right," Sarah said, looking at Olivia. "One gets solved and then another is presented in its place. How is it possible that Luke and Nate knew each other, and now they're both here at the Lodges?"

"Kismet," Mrs. Beabots said. "It takes a lot of angelic intervention to bring this much combustion into a single room on an Easter Sunday, wouldn't you say?"

"That's as good an explanation as any," Sarah replied. "Olivia, can you manage to get Mrs. Beabots to Maddie's car? My guess is that she's still outside waiting for us. I'll take the children and meet up with Luke."

"No problem." Olivia offered her arm to

Mrs. Beabots. "She's the best date I've had in a long time."

"The only date, you mean, don't you, dearie?" Mrs. Beabots asked in the honeyed tone she took when she was stating the blunt truth. "Now, I think I can help with that kind of thing," Mrs. Beabots said.

"You think… how do you know…" Olivia shook her head as if to clear her thoughts. "I mean, I see guys all day long at the deli. Lots of guys—cute young bank executives, even that new attorney who just interviewed with George. No one ever asks me out."

"And it's no wonder, what with the way you wear your hair all tightly cinched to the top of your head like you're embarrassed by it. And those sloppy clothes. Who can see your figure under those…what does one call that getup you wear all the time?"

"Poet coats. Lots of artists and photographers wear them."

"Not since 1925. And they didn't do them any good then, either."

The group gathered their belongings. Timmy took advantage of all the hustle and distractions to swipe a few extra jelly beans from the center of the table. He started to walk away and then turned and grabbed an extra candy egg and scrambled after his sister and the rest of their party.

By the time Sarah reached Luke, who was smiling and chuckling with Nate, the Barzonnis had come to his supposed rescue. Everyone was asking questions all at the same time. They didn't seem to mind that they interrupted each other constantly or talked over each other. Sarah had the distinct impression it was probably always like this with the Barzonnis.

"Hey, man," Gabe said, slapping Nate on the back good-naturedly. "Do you need a paramedic?"

"Good one," Nate grumbled back.

"Come on, Doc," Rafe chimed in. "I can get you a nice nurse. I see Sophie Mattuchi over there with some friends. She works at Indian Lake Hospital. Want me to call her over?"

"No!" Nate roared. "I don't need a nurse. I'm fine."

"Are you sure, my darling?" Gina asked, lifting Nate's sport jacket, trying to inspect his stomach.

"Mom. Please. We're in public."

"Sorry," Gina said. "I just worry."

"Who was that woman, son?" Angelo demanded, craning his neck toward the front doors through which Maddie had vanished.

"An old friend?" Rafe leaned back as laughter exploded from his chest. He had to put his hand on Gabe's shoulder to steady himself.

"Sort of," Nate replied.

Gina clasped her hands in front of her and glared at Nate. "It wouldn't take me any more than one guess to figure out who it was."

"Mother, not now. Not today," Nate warned her.

"Later, then," Gina replied firmly, letting her son know that the matter was open-ended and only tabled for the moment. "You're right. It's Easter."

"And who is this?" Angelo asked, gazing at Luke with a suspicious crook to his dark eyebrow.

"I'm sorry." Nate finally gathered his composure. "This is just about the wildest coincidence. Dad, Rafe, Gabe, Mica, Mother—this is Luke Bosworth. Luke and I were in basic training together at Great Lakes. He's good people." Nate slapped Luke's shoulder. "I can't believe you're here, man. In Indian Lake, of all places."

"You, as well," Luke countered. "It sure is

a small world. Sorry I was witness to your humiliation." Luke laughed. "But I believe you'll live. I don't know Maddie super well, but I have to say, I've never seen her do anything like that before."

Nate tilted his head closer to Luke. "You don't know anything about Maddie and me?"

"No. Should I?"

"I just thought…well, this being a small town and all. You might have heard…things."

"No, I—"

Sarah chose that moment to tug on Luke's arm.

"Hello, Nate," Sarah said sweetly, holding out her hand to Nate.

Nate offered her his most dazzling smile as he shook her hand. "Sarah. I'd say you look just the same, but that would be a lie. You're more beautiful than ever."

"So," Luke said, "you guys know each other?"

"We went to high school together. We all did. Maddie, too." Sarah stared straight at Nate.

"I know I have a lot of explaining to do," Nate said. "I just wasn't prepared for the punch." He grinned sheepishly and rubbed his palm across his flat stomach. Then dropped it as he realized the pain was gone but the sting of the loathing in Maddie's eyes would remain for a long time, he feared. "That's the thing about Maddie. You always know where you stand with her."

"That's very true," Sarah said.

Timmy and Annie worked their way through the group and stood in between Luke and Sarah. "Maddie thought you were a ghost," Timmy said boldly, looking up at Nate.

"I thought she was kidding, little guy," Nate replied.

Luke introduced the children to Nate. "This is Nate Barzonni. He was in my graduating class at Great Lakes. We go back a long way," Luke told his kids proudly.

Nate's head jerked up to face Luke. "You have kids? The last I heard, you were in Afghanistan. Or was it Iraq?"

"Both," Luke said sternly and without further explanation.

Sarah slipped her arm through Luke's.

Nate turned to his parents. "Luke was one of the ones who spent most of his tour of duty overseas and seeing the world."

Luke rubbed the back of his neck. "Yeah. I did. I don't know if that was lucky or not.

Came back alive. Nate, these are Jenny's children. She died several years ago."

Nate felt sincere remorse for his friend as the weight of Luke's information rolled over him. "Oh, God. Luke, I'm so sorry. I liked her. Jenny was so beautiful and so much fun. Gosh, I just…" Nate raked his hand through his hair. "I just didn't know. I'm sorry. Jenny was great."

"She was," Luke replied in a low voice, and then he brightened as he put his arm around Sarah. "But I've been blessed again. I found Sarah, or she found me or something. Anyway…"

"We're getting married in June," Sarah said before Luke could finish his thought.

"Wow. You're kidding!" Nate was happily surprised and shook Luke's hand again. "This is great. Congratulations. Sarah is one of the best friends I had in high school. Remember, Sarah?"

"I do," Sarah replied.

Nate saw pain flash in her eyes. He realized that when he'd left Indian Lake without telling anyone, he'd hurt Sarah, too. Maddie hadn't been the only one.

"Nate, dear," Gina urged politely, touching her son's sleeve.

"Oh, sorry, Mom." Nate turned to Luke. "Listen, we still have our brunch, and I'm sure you guys have your Easter plans, as well. Why don't we get together one day soon." Nate patted his pockets. "Ah, here. My new card. That's my cell phone. Give me a shout. We'll catch up. Okay?"

"Absolutely," Luke replied, and shook Nate's hand one last time. "Come on, kids. Let's check on Mrs. Beabots."

IN THE PARKING LOT, Maddie was furiously tapping her Italian high-heeled shoe against the gravel.

"Are you okay, Maddie?" Sarah asked as the kids piled into Luke's pickup.

"I'm contemplating the purchase of some brass knuckles at the moment," she fumed.

Olivia helped Mrs. Beabots into the passenger's side of Maddie's car. "You did great, dearie," Mrs. Beabots commended her, giving her a thumbs-up.

"Thank you," Maddie said, and blew the elderly lady a kiss.

"Listen, Sarah. I'll take Mrs. Beabots home, and then would it be okay if I came over and talked to you this afternoon? Or are you fixing a big dinner or something? I won't be intruding, will I?"

"I'm cooking dinner, and you can help me. Mrs. Beabots is making her sugar pie. Please come over. Luke can tell us both about his days in the navy with Nate."

"His what?"

"Oh, right. You left before you heard all that. Seems Luke and Nate graduated boot camp together at Great Lakes."

"Nate went to the navy? That's where he's been?"

"Apparently. Come over later and let's see what we can piece together. Something tells me we'll both learn a lot."

"Sarah, you're the best," Maddie said, hugging her friend.

CHAPTER NINE

MADDIE SAT AMID the family chatter and kitchen clamor as Sarah placed a leg of lamb in the oven and yelled for Beau to come eat his dinner. Maddie's only job was to whip the cream that would top Mrs. Beabots's sugar pie. She got up from one of the new bar stools Sarah had placed around the maple-topped island and plugged in the industrial-size mixer. She poured the cream into the bowl, attached the whipping blade, covered the mixer with a kitchen towel to catch the splatters and turned it up to top speed.

Timmy and Annie were helping Luke put dessert plates, forks, spoons and wineglasses on the dining room table. They marched in and out of the kitchen gathering napkins and serving pieces.

Maddie was amazed at how quickly the entire family had melded together. "As if it were meant to be," she whispered to herself.

All afternoon, Maddie had staggered

numbly through the minutes and hours as if she'd been injected with a narcotic. She'd experienced shocks before. Well, only once before. And the shock had been delivered by Nate that time, too.

It had taken her years to work through that minefield of pain, and now she had a new one to deal with. His out-of-the-blue appearance at the lodge with his entire family, as if they'd all been together every Sunday for the past decade, made no sense to her.

Unless his family had known his whereabouts all along.

Was that the answer? The Barzonnis were a tight-knit family. Everyone in Indian Lake knew that. Even though she'd dated Nate for a year in high school, she'd only met Gina and Angelo once, and that had not been by design but by accident.

Many were the nights since their breakup that Maddie thought about their romance and what had gone wrong. What had she done wrong to push him away? She'd also thought about what *he'd* done wrong, and the things he could have done that would have made a difference.

One of them was that he'd never taken her home to meet his family. He'd never presented her as his girlfriend. Granted, they were only in high school and they weren't officially engaged, and she'd never pressed him for an introduction. Perhaps that had been wrong of her.

She had to admit that Sarah's observation that some of her actions belied her lack of self-esteem was true, at least in this case. At the age of seventeen, Maddie hadn't wanted to meet Nate's parents. She hadn't wanted to face the usual battery of questions about her past and her family. She didn't even talk to Nate about her upbringing—ever.

She wanted him to believe she was the person she had finally invented once they were in high school. She wanted him to think of her as bright, accomplished, fun to be with and popular.

Maddie didn't force any real issues with Nate. Secretly, she was thrilled that he had chosen her, a white-trash kid from the wrong side of the tracks in disguise, as his girlfriend. She remembered the envy in the other girls' faces when Nate would walk her to class or meet her under the bleachers after the football and baseball games. She had been his one-and-only girlfriend that year, and it never occurred to her that anyone would dispute it.

She'd assumed that he told his family about her, but maybe he hadn't.

She couldn't fault him. She never discussed Nate with her mother. Babs would only mock her and make fun of her new "puppy love." Her mother loved to go on about how she was so much wiser about men than Maddie, how she knew what they did and did not want. Most of these conversations ended in so much vulgarity, they made Maddie sick.

"Maddie?" Sarah's voice drifted to her from across the kitchen. "Earth to Maddie. I think the whipped cream should be churned enough by now."

"Huh?" Maddie looked up at Sarah, who was standing at the sink peeling apples. Sarah glanced down at the mixer.

Maddie followed her gaze. "Oh, right." She turned the mixer off and removed the towel. "Sweet, not so sweet or super sweet?"

"Not too sweet. The crisp is very rich and sugary."

"Got it." Maddie added two heaping tablespoons of white sugar to the cream. She turned the mixer back on for a few more seconds, until the whipped cream was well blended. She stuck in a spoon and tasted it. "Perfect."

Sarah smiled brightly. "I expect no less from my master pâtissier."

"Thanks." Maddie unhooked the whipping blade.

"How are you doing?" Sarah asked, plunging a pink rubber spatula into the cream and transferring it into a gold-rimmed china serving dish.

"Do you think Nate's family knew he went to the navy?" Maddie asked Sarah.

"They do now," Sarah replied. "That's not much of an answer, but until you talk to Nate, you won't know the real truth of any of it."

At that moment, Luke walked into the kitchen. "What about Nate?" He stuck a finger into the bowl of whipped cream and scooped a large dollop into his mouth.

"Did you know Nate's family when you were in boot camp?" Maddie asked.

"Not that I remember. He and I were in the same division, of course, but because our last names both begin with a B we were placed together a lot. In the fourth week, we did weapons training. Nate really sucked, and I spent some extra time giving him some tips."

"You were good at that?" Sarah asked.

"My dad was an ace!" Annie said, whisking past the island and going to the backdoor, joining in the conversation as easily as if she'd been involved all along...or eavesdropping from the dining room. "Come on, Timmy. Let's make sure we got all the eggs Sarah hid."

"Check the cherry and apple trees. You never know," Sarah called out as the children pounded across the kitchen floor and down the porch stairs to the yard. Beau lifted his head from his doggie bed and jumped up, rushing after them.

Luke continued, "By that time we had all pretty much learned how to live our lives and do things the navy wanted us to. I certainly knew I'd changed. The restricted diet alone was killer. Everything was so fast-paced and every hour seemed to go by in a rush. We were in classrooms and then out. I didn't have much time to notice anything anyone else was doing. I had a hard time keeping myself from exhaustion and just going and going. I wanted to be the best of the best."

"What does that mean?" Maddie asked.

"Back then, I wanted to be a navy SEAL."

Sarah sucked in a breath. "You didn't tell me that."

"It's in the past. And yes, I succeeded. That's why I was in Iraq and Afghanistan, which I don't like to talk about. Maybe another time," Luke said with finality.

"Okay," Sarah said reassuringly.

Luke took her hand and kissed it, then turned back to Maddie. "So, as I was saying. By this point, we trusted the other hundred guys in our division. They'd been strangers only a month before, but now we all knew we were each other's lives. We were a team. Then we went into firefighting and shipboard damage-control classes. By the end of this training we all had to go inside a tear gas chamber. While we were exposed to the gas, we had to recite our names and social security numbers. It was quite a test to see who could last and who couldn't."

"Some didn't make it?" Maddie asked. "Even after all that training?"

"Some didn't," Luke answered. "Then we had Pass and Review, which was when we received our caps. It was our graduation, essentially. My parents were very proud. Jenny was there," he said with a smile born of fond memories but without the old grief and pain Maddie used to read on his face.

"But you don't remember if Nate's family was there?" Maddie inquired, too much hope riding on this fragile piece of Luke's memory.

As far as she was concerned, that one bit of information would tell her if Nate's disappearance had been a family conspiracy.

"I was so involved with my own triumphs that day that, honest to God, I didn't pay attention to any of the other guys. We had all been living out of each other's pockets for so long that I think on that one day, I just wanted to focus of my other life."

"I understand," Maddie said. "And you deserved that. It's a huge accomplishment to make it through any military boot camp. And if I haven't said it before, thank you for your service, Luke."

"You're welcome."

Maddie looked down at her hand. "I guess I shouldn't have punched him, huh?"

Sarah and Luke were silent.

"If I'd known all he's been through, I would have thanked him as well."

"But you didn't know," Sarah reminded her.

"Was he in Iraq or Afghanistan with you, Luke?"

"No. When we were in classes during boot camp, he was in medic training. He's a doctor now."

"A doctor?" Maddie and Sarah exclaimed in unison.

"That's what the business card he gave me says."

Maddie wiped her face with her palm. "That's a big piece of my puzzle, Luke."

"It is?"

Maddie nodded. "Nate told me he thought he wanted to be a doctor, but I suppose I didn't put much stock in it at the time. We all changed our minds every month about what we wanted to do after graduation. He was all set to go to Purdue and study agriculture. So, I just figured he really hadn't made up his mind yet. Frankly, we didn't talk about much that was all that serious back in those days. We were too busy—" She turned around and glanced out the window to make sure the children were still outside and out of earshot. "We were too busy kissing and hugging each other." She smiled to herself. "Anyway, I do remember him telling me that when he was thirteen or fourteen, he'd seen one of his father's horses give birth and nearly die. Ever since then, he'd been hooked on the medical field. Apparently one day he just knew he was meant to be a heart surgeon."

She stopped abruptly and thought deeply

about what she'd just said. She hadn't remembered that incident with Nate all these years, and now it had come back to her in a very clear flash. She wondered how she could have forgotten it.

"But the Barzonnis are all farmers and businessmen," Sarah mused.

"It's pretty obvious that Angelo wanted his sons to work on their farm. He demanded that Nate go to Purdue just like Gabe and Rafe. Just before he left town he told me that he had everything set for his freshman year at Purdue. There was so much that Nate kept to himself. I just can't remember if we discussed his father being an impediment to his dream."

Luke picked up a slice of apple and munched on it. "So what did you want to be, Maddie?" he asked her.

"I didn't have a goal, really. I knew I wanted something better for myself than just working the line like my mother. I did dream of being my own boss and having my own business, but I didn't have any real concept of what I would do. I knew I wasn't going to college, so I tried to cram as much knowledge and experience into those high school years as possible. But I knew that education was incredibly important for both me and

Nate. So, I suppose when Nate talked about his dreams, I must have been supportive. I just wish I remembered." Maddie looked up at Sarah and Luke. "You know, guys, this has been really good for me. For so long, all I've done is stay angry at Nate for abandoning me. Instead of trying to learn what really happened, it was easier for me to just hate him and blame him for our breakup. I can see now that there were all kinds of issues going on with both of us. He was incredibly focused. To be honest, Luke, I would have to say that my goal back then was to be Nate's girl. It's a seventeen-year-old's dream. And I've clung to it far too long."

Luke gave Maddie a compassionate smile. "I can tell you one thing—the navy changes boys to men. The Nate you knew is probably not the one I knew, and he's not the one you saw today at the lodge. Even I don't know this guy. I haven't seen him in ten years. I went to war and came back. Got married, had kids and lost my wife. Now I'm starting a new life. So much can happen in ten years, Maddie."

"So you're saying?"

Luke inhaled deeply. "Here's his cell-phone number," he said, reaching into his pants' pocket for Nate's business card. "Call him.

Talk to him. I have no idea if you'll even like this new guy. He could be married, divorced or even a widower like me. There are a million things that could have happened to him."

Maddie looked down at the card that somehow swam before her eyes. A tear fell from her eye. "And all that while I stayed shut off in a time warp of my own making. I didn't do any of those things."

"That's not true," Sarah retorted. "You built your business and you have all kinds of friends. You helped Luke and me with the renovation of St. Mark's. You have a national franchise all put together. I think that's quite a lot."

Maddie looked at the card again. She took out her phone and typed Nate's number into her contacts list. She handed the card back to Luke. "Thanks. I...I'll have to think about it. Maybe I could send him some flowers to apologize for punching him and be done with it."

Sarah pursed her lips. "Where's that Maddie spunk we all love so much? You're always willing to take on an argument for argument's sake just because you like the energy of the fight. I'm with Luke. Call him. And while you're at it, ask him how it was that Gina knew exactly who you were."

Luke turned away from both women. "Okay. I think I'll check on the kids." He headed out the backdoor.

"Come again?" Maddie asked.

"When Gina and Angelo came to Nate's rescue after you stormed out of the dining room, Gina suggested that she knew who you were. If his family never knew a whole lot about you, then why would she instantly guess, after eleven years, that Maddie Strong was the one woman in Indian Lake who would cause a scene with her son?"

"We never had sex."

"I know that."

"But that was the problem."

"Excuse me?"

"On the night he left me, he begged me to run away to Kentucky and get married so that we could sleep together, but…"

Sarah leaned closer. "But…what?"

Maddie clamped her palms to her cheeks. "I told him we couldn't just run away. I told him…" She ran her fingers across her forehead as if making deep trenches there would unearth the long-buried truth. "I told him that he had to think about his career in medicine.

Deep down, I knew it was what he really wanted. I remember the look on his face. It was as if I'd speared him, gutted him. He went pale right there under the porch light. He told me he couldn't go on any longer the way we had. But I was terrified of getting pregnant. I didn't want to be like my mother. I did dream of a big wedding with all the Barzonnis there giving us their blessing. I wanted it all. I told him nothing had to change. I told him I was happy with the way things were."

"You said that?" Sarah asked incredulously.

"I did."

"So, in fact, Maddie, you turned *him* down. You said no to his proposal."

Maddie shook her head. "He left me. He abandoned me."

"Only after you rejected him."

Maddie wasn't quite sure she'd heard Sarah correctly. Had she really rejected Nate? Had he really been serious about running away together? At the time, she had thought it was just another line to coerce her to give in. He was out of high school now, life was changing for him and soon he'd be going away to Purdue. She still had senior year left. He hadn't given her a ring. He hadn't gotten down on his knee. Very little of it felt like a real proposal. Was Sarah right? To Nate, had his real marriage proposal been real? He'd been the one who had always said he didn't want to get married. He wanted to travel and go to college. That's all he'd talked about. Maddie hadn't taken him seriously.

Not at all.

"Oh, God. I can't breathe," Maddie said, grabbing her stomach, then her forehead.

"You want some water?"

"How about straight hemlock?"

Sarah went to the sink and drew a glass of filtered water from the narrow spigot. She handed it to Maddie. "Want a slice of lemon for that?"

"No, thanks. It's sour enough without it."

Sarah sat down on the stool next to Maddie and took her hand. "All this time, you didn't remember your part in this legendary breakup of yours?"

"I didn't. Or worse…I blocked it out," Maddie continued, "But he never called me after that. Not once. I was worried silly for over a year about him."

"I would truly think through everything you want to say to Nate when you do talk to him. I'd be prepared for everything, like Luke said. That includes the possibility that he's got a wife somewhere. I don't think there are any children because he seemed shocked that Luke had kids already. So, that's probably not an issue."

"Kids? I can't imagine myself with kids. I mean, someday, maybe. But not yet."

"Really? You haven't thought about it?"

"I told you. I've been stuck in a time warp. I still think of myself as seventeen." Maddie delivered her statement with a jaunty flip of her hand through her short hair, but the gesture died awkwardly. It was time to stop fooling herself.

"Then this has been a very good day for you, Maddie. The truth is, you're not seventeen anymore, and now you can see that clearly. If you continue to think of the past and what happened with Nate the way you have been, you could miss out on the greatest opportunities of your life. Don't you find it interesting that at the same time as you're expanding your business, and even considering a move to Chicago, Nate appears here in Indian Lake after all this time like a…"

"Ghost?"

"A sign from God was what I was thinking."

"What does the sign say, Sarah?"

"Know all your options. Weigh them carefully. Choose wisely."

A cloud of gloom settled over Maddie. "I thought signs were supposed to make things easier."

"Who told you that?"

"I think I read it on a needlepoint pillow at Celebrations To Go."

"Well, there's always the other route to take," Sarah offered.

"What's that?"

"Don't deal with Nate at all. Don't call him. Don't rehash the past. You've now dredged up the truth for yourself. You now remember exactly what happened that night. I'm sure he remembers it that way, too. The two of you ran into each other at the lodge by accident. You had an encounter...of sorts. And that's it. Finis."

Maddie considered Sarah's advice for a long and careful moment. "But what about the other time?"

"What are you talking about?"

"I saw him watching me when we were at the Bridal Corner. That was no accidental meeting. It was as if he had been following me."

"I forgot about that," Sarah replied, chewing her lower lip. "That's a very big point. Big."

"You know what that tells me, Sarah?"

"What?"

"I think Nate wants some answers from me."

"Oh, Maddie. I think he wants more than just answers."

"Yeah? Like what?"

"The first thing that comes to my mind is what you wanted this morning when you saw him."

"What's that?"

"Revenge."

CHAPTER TEN

THE MONTH OF May moved into Indian Lake on the strains of romantic ballads playing on the local radio station. Once the tourist season began the first weekend in May, most of the merchants in town piped the same music through their businesses because the nostalgic tunes kept the tourists shopping and spending money inside the antiques stores, restaurants, dress shops and local art galleries. As far as Maddie was concerned, every cup of coffee tasted better when one was listening to Frank Sinatra or Josh Groban.

Maddie lugged a commercial-size trash bag filled with empty sugar and flour sacks, egg cartons, butter boxes, milk cartons and dozens of other containers that had held the ingredients she'd used over the past two days. She'd received a plethora of orders, from prom parties to baptisms, family reunions, birthdays and anniversary celebrations. And she still had to manage her increasing daily business at the café.

Maddie was more than surprised at the number of catering orders she was receiving this year compared to last. When she asked her new customers how they'd heard of her, eighty percent of the responses were always the same. "We bought your cupcakes at the St. Mark's Summer Festival last year. We never forgot them."

The St. Mark's Summer Festival had been Sarah's brainchild to raise money for the renovation of St. Mark's Episcopal Church, which had been in deplorable shape. Sarah had talked many of the merchants in town into renting booths at the festival, then donating their profits to the church. It had been the best move Maddie had made, marketing- and advertising-wise, for her business. The festival had been held right after the Fourth of July parade. For the past thirty years, Indian Lake had drawn twenty thousand or more visitors to the town for the parade, and that number was likely to rise with the added attraction of the St. Mark's Summer Festival. Maddie had customers she'd never seen before. They came from a five-countywide area, and a great many of them had been from Chicago. She had also picked up three new vendors for her cupcakes in New Buffalo. One was another café and the other two were restaurants. Now she was baking and filling orders to beat the band, and she was making good profits.

She had worked until one in the morning the previous night, then woke up at five and worked another two hours this morning.

Like most single people in Indian Lake, Maddie lived in a renovated portion of one of the old Victorian mansions on or around Maple Avenue. Maddie lived with eighty-five-year-old Hazel Martin, a friend of Mrs. Beabots, who was as kind as Mrs. Beabots but not nearly as intriguing a character. Hazel's house was on Lily Avenue, and had been divided into three apartments back in the seventies. Hazel lived upstairs, where she could sit in her "Florida sunroom," a room with three walls of beveled-glass windows that looked out over the glorious trees of stately Maple Avenue and the equally lovely Lily Avenue. The house was three stories high, complete with a widow's walk and wraparound, turn-of-the-last-century porch. Maddie knew for a fact that Mrs. Beabots envied that porch a great deal. Hazel still hosted summer dinners on her porch and late-night bridge parties in the screened enclosure on the north side. Maddie had her own backdoor entrance and parked her van in the driveway so she could come in late and leave early when need be without disturbing Hazel or Gladys Wright, the piano teacher who lived in the smaller apartment next door. Fortunately for Maddie, Gladys gave all her lessons during the hours when Maddie was at the café.

Now that Maddie was on the verge of making some real money, she'd vaguely thought about moving. Uncle George had spoken to her about buying a house for the tax write-off, now that she needed to be concerned about such things. He'd suggested buying a Victorian so she could rent out several apartments, but what Maddie really wanted was a condo in Chicago.

She knew she didn't have enough money yet to even rent a second home, much less buy one, but still she dreamed about it. If she were in Chicago, she and Alex could meet with investors whenever necessary. They could go to lunch together and meet at the theater doors for an afternoon matinee. They would window-shop together and perhaps duck into a wine bar...

A gust of warm spring wind clawed at her pants' leg and then pushed the plastic recycle-bin top closed, bringing Maddie back to the present. Her thoughts had kidnapped her once again.

Maddie secured the trash-barrel lids and went back into the café, locking the backdoor behind her.

"Where to start?" She scratched the back of her neck and shook her short hair. She walked over to the line of six mixers, each a different jewel color to help her remember which cake was which when she was making up the batters.

She dumped sticks of salted butter into each stainless-steel bowl, lowered the beaters and turned on the machines to cream the butter.

As she measured out sugar, placing each measuring cup beside each mixer, she wondered just how much being a franchise owner was going to actually change her life.

Right now, her psyche was a tangled ball of string that rolled around in her belly, keeping her awake at night. Being honest with herself, she had to admit that she used her business to explain the fact that she couldn't sleep and hadn't slept the whole night through since Nate left Indian Lake.

She'd come to rely on her ability to blame Nate for all the pain in her life. Frankly, she should have meted it out a bit further. Her mother's lack of love was to blame for her feelings of inadequacy. Yet at the same time, because Maddie was so fiercely driven to prove she was better than her mother, that she could have a better life than her mother, her success was in part due to her mother.

Nate's impact on her life was the fuel she needed to push herself beyond her limits and take risks she might not have taken otherwise. She'd jumped at the chance to open the café with Ann Marie's help. She'd pursued each of her trademarks and patents with a vengeance. Buried deep in her heart had been the absolute necessity to prove herself to Nate. Secretly, she'd always known she would see him again someday. In those first weeks and months, even years, since he'd left Indian Lake, she'd looked for him down every street and at every gathering. She'd thought he would come back for her. But he never had.

And now, here he was.

But for what purpose?

He hadn't rushed to see her or call her. He'd spent more time talking to Luke than anyone else in town. Of course, after that punch she'd delivered, he'd probably never speak to her. She was surprised that she still felt a small pinch of rejection at the edges of her heart. She was surprised that he could still hurt her. She didn't know why his actions would elicit any response from her at all.

It made no sense.

Maybe she needed to see a counselor as Sarah had done when she went to the bereavement group. Maybe a trained professional could explain the psychology to Maddie. Yes, that was what needed to be done. Then she could check Nate off her list for good.

Maddie, you fool. You thought you were over Nate years ago. She swiped her palm over her face. *Seventeen. What does anyone know at seventeen?*

Being excruciatingly brutal about herself, Maddie accepted that back in high school, she had loved Nate. She had loved him completely, utterly, naively, with that kind of first love that only the young experience. The kind of love that allows the young to dive head, heart and soul first without reservation or experience to throw off caution and red flags.

It was this young love that Maddie had read about in poetry and the romantic novels in high school. Perhaps her studies had meant so much to her back then because that world of emotion was the world in which she was immersed with Nate.

It was a childhood thing.

But not a *childish* thing, she had now come to realize.

She and Nate had both gone their separate ways, growing and changing their views of the world. Or maybe they hadn't changed so much.

The fact was that Nate had come back here to Indian Lake.

Nate was a doctor now. He'd fulfilled his dream, and she was happy about that.

Maddie hauled a twenty-five-pound bag of flour out of the bottom cabinet. She felt the muscles strain in her lower back.

Maddie had to admit she couldn't keep up this pace for much longer. She was going to need her rest or she'd get sick. For the first time, she seriously considered hiring someone to help her do the night baking. If she had a helper, she could get her own baking done between five and seven, have a normal dinner, maybe even with friends, and be in bed by nine. It was doable.

She looked out the small kitchen window and realized the sun had just broken the dawn. It was another day. A new day.

That meant she had another twenty-four hours during which she would wrestle with herself over the problem of what to do about Nate.

Blunt self-honesty told her that the real reason she pushed herself so hard was that if she was working ninety to nothing, then she didn't have to think about Nate. And right now, the last thing she wanted was to be reminded that she had Nate Barzonni's cell number in her phone. And she still had not called him.

Since Easter Sunday, when she'd delivered her much-gossiped-about punch to his stomach, her one constant thought was that until she picked up the phone and called him, she would not have her answers.

Oh, she had tried.

With her hand shaking, she'd picked up the phone a dozen times to place the call. She'd chickened out every single time.

Though she'd rehearsed what she would say to him, she kept changing her mind. Her conversation with Sarah on Easter Sunday had replayed so many times in her brain, the tape had been stripped of all meaning, until she didn't know what was conjecture and what was real.

The bottom line was that she would never know the truth until she talked to Nate. Her decision now was whether she wanted to do that at all.

She was terrified that Sarah had been right. If it was true that she had pushed Nate away, that he hadn't abandoned her as she had told herself he had for eleven years, then she had based her entire adult existence on a self-inflicted lie.

"Self-inflicted" was the operative key.

She had to face the fact that the Maddie she had chosen to believe she was wasn't the real Maddie at all. Maddie had been holding a self-sabotaging pity party for herself since high school, and she had blamed Nate's abandonment on her family and social status. Deep down, she hadn't thought she was good enough.

Maddie longed for a new start. *In Chicago? With Alex?*

Thinking about Alex, Maddie realized all too clearly that while she did want to be successful, mostly she wanted a life filled with joy and friends and good times. Maddie couldn't help wondering what her life would have been like if she had faced up to her participation in her breakup with Nate back when they were seventeen. Would she have left Indian Lake? Would he have had to leave the way he did, surrounded in mystery and secrets?

Maddie added the eggs and flavoring to the sugar and butter, then slowly folded in the sifted dry ingredients.

She placed colorful paper cupcake holders in greased muffin tins, then measured the batter into each holder. She placed the first batch of cupcakes into the oven and set the timer.

Maddie went to her office and checked the phone for messages.

"Hi, Maddie. Jake here from New Buffalo. Say, we had a killer crowd this weekend already. So, I'm going to ramp up our standing order. I'm going to need three dozen cupcakes on a daily basis. Then eight dozen for Saturday and Sunday. Sorry, I mean sixteen dozen for the weekends. Let's see how that works out. Give me half chocolates of various kinds. Your choice. Then lots of lemon and strawberry. Nothing healthy. Surprise me. They all sell, so it doesn't matter. If there's a problem, give a ring. Ciao."

"Are you kidding me?" Maddie smiled as she scratched notes into her order binder. The next message came on. "I'm trying to reach Maddie Strong of Cupcakes and Coffee Café. This is Mia at Alex Perkins's office. I'm calling to confirm your appointment with Alex on Tuesday with both Alex and Mr. Stapleton. Alex told me to tell you that he expects the meeting will take about three hours and he is looking forward to seeing you. He will call you personally as well."

She hit the recorder again. This time it was Alex's voice. "Hey, beautiful. I left a message on your cell, but it must not have gone through, so I'm trying the café. I'm going to send a car for you on Tuesday. I'll give you details later. Call me when you can. I'll be in the office at eight. Take care."

The recorder beeped.

Maddie sank into her office chair and ran her fingers through her hair. "Wow. A real investor." She stared at the phone. *Alex.*

She felt the blood in her veins turn to ice as she faced the unknown. She balled her fists. "I can do this," she told herself and glanced at herself in the antique gilt mirror she'd hung on the wall next to her desk so that she could always check her hair and lipstick before greeting customers. "I can do this. I want to do this. I will succeed in doing this."

Her gleaming green eyes stared back at her. The girl in the mirror seemed genuinely confident. It was not bravado. She believed what she said.

Maddie rose from the chair and went to the front of the café and turned the closed sign around to open. She unlocked the door and started back toward the counter to finish preparing the coffeepots for the self-serve counter.

She passed by her vintage Vesubio Espresso Machine, which she'd won on a bid on eBay. The machine was her pride and joy, and truly a focal point of the café's decor. The top, which was emblazoned with an eagle motif and the name of the unit, lifted off to reveal the basket for the coffee inside. The copper-and-brass unit was heavy, impossibly well made and fourteen inches tall and about six inches wide. She hoped she could convince James Stapleton that it would be a signature move to install Vesubio espresso/cappuccino machines in all her franchise shops.

Maddie took a deep breath, remembering George's warning that all negotiations were a matter of compromise, and not to get her heart set on any one detail. The moment she did, the deal would be dead. She knew she'd have to make a lot of compromises in order to turn profits because that was what investors cared about.

As always, the unit heated up quickly. The first cup of coffee she made each morning was for her personal consumption. There was always enough steam left over for the milk. Because all espresso machines held the danger of building up too much steam and exploding, she never let Chloe use the machine. If someone wanted espresso, cappuccino or latte, Maddie was the barista.

Although, if James did invest in her franchise, Maddie would be expected to help with the opening of the first cafés. Circumstances would force her to loosen the reins. Chloe would be the barista in Indian Lake.

So many changes.

She took out one of her oversize, white stoneware cappuccino cups and saucers, still warm from the industrial dishwasher, and started her cappuccino.

She steamed the milk and spooned it on top

of her coffee, then drew a leaf design through the foam. It was an unnecessary touch that she, as the owner, probably shouldn't spend the time doing, but Maddie wouldn't have a minute to herself for the rest of the day. This was her treat.

As she finished the leaf design, the little bell over the café door jingled.

"Be right with you," Maddie said without looking up from her pretty cappuccino.

"Maddie?"

His voice struck her heart with a strong hand, like that of a Greek god who came to earth to enchant humans and make them dance to his will.

She continued to stare at the dissipating foam in her coffee. He couldn't possibly be here. Not here, on her sacred ground.

"Can I talk to you?" Nate asked.

She raised her head slowly and gazed at him.

His blue eyes were like long-remembered azure summer skies so crystal clear, it stung to look at them.

"No," she heard herself reply.

She walked up to him and without another word, she kissed him.

CHAPTER ELEVEN

FROM THE INSTANT her lips touched his, they were like kids again, so intensely in love there was no room in their world for anything else. Time seemed just a tick off, a second slower than real time. Their love was familiar, it was safe and they'd found it again.

Nate's arms went around Maddie's waist and to the small of her back. She held the nape of his neck, let her fingers remember his strength. Tracing the slope of neck where it met with his shoulders and back, just under the collar of his jacket and shirt, her fingers settled into their familiar grooves, comforted by the sameness of it all. She tilted her head and slanted her mouth over his again, taking in his smell of vanilla and spice. He held her so tightly, she thought she would never breathe again.

She hadn't asked any of the right questions of him. But she'd been through so much confusion in the past few weeks, the truth to her was that the angels were blessing her in this moment. She had wanted to see him, she understood now. To be with him. She wanted to pretend the past eleven years had never happened. She wanted to know if his kisses would ever be, could ever be, how she remembered them.

And they were.

And more.

She honestly didn't know how she was standing on her own legs without the support of his arms. Reining herself in was absolutely out of the question. This moment might never come to her again. She let the last of her recalcitrant emotions out of her heart. The kiss was thrilling and reckless and frightening.

Just then, the bell over the front door dinged. "Hey, Maddie!" Chloe Knowland said as she shut the door behind her.

Maddie jerked out of Nate's arms in a flash. She smoothed her hair. Nate swiped his palm over his face.

"Hey, Chloe. Good morning," Maddie said. "Cappuccino's up. You want one?"

Chloe looked at Nate, nodded as she would to any stranger, and walked past him to stash her purse and jacket in Maddie's office. "I'll pass. Maybe a latte later. I'll get busy on the cooked icings."

"You do that. I was just getting a cappuccino for…" Maddie caught Nate's eye and smiled. "Our customer."

"Cool. Did you get the cash drawer out yet?"

"No." Maddie continued to stare at Nate. His eyes delved into hers.

"I'll do it," Chloe shouted from the office.

Nate took a step closer to Maddie. He smoothed the back of her hair. "I still want to talk to you," he said.

"Yeah?" She felt her mouth go dry. Suddenly, she was so nervous. She felt like a robber who'd just been caught during a jewel heist.

"Should I come over to your house tonight?" he asked.

"My mother's house by the tracks? I don't live there anymore."

He stuck his hands in his pockets. "Stupid. Of course you don't. That was a long time ago."

"Yeah. Long time." She looked down at the floor. She felt so shy she almost didn't recognize her own reactions. Two minutes ago she was kissing him, and now she was tongue-tied and couldn't think of a thing to say.

"How about lunch?"

"That's my busy time. It's just Chloe and me, and we get a good crowd for our bagel and croissant sandwiches."

"Okay. You name it. Tonight, dinner—I don't care. But Maddie…" He took her hand. "Can we make it soon? I'm only in town for two days."

Her head snapped up and she stared at him. "You're going away again?"

"It's a long story. But I'll be back soon. And I need to talk to you first. Tonight. I can meet you."

"Well, okay. Seven o'clock. Come back here. But only if you answer one question first."

"What's that?"

"Did you, er, I mean, you've been gone a long time. Are you married?"

Nate peered blankly at her for a long moment, as if he hadn't heard the question right. "Me?"

"Yes. You."

"But you're the one getting married," he countered with a distinct grimace of loss.

"Where did you get that idea?"

"I saw you. Through the window at the Bridal Corner. You were wearing a wedding gown. When is the wedding?"

A vengeful smile played across Maddie's lips, but she quickly licked it away. In her new life, she wasn't going to allow even minuscule flutters of sabotaging emotions to take root in her psyche. The new Maddie would be built on truth and understanding, respect for others, honesty and fairness. She wasn't going to play games in any of her relationships. "I'm not engaged and I'm not getting married. I was trying on the dress for Sarah. We're planning her wedding. It's at the end of June. It's going to be—"

"You were beautiful," he said, interrupting her. "I thought you were the most beautiful woman I'd ever seen. I swear, my heart fell right out of my chest when I saw you."

"Really?"

"Yeah. There's no one for me, either," he said.

She pursed her lips. "I know there isn't," she said confidently.

"Oh, ho. How's that?"

"A man who kisses a woman like you just kissed me cannot possibly be with anybody else."

"I was thinking the same thing myself," he said and kissed her very soundly on the mouth before leaving through the front café door.

CHAPTER TWELVE

AT THREE MINUTES to seven, Nate rapped on the café door and Maddie, who had been waiting anxiously, unlocked it for him.

"Hi, Nate," Maddie said, gazing into his handsome face. His blue eyes blazed right through her like early dawn striking the horizon. She stood back for him to enter.

She was still wearing her work clothes, though she'd freshened her makeup. He leaned over and kissed her cheek. Just the feel of his lips on her skin made her tingle all over. She didn't know if she'd just shivered, but she should have.

She just knew her cheeks were flaming.

I could have laid off the blusher, she chided herself.

"How are you tonight?" she asked.

"Tired. Can we sit?"

"Sure."

Nate took a step back and Maddie led him to the little round table in the corner by the window. He gently placed his hand on the small of her back, just as he used to when they walked anywhere together. She had forgotten this simple gesture, forgotten how protected, even cherished, she had felt when he did it. She wondered now if he treated all women that way, or if it was a special gesture, meant only for her. She had to guess there had been dozens of women for him over the past decade. Maybe more.

While Nate sat, Maddie pulled the café curtains closed.

"Afraid of being seen with me?" he said with a wry smile.

"No one needs to know we're here," she replied, moving nervously toward the counter. "I'll get us a cappuccino."

"It's okay," he said. "I came to see you."

"I know, but you look like you're asleep on your feet." She ground the beans and steamed the milk, then drew tall pine trees in the foam. She grabbed two yellow cloth napkins and two spoons, then placed the coffee in front of him. "Here's some natural sugar if you like."

"Thanks," he said, adding a spoonful to the coffee. "This is gorgeous." He cast her an appreciative eye as he took his first sip.

Without a word, he sipped three more times. Putting down the mug, he exclaimed, "Even in Italy I haven't had cappuccino this delicious. How—"

"I buy my beans from a great Italian supplier in Chicago. Giovanni is the best. He's shown me a lot of ropes," she said, tasting her own drink.

"Maddie, I'm sorry."

She froze. "What?"

He grabbed her hand before she could hide it in her lap. "I should have told you everything."

The old Maddie would have thrown her napkin in Nate's face and stormed off without allowing him to talk. But the old Maddie hadn't gotten her too far with Nate. In fact, she had now backtracked all the way to the beginning. They did have a lot to talk about, and because she had absolutely no clue how any of this would turn out, she did the one thing she had never truly done before. She listened.

"I should have told you where I was going," he said.

"The navy?"

"Yes. The navy." He took a very deep breath and took a drink of his cappuccino.

"That year was a hard year for me, Maddie. Torture, in some ways. A lot of ways. There was more going on than I ever told you about. I don't know why I didn't talk to you about it…"

"Nate. Be honest. We didn't do much talking." She laughed.

"I guess you're right. Still, in so many ways, you were my best friend."

"I was?" Maddie sat back in the chair. She hadn't expected praise.

He nodded. "All my life, my parents— my father, especially—talked about how we brothers would inherit different parts of the business. They expected every one of us to go on working for them, and only them. They never asked Gabe or Rafe or Mica what they wanted to do. They sure never asked me. They had our high school years all planned out. They wanted each of us to go to Purdue and major in agriculture or business and then be indentured to them for the rest of our lives. They expected us to keep the business going for the next generation and the next."

Nate raked his fingers through his hair and his words tumbled out at a quicker pace.

"Mica tried to stand up to them once, but he got blasted back so fast I don't know if he's ever had the guts to face them down again. I'm not sure what it was all about, because he won't talk about it even now. But there's some kind of fire in his belly and it has nothing to do with the Barzonni millions, I can tell you."

"And you? You told me you dreamed of becoming a doctor."

"That's just it, Maddie. I never told anyone else. Nobody. Not the school's guidance counselor. Not my brothers. Definitely not my parents. No one. You were the only one who knew. And then, my senior year, life as I knew it was coming to an end. Once I graduated, I was going to have to go to Purdue and learn even more about tomatoes. I knew I was capable of more than that. I wanted so much more. I did want to see the world. I wanted to go places and learn things. I wanted to be a doctor. And I wanted to do it all on my own without owing my parents for my education."

Maddie folded her hands around her untouched cappuccino. She looked at the coffee with her foam artwork still floating on top. Unattended. Unappreciated. "And I was part of the problem. I was keeping you from your dream. Or was proposing to me part of your escape plan?"

"Honestly, it was both. But you were never the problem."

Maddie hated the fact that a tear fell from her eye and onto the table before she lifted her face to his. She'd always thought tears were weak, used to manipulate men into bending to the female will. All her life, she'd been able to bat them away, deny them, swallow them.

"When I look back on our relationship, I can see how I would have been a problem. A big problem. Especially if I'd have gotten pregnant."

"You were right then, and I thank you for it now. You were smarter than me."

Maddie snorted. "I doubt that."

"Think about it. Us. Back then. I was ready to grab you and drive all night to Kentucky. I would have given up all my dreams just to have you, Maddie. Everything. That's how badly I wanted you. But when you refused my proposal, that was the dousing of ice water I needed. You told me we had to think about our careers. You knew what I really wanted. You knew how many years it would take to go to college, then med school, internship and residency. You had the guts to do what I couldn't do."

"But Nate, I didn't realize what I was saying. I just didn't want us to sleep together. That's all. I thought I would see you the next day and the day after that. I didn't know I was pushing you away forever. That's not so brave, if you ask me."

"Your soul was brave. Your heart was brave, and you listened to your heart."

She shook her head vehemently. "You don't understand. Please don't be so nice to me. For eleven years I've hated you for ditching me that night. I told all my friends what a low-life creep you were. I've based this entire portion of my life on my hatred for you. I strove to succeed in my business so I could show you up. The thing is, I can almost understand why you might have wanted to break up after that night, but to just leave with no explanation? There was no way to get ahold of you. None of us knew where you went."

"I know. And I'm sorry. That was wrong of me. All I wanted was to escape and hide for as long as possible."

"Well, you sure did that." Maddie felt the old anger gnaw at her belly. She grimaced. "Did you tell your parents where you were going?"

"No way. They would have talked me out of it."

"When did you let them know?"

"I left them a letter telling them that I was fine—not kidnapped or anything—but that I had to go away for a while. I told them I would contact them after the summer was over. I knew that would give me time to get through boot camp."

"And?"

"I called them the night before graduation at Great Lakes. I figured that they and my brothers would never forgive me if they weren't there for the Review."

"Did they come?"

"Yes."

"So, your family has known your whereabouts for over a decade."

"Yes. Part of the reason they never said anything to anyone was that they were embarrassed. Well, my father was. He thought I'd brought shame on the family, not following the family tradition and all that. My brothers were happy for me, but they never said that to Mom or Dad."

"And how are they now?"

"My mother's resentment is totally gone. My father is another issue altogether. I think he's angry because I defied him. I proved that he didn't have control."

"So, you don't owe them any money. They still have three sons to run the farm and business. Yeah, I guess they would probably think they'd be pretty foolish not to let you back in the house. Better to have some relationship with their son than none at all."

"I guess that's what they figure," Nate said.

Nate finished the last of his coffee. "Maddie, I think you should know that I came back to Indian Lake to take a position with the Indian Lake Hospital."

Maddie blinked. She thought she'd heard him wrong. "You're moving back here?"

"Yes."

"When?"

"Right away. I just signed the contract today. This is a major opportunity for me. If I can excel here, I've got a real shot at my dream."

Maddie swallowed hard, feeling as if she was at the top of a roller coaster, about to plunge to the very bottom. "Your dream?"

"I want to go back to the Indian reservation where I worked for a year. They desperately need doctors."

"Where is that?"

"Arizona," he replied.

"That's...a long way from Indian Lake," she mused. *So, he* will *be leaving again.*

"Yeah. It is." He paused for a long moment. "It's a special place for me, Maddie. When I was there, I felt like for the first time in my life, I fit in. I can help so many—"

"That's a very big dream," she whispered. "Mine pales in comparison."

He looked around. "Your café?" Then he stared into her eyes. Slowly, he shook his head. "This isn't the end of the dream train for you, is it?"

"Not by a long shot. Let's just say I have some irons in the fire," she said proudly.

"That's cool," he replied, disappointment shadowing his eyes. He had hoped she would confide in him the way he had with her.

"I can't talk about it yet."

"I understand. Well, good luck, Maddie. You deserve it all, whatever it is."

"Thanks, Nate." She replied and paused for a moment looking at him quite seriously. "I'm sorry about hitting you."

Nate tried to hide his grin. "Uh, huh. In front of my family. And half the town."

"I shouldn't have done that," she said sheepishly. "I'm really sorry."

"But at the time you felt I had it coming,

right? I bet you felt better afterward," he offered.

She looked up at him. "But that's just it. After I calmed down, I felt terrible. Really bad."

He touched her cheek. "It's okay, Maddie, girl. I've had worse. And to be honest, it hurt me to realize how much pain I'd caused you all these years. I'd been selfishly going about my career and my life and I never tried to contact you." He peered deeply into her eyes. "You deserved better from me. I'm sorry, too."

Maddie felt her breath catch in her lungs as something inside her wanted this moment to stretch on for eternity. It was just like it had been when they were kids. Their hearts had barely been used, they were shiny and new and untouched by betrayal. Back then, Maddie thought she could see forever in Nate's eyes and at this moment, she felt exactly that. She couldn't imagine her world without Nate in it. But Nate had just said he wasn't back here to stay.

"Can I ask you a question?" She scanned his face, searching for the truth.

"Sure."

"Just when did you decide to sign the contract at the hospital?"

"I knew the job was mine, and like I said, it's a stepping stone…"

"Nate…when? Exactly?"

"Today. Shortly after I saw you this morning."

Pleasure lifted the corners of Maddie's mouth. "You mean, after I kissed you."

He snickered. "I thought I was kissing *you*."

She rolled her bottom lip between her teeth to keep her glee from filling the room. If she'd ever wanted revenge, this, whatever this was, was better.

"It's a one-year contract with a renewal every year if I want it."

"What will you be doing?"

"Cardiac surgery."

Maddie's eyes widened. "A heart surgeon? Open-heart surgery and all that? You can do that?"

"Yeah." He grinned.

"I just didn't think…"

"What kind of doctor did you think I'd be?"

She flipped her hands in the air, trying to knock away all her preconceived visions of Nate. This was not the boy who'd left her on the Fourth of July. This was a new Nate, a person she didn't know whose depths appeared to be vast. He'd spent his time away from her growing, improving himself, making things happen in his career. He'd defied his parents, served his country and now he was helping to save people. How many ways could she spell "hero"?

She tilted her head and shot him an assessing gaze. "I don't know, exactly. When you used to talk about being a doctor, I was thinking the normal stuff—coughs and colds and writing prescriptions for gout."

He shook his head. "You should know I would never do anything that was ordinary, Maddie."

"How would I know that?"

"I fell in love with *you* once, didn't I?"

CHAPTER THIRTEEN

Miss Milse, Sarah's middle-aged German housekeeper, carried a hot dish of potato, cauliflower and cheese casserole to the dining room table. Sarah was setting out an impromptu buffet supper for her girlfriends so that Maddie could share the exciting news about her upcoming meeting in Chicago. Aunt Emily was in the kitchen spreading a third coat of brown-sugar glaze on a baked ham. Charmaine Chalmers had brought several bottles of wine and champagne to celebrate. Sarah and Charmaine had pitched in to do the elevations, drawings and interiors of the proposed cafés, but Maddie had kept the news about her investor to herself. So anytime there was cause for celebration, Sarah and Maddie jumped at the chance to throw a party.

Luke, Annie and Timmy helped Maddie bring in four dozen cupcakes for their dessert. The kids were the first to notice the new pineapple upside-down-cupcake recipe Maddie would be testing on their guests that evening.

Mrs. Beabots tossed a green salad with red onion, strawberries, almonds, crisp, apple-smoked bacon and her own homemade hot-bacon dressing. Mrs. Beabots always made it a point to offer to make the salad herself, so no one ever really knew all the ingredients she put in the salad or the dressing.

Miss Milse's oxford shoes clomped against the kitchen floor as she walked up to Sarah. "You want your mudder's china plates or the kitchen plates?"

"Oh, that's a lovely idea, Miss Milse. This is a once-in-a-lifetime night."

"It is?" Miss Milse looked at Maddie, who was stacking cupcakes on a special, multi-tiered display tree.

"Very," Sarah whispered. "Maddie's store is going to become famous."

Miss Milse's small blue eyes brightened. "Famous? Like Justin Bieber?"

Sarah's jaw dropped. "You can't possibly know who Justin Bieber is."

"Yeah. I do. I like him. I hear his songs on the bus. The driver plays Justin Bieber. I ask him. He tells me that Justin Bieber famous."

"Well, Maddie won't be that kind of famous, but I suppose for Indian Lake, it might be a little bit like that."

"I understand," Miss Milse said as she hoisted the ham and carried it to the dining room table.

Maddie turned to Sarah. "I think I hear car doors slamming," she said.

"Why don't you get the door with Beau and the kids. Luke and I will get things done in here."

Maddie looked at Sarah. "Make sure Mrs. Beabots sits in that nice aqua French chair your mother always liked. I want her to be comfortable."

"Absolutely."

"Come on, Annie. Timmy," Maddie called. "Let's go see who's here."

Beau jumped from his sleeping bed and raced across the room with them.

Charmaine was setting up wineglasses and placing the wine in a special silver bucket that had been Ann Marie's. "Maddie, this is so exciting," Charmaine said as they passed through on their way to the door. "I'm just like everyone else. I can't wait to hear the details."

"I still can't believe it," Maddie said.

Charmaine cast an affectionate smile on

Maddie. "Anytime you need my help, you just ask. I'm so honored to be even a small part of your dream."

"Thank you for offering," Maddie replied.

Maddie continued to the door, where Olivia and Isabelle were waiting. They were quickly followed by Cate Sullivan, Chloe Knowland and Liz Crenshaw. They all began chatting happily on the porch steps.

Maddie and Sarah urged everyone to start the buffet, and Charmaine served the wine. Once they'd all filled their plates, Sarah asked everyone to gather in the living room, where Maddie would make her announcement.

Maddie stood at the fireplace and looked at the faces of all her dear friends beaming up at her with pride. Annie and Timmy sat on the floor at her feet, petting Beau. She noticed that Timmy was allowing Beau to lick the icing off his cupcake.

"As you all know, I wouldn't have gotten as far as going to Uncle George with my idea if Sarah and Mrs. Beabots hadn't pushed me so much over the past year to put my ideas down on paper, trademark my company and protect my recipes, and then finally put together a business plan."

"That took a lot of work!" Sarah interjected.

Maddie smiled. "Prodding me to do it or the paperwork and filing?"

"Both!" Sarah laughed, and everyone joined her.

"So true," Maddie admitted. "Once George came into the picture, things really started rolling. He told me how to improve the business plan since there were a few details missing from the research I did online. Anyway, George made some phone calls to his friends in Chicago, who steered him to Ashton and Marsh, and so now, here we are."

Cate Sullivan, always the businesswoman and always expecting specifics, asked, "So, is this truly a national franchise they are talking about?"

"Yes and no. My first and only investor at this point is from Chicago. He intends to open two locations. If they go well, he'll buy four to six more."

"And is it going to be just like your place here?" Liz Crenshaw asked.

"Somewhat. Sarah, Charmaine and I worked on some ideas that would be easy to incorporate into any space the new owner wants to try. We do have several signature

pieces, such as the Italian theme, a real cappuccino machine, the blend of coffee beans
I put together myself. Believe it or not, the
stainless-steel rack I hang my icing bags on is
a signature piece, as well as the display coun-
ters. And I want a yellow-and-white-striped
awning to hang over the entrance."

"You need to get one for Indian Lake first!"
Cate laughed.

"You're right. It's been something I've
wanted all along, but I've been so busy, I
never got it done."

"We forgive you." Cate laughed merrily
again.

George stepped up to Maddie and put his
coffee cup and saucer on the mantel. "May I
add something here?"

"Of course." Maddie stepped aside.

"I've only glanced over the documents
Maddie brought back from Chicago. Everything seems to be in order, but I want to study
them. The details shouldn't be shared with
anyone until after everything is finalized. But
I think it's safe to say that Maddie's Cupcakes
and Coffee Café is in the beginning stages
of becoming a franchise." George turned to
Maddie. "You have another meeting with
these people on Tuesday, is that right?"

Maddie nodded. "Yes. I'm meeting with Alex Perkins and the investor himself in downtown Chicago. They're sending a car for me."

Olivia gaped at her friend. "A car? You mean a limo? All the way from Chicago?"

"I don't know. I didn't ask. I was too stunned. Alex had a Lincoln Town Car that drove us to the restaurant last time."

"You had lunch? Where?" Isabelle asked.

"Bandera, I think. It was really nice. It was on the second floor so you could watch all the shoppers."

"Cool," Olivia muttered.

George cast a sideways glance at Emily, who caught his gesture. She rose from her chair. "Maddie brought cupcakes for us all and I have fresh coffee that was just brewed," she announced, then she turned to Maddie. "Let us all say, congratulations, Maddie! You deserve this success!"

"Yea, Maddie!" The cheer went up from the group.

Then the flurry toward the desserts began.

Maddie noticed that Annie and Timmy remained on the floor petting Beau and did not scurry quite as quickly as she would have expected. "Hey, guys. What's up? You don't want dessert?"

Timmy was sitting cross-legged with his little hand on Beau's head, stroking the golden retriever lovingly. "I don't want to disturb Beau. I don't get to see him as much as I'd like."

"And how much would that be?"

"Every day," Timmy replied.

"All day," Annie added as she looked up at Maddie. "Besides, we already snuck our cupcakes, and my dad would be mad if we ate more than one."

"Yeah, especially since it's nearly our bedtime," Timmy added sadly. "I wish our bedtime was at ten o'clock so I could pet Beau for a couple more hours. See how much he likes it?"

"Yes, he does," Maddie answered. "But before you know it, your dad and Sarah will be married, and then you'll be living here and you can pet Beau all night long if you want."

Timmy sunk his cheek into his palm with a very glum look. "It's taking forever for them to be married. I keep waiting and waiting. I don't see why we have to wait anymore. This is just stupid."

Annie exhaled deeply. "It's because of the

wedding. They have to finish planning the party and everything. It's a lot of work."

Timmy gazed up at Maddie again. "I don't need to have a party. I just want us all to be together and be a family."

Luke, who was listening to the entire exchange from the entrance to the dining room, walked over to them. "I agree with you, Timmy. I wish we were all together already, as well. But see, this is Sarah's wedding, and she wants it to be very special. Do you know why?"

"No."

"Because we're very special to her. We are a unique situation, when you think about it. She's not just getting married to some guy, she's getting a whole family all to herself. She'll have me and Annie and you. And I can't think of anything more wonderful than that, can you?"

Maddie stared at Luke with tears in her eyes. In all her life, she'd never heard a parent talk to a child the way Luke just had. And she'd never seen so much love and sincerity come from a man. Sarah was more than lucky to have found Luke.

Maddie had grown up without a dad and had seldom reflected on what a father's role should be. Watching Luke, she realized that someday, she actually would want children and a real home…and a man who truly loved her and cared for her.

What's happening to me? I've never had these thoughts before. Is it because of Nate?

"No, Dad," Timmy said. "I guess that does make us very special. But I still don't see why a party has to take so long to get here. Maddie and Sarah made this party in just one day and I think it's a really good one," Timmy said.

Luke looked up at Maddie and saw her tears.

Quickly, she wiped them away with her fingertips.

You okay? he mouthed.

She nodded. "You just have the most wonderful kids. And Sarah is so blessed to have you."

A smile born of understanding and humility curved his lips. "I'm the lucky one here. And there's no question in my mind that Sarah was heaven sent to me." He looked down at Annie and Timmy who were watching him. "No question."

Just then, Maddie's cell phone rang. It was Alex.

"Hey, beautiful! Excited about tomorrow night? I am," he said breathlessly.

"I am. I just told my friends you were sending a car. They're very impressed."

"Really? Good. I'll send one every week. That should bowl them over. Anyway, I just wanted to check in and see how you're doing."

"You're working?"

"On your deal. As always. Nothing I wouldn't do for my beautiful girl."

"Thanks, Alex," she said with a smile as Sarah walked by. Maddie turned away from Sarah's probing eyes and went to a corner to finish her call. "Listen, I have to go."

"Call me after you're in the car and on your way. We can talk then. Have a good time tonight," he said. "Be well."

"Good night." She hung up, looking down at her phone. Alex was truly going the extra mile for her. She wondered if he worked this hard for all his clients, or whether his dedication was tied to the crush he clearly had on her.

George walked up to Maddie and placed his hand on her elbow. "Could we step over here? I'd like to have a word."

"Sure. What's wrong?" Maddie asked.

George led her to the far corner of the

living room near a pair of upholstered club chairs and an English Hepplewhite table with a crystal lamp on it.

"Before you go to Chicago and meet the investor, I want to see you to go over a few points in the contract."

"Is there anything wrong?"

"Not wrong. But I want to make certain you understand the particulars. Mostly just legalities."

"Okay."

"When you meet with him, you ask any questions you feel like. From this first investor, all others will come. He needs to believe that you're not desperate or needy in any way."

"But I'm not."

"If he were to meet with you and decided he didn't want to go through with the deal, would you be disappointed?"

"Yes. No. I…" She looked around the room at her friends who were all chattering about her news. She turned back to George. "I would go back to things as they were."

"Precisely. And we would try to find another investor. That's the truth of it. But the other side of it is that it might never happen again."

Maddie looked down at her wineglass. "I see what you're saying."

"Maddie, I also think you should pay Austin McCreary a visit."

"Austin...."

"If Ann Marie hadn't gone to him and talked him into putting up the loan money for you to start your business, you wouldn't have Cupcakes and Coffee at all."

"I've paid him back in full. You know that, don't you?"

"Yes, you told me when we worked on the business plan. He never signed any kind of paperwork that entitles him to your recipes or concepts, so legally, he can't sue you for any of the money from the franchise. But anybody can sue anybody for anything. Winning is another matter."

"Sue me?" Maddie's eyes flew wide open. "Why in the world would he do that?"

"Greed. I don't know how his family actually made all their money. It's none of my business."

"A lawsuit." Maddie put her palm on her flaming cheek. "Uncle George..." She was once again filled with fear of the unknown.

"All these issues are part of the world you enter when you become a big business.

You've been lucky that someone hasn't pulled a lawsuit on you already, blaming you for an allergic reaction to a cupcake or coffee that was steamed too hot. Remember that lawsuit against McDonald's? The woman who spilled the brew on herself? She won."

"Oh, God."

"I'm just saying these are all situations that can happen to you, so I want to make very, very certain you're legally protected all the way around."

"I understand." She nodded.

"Try to see Austin soon so that he hears about the franchise from you and not from Helen Knowland. I like Helen, but she is such a gossip." He shot a glance at Chloe, Helen's granddaughter.

"You won't believe this, but I had Chloe sign a letter of agreement that any conversations she overheard at the café, or anything I said on the phone with my suppliers or anyone else, had to remain private or she would be fired instantly."

"You did that? And she signed it?"

"Yes. She wanted the job."

"Good going." George smiled and put his arm around Maddie's shoulder.

Emily approached with a cupcake on a dessert plate. "May I interest you in a cupcake, George?"

"Actually, I had my eye on one of those red velvet ones. Excuse me," he said and walked away.

Emily smiled at her husband and then focused her gaze on Maddie. "We are all so happy for you, Maddie."

"Thanks. I think." Maddie sighed heavily.

"Oh, George does that to everyone when there are legalities involved. Enjoy the moment. All the rest will be work, and you know that. But I was curious about one thing."

"What's that?"

"I noticed all your friends were here. I was surprised you didn't invite Nate."

"Nate?" Maddie stared at Emily blankly.

"Did you forget about him?"

"No, I didn't forget. Believe me. But he hasn't been here for the past eleven years, while I've scrimped to make all this happen. He hasn't been part of my crowd, I guess. I thought I would talk to him privately."

After their conversation at the café, she'd been surprised at how easily their friendship had returned. But she'd held back from inviting him. Was it because she knew he was only going to live in Indian Lake for a year?

Or was it because she wanted to keep him as a friend and nothing more? Each time she thought about Nate, she was more confused than ever.

"Good. One-on-one is very good," Emily replied, then bit into her chocolate-fudge cupcake.

CHAPTER FOURTEEN

NATE FINISHED HIS morning rounds by seven o'clock and began a scheduled ablation procedure at seven-thirty. His surgical nurse was Sophie Mattuchi, whom he'd known since high school. He hadn't heard a thing about her skills or reputation, but he made it his business to read over her file. Sophie had signed on at Indian Lake Hospital as a registered nurse out of Bronson School of Nursing in Michigan, and she'd gone to Indiana University Hospital–Indianapolis for two years for further training. She'd been back in Indian Lake for the past three years and everyone on staff liked and respected her.

From a private interview with Sophie, he discovered that she had helped care for Ann Marie Jensen in her off-duty hours during the woman's last days.

Sophie had thirty ablations under her belt by the time Nate was hired at the new cardiac center. Her experience at this point wasn't much more than his.

Though Dr. Caldwell believed that this procedure would take approximately three hours, Nate wasn't quite so sure. The patient, fifty-year-old Gwen Petrowski, had undergone a triple-bypass surgery seven years earlier. She'd had two angioplasties and one stent put in. Studying the patient's records and X-rays, he saw that she didn't smoke or drink, which was encouraging. Unfortunately, she had a great deal of heart disease in her family history. Until eighteen months ago, her arrhythmias had been somewhat controlled by medication. But recently they had increased in intensity and length according to the readouts from her Holter Monitor test.

After scrubbing in and donning his sterile face mask, surgical gown, cap and booties, Nate entered the O.R. The nurses wheeled the gurney in and moved the patient onto the operating table.

Nate stood over his patient wearing his face mask, surgical gown, cap and booties. "Gwen, can you hear me? They gave you something to make you very drowsy. You're in the EP lab now. You won't feel anything as I insert this catheter into your groin and then as it goes into your heart."

"I'm scared," she said, trying to move her hand, but it had been strapped down.

Nate leaned over and peered into her frightened eyes. "You're going to be fine. Everything is going to be just fine." He touched the top of her head, which was covered in a surgical bonnet. "You believe me, don't you?"

"Yes," she replied, closing her eyes slowly. "I believe you."

The anesthesiologist injected the drugs into Gwen's IV.

Nate turned to Sophie. "Do you have the catheter ready?"

"Yes, Doctor," Sophie answered. She stood at his side waiting for further instructions. "You just lead the way."

Nate looked down at his patient. "You relax, now, Gwen. We're going to fix this heart up for you. You'll feel like a young girl again."

Gwen tried to smile, but she was already falling asleep. "Promise?"

"I promise you that," Nate said.

Nate began the procedure by numbing the area of Gwen's groin where he would insert the thin guide wire. Along with the catheter and guide wire was an intravascular ultrasound catheter that Nate would direct up the blood vessel and into Gwen's heart. He used a special dye that would help him place the catheter in the right spot.

"Sophie, I need another catheter here," Nate said, extending his right hand.

Sophie placed another catheter wire in his gloved hand.

Nate went back to work, watching his progress on three different screens.

In an adjoining room were twelve computer screens that helped other nurses and assistants chart the procedure.

"Sophie, I want pictures of everything here. I think we have an upper-valve problem that may be trickier than we'd thought," Nate said, studying the monitor.

"I'm sorry. I thought we were doing this procedure because the lower chambers of the heart were in question."

"That's my point. We may have to do both."

"I understand, Doctor."

"This is going to take all morning, if not longer. So buckle up, boys and girls," Nate said with a low laugh.

For the next several hours, Nate used the electrodes at the end of the catheters to stimulate the heart. Once this was done, he could locate the exact position of the problem areas. Using a mild radiofrequency heat energy, Nate destroyed these areas, or "the mischief makers" he told the nurses he called them. Once this tissue was ablated, the abnormal electrical signals that had created the arrhythmia in the first place could no longer be sent to the rest of the heart.

Four hours into the operation, Nate took a break and went to the adjoining computer room and checked all the screens. The intravascular camera was excellent and revealed to Nate just what he knew he would have to do.

He went back into the surgery area and took the guide wires and catheters from Sophie's capable hands. "I have it now, Nurse."

"Yes, Doctor," she replied and stepped aside.

For two more hours, Nate worked on the area at the top of the heart near the aorta, trying to ablate as much of it as possible. Nate knew that if this had gone untreated, Gwen would have found herself a stroke victim, or worse.

By the time the procedure was over, Nate was tired, hungry and thirsty.

He peeled off his surgical clothes and threw

them in the large trash bin in the scrub room. "Sophie, did you talk to the family?"

"Yes, I did, but they're waiting for you."

"Good." Nate pushed the swinging door open and strode toward the family waiting area.

Nate knew that the chairs in the narrow room with windows looking out onto the hospital courtyard could only be comfortable for an hour. Certainly not all morning long. Gwen's husband, a thin man wearing jeans and a Green Bay Packers windbreaker, stood up the minute he saw Nate. Two teenage girls were immersed in playing games on their iPads.

"Doc!" the man said. "How is she?"

"She's just fine. She came through like a champ." Nate shook his hand. "I want to tell you, Mr. Petrowski, we did a lot more than we had originally planned, but I think I got it all. The procedure was twice as long as we had expected, but I found a great deal of damaged area at the top of the heart. That was pretty tricky, but I think it's really good now." Nate smiled confidently.

"You're happy. I can see it in your face," Mr. Petrowski said.

"I am. Happy for you. She's going to be fine after her recuperation, of course."

"When can we see her?"

"They're taking her up to the room now. You can go with them, if you like. She has to lie completely still for six hours. She's pretty groggy, so it won't be a problem. She'll stay all night, and then I'll check on her in the morning and we'll release her as long as there aren't any complications. Probably about eleven, I would think."

Mr. Petrowski shook Nate's hand again. "I can't thank you enough, Doc. Gosh, this is just, well, a miracle."

Nate nodded. "It is pretty miraculous. Even I think it is." Nate stepped to the side as the girls rose from their chairs and smiled at him.

"Thank you, Doctor," they chimed.

"You're welcome," Nate replied and then went back into the surgical area.

NATE HAD AN hour and a half until his next surgery. He knew just what he wanted to do with that time. He walked out the hospital doors toward the employee parking lot, and spotted Sophie at the entrance.

"Good job, Doctor," she said brightly, pushing back her curly dark hair. She had lipstick on, and some blush, and she was wearing her street clothes.

"You going home?" he asked.

"Yeah. Carrie will assist you this afternoon."

"Carrie. Hmm. I met her last week, but I can't remember her."

"Petite. Strawberry blonde." Sophie smiled and then began rummaging through her purse.

"Ah, I remember Carrie," he said.

Sophie tossed her curls away from her face and flashed him a provocative smile. "Well, see you Thursday."

"Yeah," Nate replied. She looked back over her shoulder as she walked away, and she waved to him and smiled again.

He waved back, scratched his head and bounded across the parking lot toward his car. Nate wasn't quite certain, but if he didn't know better, he would guess that Sophie was flirting with him.

Nate stuck his key in the ignition, turned the Hummer on and pulled out of the parking space.

Nate walked into Cupcakes and Coffee and found a line of over a dozen people. Chloe was waiting on customers as quickly as she could. Looking over the heads of the others in line, Nate noticed that Emily Regeski, Sarah's aunt, was working the cash register. There was no sign of Maddie.

"May I take your order, sir?" Chloe asked when he reached the front of the line, blowing a lock of dark hair from her eyes. "Hey, you're that guy."

He leaned over the counter. "I am." He chuckled. "But exactly what guy are you talking about?"

"The one who was here with Maddie the other morning." She winked at him.

"Guilty," he said.

The patrons who had been in line in front of him had all been served, and as no one else had entered the café, Nate was now the only one at the counter. Emily closed the register after he paid.

"Nate Barzonni! How are you?"

"Just fine," he offered.

Emily walked out from around the counter and up to Nate. "I didn't get a chance to hug you at Easter."

"Yeah." He patted his stomach. "I was preoccupied."

She hugged Nate and then held his arms and scrutinized his face. "I can see the years away did you good. Handsome as ever. No, I take that back. More handsome."

Chloe, not to be left out, jumped into the conversation again. "So you know Sarah, too?"

"Yes. Maddie, me and Sarah, we all hung around together back in those days." Nate looked at Emily. "I thought maybe Maddie would be here today. I just finished a surgery and have an hour till my next procedure."

Emily's face brightened. "That's right, you're at the hospital now, aren't you?"

"Yes, ma'am."

"Maddie told us," Emily informed him. "Oh, but I'm so sorry. She's in Chicago all day."

"Chicago?"

"She didn't tell you? She's having a meeting with a mergers and acquisitions company for her franchises. George helped set it up for her," Emily said proudly.

"Franchises."

"Yeah," Chloe chirped. "Cupcakes and Coffee Cafés will be everywhere, just like Starbucks."

Emily shook her head. "Let's not get ahead of ourselves, Chloe. It's just the first meeting with the investor. We have no idea what the terms of agreement will be. But it's all so exciting, isn't it?" Emily asked Nate.

"It is," he said morosely, but both Emily and Chloe were so excited for Maddie that they didn't pay attention to his response. "Well, I guess I'll just call her tomorrow."

"That would be great," Chloe said. "I know she'll be wanting to hear from you." Chloe nodded so forcefully that Nate was reminded of a bobblehead doll.

"Thanks, Chloe. I'll do that."

"You have her cell number, right?" Chloe asked.

"Uh—" he patted his pocket for his phone "—I don't. Just the number here. I should put it in my contacts."

"Absolutely," Chloe said and scribbled the number on a paper napkin. "Here," she said. "Gosh, I almost forgot. What can I get for you?"

"Can I get a coffee to go? And I'll try one of those turkey croissant sandwiches over there."

Emily whispered, "I'll put it in our new Panini machine with a slice of Gruyère. It's one of Maddie's inventions. Fabulous."

"Okay, I'll try it."

Nate paid and waited for Emily to wrap up

the hot sandwich in foil, then left the café and got into his car.

Staring at the little house that Maddie had turned into a warm and friendly spot to enjoy coffee, friends and a sweet treat, he marveled at all she had done. He couldn't be more proud of her if she'd won some major award. She'd had an idea, and she'd believed in her dream long enough and hard enough to make it come true. He considered her to be a genius because she'd made something out of nothing. That was the definition of genius to him. An idea was only ether and energy until someone put faith in it and molded, coddled, loved and forced it into existence.

She was a marvel to him and he hadn't had enough time yet to tell her.

That was something he intended to rectify—soon.

He pulled the lid off his steaming cappuccino and took a sip. He took another sip. Then he whistled with appreciation. "Darn, that's good. Really good."

Nate was a coffee lover, and to his recollection, Maddie's coffee was the best he'd ever tasted. The drink the other night wasn't just a fluke. Maddie's blend was exceptional. Was it possible that Maddie had bested the gourmet restaurants in Chicago and New York he'd visited? Was the milk different? Had she found better beans? What other tricks had she discovered in the years they'd been apart?

He tasted his sandwich and found it was remarkable as well. It was just a simple turkey sandwich, but the meat was better, not the usual commercial sliced meat sold to restaurants. Nate had a sneaky suspicion that Maddie actually baked this turkey herself. The cheese was high quality and the croissant was especially buttery. She'd told him she made all her baked goods in-house, which was why she worked late at night. Maybe she made the croissants and brioches, too.

Nate was hooked. He knew where he'd be getting his lunches now that he was living in Indian Lake.

Digging in his pocket for his keys, he sat back in his seat. If this was such a big meeting in Chicago, why hadn't she told him about it? Nate felt his earlier exuberance deflate.

He knew why.

She didn't trust him.

Maddie was still angry with him for leaving her the way he had. She had always impressed him as a person who was loyal. But the flip side of that loyalty was a person who would hold a grudge forever.

Despite the fact that she had kissed him as if she thought he was the last man on earth, the fact remained that Maddie didn't trust him.

And without trust, there couldn't be love.

Either way, Nate, old man, you're done for.

CHAPTER FIFTEEN

MADDIE SAT IN the back of the Lincoln Town Car as it cruised up North Michigan Avenue toward Spiaggia, the restaurant where she was meeting Alex and the investor. It was after six, and all the lights had come on. The apartment and office buildings glowed as they reflected the setting sun, and Lake Michigan glittered as if the stars had fallen from the sky and were dancing on the surface.

"It's like a dreamland," Maddie said to herself, falling back on the soft leather cushions.

"We're here, miss," the driver said as they pulled up to the restaurant. The facade was granite, glass and brass, much like most of the buildings along the Magnificent Mile. The driver came around to her side of the car and opened the door. "You just go up the stairs and Spiaggia is on the second floor. You can't miss it," he said. "Mr. Perkins is there waiting for you."

"He is? But I'm still fifteen minutes early."

"He's earlier," the man replied.

Maddie had worn a slim, black linen sheath with long sleeves and a V-neck. A simple cameo on a gold chain hung around her neck. In her ears were pearl studs. Black stockings and black pumps completed the outfit. She carried a vintage silver-mesh evening bag that Mrs. Beabots insisted she borrow.

When Maddie walked up to the reservations desk, she realized that the restaurant was very crowded. The women were beautiful and animated and the men were handsomely dressed, chatting and laughing with each other. There were no children allowed, and Maddie could see why. She knew for a fact she'd never been in one place with so many beautiful, sophisticated people. The restaurant itself was a magnificent orchestration of luxe Italian design executed in tall black marble pillars, glass walls and partitions and gleaming granite.

"I'm meeting my party here. I'm with Mr. Perkins," Maddie told the hostess.

The tall, auburn-haired hostess smiled. "You must be Miss Strong. Alex is waiting for you at the table. If you'll just follow me," she said.

Maddie wondered if Alex came here a great deal.

She was ushered to a linen-covered table for four. Alex was talking on his cell phone and had a martini in front of him. As she approached, his face brightened with a wide smile.

"You look good enough to eat with a spoon," he said, hanging up his phone and shaking her hand.

"I bet you say that to all your clients," she retorted as he held her chair for her. She wondered if he could smell her perfume. She'd worn Chanel No. 5. Classic, understated and rich. Or so Mrs. Beabots had told her.

"Trust me. None of my clients look like you." He sat back down and leaned over conspiratorially. "Our investor is on his way up. My advice is, be yourself. And ask for the moon."

Alex's cell phone buzzed. He answered it and hung up quickly. "He's at the podium."

"That was the hostess? Calling your cell?"

"Yeah."

"They do that for everybody?" Maddie took a mental note. It was good customer relations. She could use an idea like that somehow.

"No. I tip big," he said, gazing past her shoulder. "James," he shouted over the mounting din and walked a few steps away from the table toward Maddie's investor.

She turned around in her chair so she could get a good look at the man who was to be her investor. James Stapleton wasn't what she'd expected. He was shorter than she'd imagined. Weren't all angels supposed to be tall? He was probably only five foot eight, quite portly and, judging by the lines around his eyes and his heavy jowls, definitely over sixty. His grey hair was thinning on top and he looked as if he needed a haircut. His suit was a brown glen plaid, which did nothing for his rotund physique. But his shirt was snow white, crisp and starched, and he wore a striking blue-patterned tie that helped to accentuate his eyes.

"Well, well, Miss Strong. Happy to meet you," James said, thrusting his large hand at her. She took it and rose as he moved closer. He placed his other hand over hers, gave their hands a sharp shake and then let go as if they were going out onto the gridiron.

"It's my pleasure," she answered sweetly, sitting back down.

James sat opposite Maddie at the table.

Alex remained in his seat so that he was positioned between the two of them.

"I trust you had a nice trip into the city," James asked Maddie.

"I did. It was a lovely night and the sunset on the lake was spectacular."

James smiled and nodded. "Ah. My favorite sight myself. My wife and I have had a little hole-in-the-wall condo downtown for years so that we can enjoy the lake views."

"Really?" Maddie's eyes flew open. "I've always dreamed, I mean wondered, what it would be like to live in downtown Chicago."

"Take my word for it, nothing like it in the world," James said.

Just then, a waiter appeared to take their drink orders. Alex motioned with his open palm to Maddie first.

"Just a white wine for me."

The waiter looked at her curiously. Then he glanced at Alex, who shook his head. "Bring her a Kir Royale to start and then I'll take a look at the wine list. James?"

"Do you have Port Ellen?

"Talisker, sir," the waiter said. "And I believe Mannochmore. There might be some other single-malt scotch, but I'll take to ask."

"Don't bother. Mannochmore." James nodded. "Neat."

"Yes, sir." The waiter left.

Another waiter arrived and brought bread, olive oil, Parmesan cheese and herbs and mixed their dipping sauce for them. Their dinner waiter arrived and without looking at the menu, Alex ordered a smattering of appetizers for the table.

"Maddie," Alex said as the bar waiter returned with their drinks, "I gave James all your drawings and elevations for the cafés, and we thought, if it was all right with you, we would start there."

"Sure," she said sipping the pink cocktail in a frosted champagne flute. It was sweet and tasted like raspberries mixed with the champagne. "This is good," she whispered to Alex.

"I thought you'd like it." He winked.

James clasped his hands together. "I thought it best for us to meet so I can tell you what my concept is to see if this is a good fit for us."

Maddie was reminded once again that her business deal was by no means a sure thing. Her investor wanted to see if they were a good "fit," and she knew what that meant.

She'd be the one capitulating, and as a general rule, Maddie Strong didn't give in.

However, this wasn't a family argument or a disagreement with one of her suppliers. This time, there was more at stake. This man was her key to a large bank account and the chance at her dream of living a life in the city just like all these beautiful and very happy people.

"Here's the main thing. I've decided—just recently, by the way, Alex—to go ahead and put the cafés in downtown Chicago."

Alex's eyebrows cranked up in surprise, and though Maddie could tell he was trying to quash his reaction, this announcement meant something to him. And Maddie guessed that it wasn't good for her. Or Alex.

"This is very expensive real estate, James. When we first talked about it, you said you wanted to go to Evanston and Lincoln Park first. Then, if those worked, on to Kenilworth, Deerfield and even Highland Village. We were going to do one downtown café, but much later."

James smiled broadly. "I like this young woman's idea, and I think the downtown crowd will go nuts for her cupcakes. My wife tried that cappuccino blend you sent to

Alex. She said it was the best she's ever had. She's convinced you're Italian. I told her you weren't."

"No…" Maddie said.

James never took a breath. He just kept talking and didn't let Maddie or Alex interrupt or slow him down. "I think the downtown crowd is more sophisticated by the minute. Check out these women. They never looked like that back in my day. They want the best and they're getting it. That's what I want to push. We have really unique sweets—incidentally, I even thought of changing the name to that. I think it's genius—and a coffee that's better than anything else on the market. Everyone is waiting for that. You gotta come here, to Spaggia's, to get good cappuccino, and what do they charge? Six bucks? Eight? These people will pay anything for the best of the best. So, I think Maddie's idea of the Italian theme is perfect for Chicago. But downtown Chicago."

Alex shook his head. "I don't want to slit my own throat here, but James—the build-outs will be murder."

"I've got a guy who's working up bids for me now. He did my last two restaurants in Naperville. I put together my own numbers on the ad campaign and how much it will cost to launch the cafés. So, I thought, maybe I should just jump in there with the half-dozen cafés off the bat."

"Six?" Alex reiterated.

"Yeah." James took a drink of his scotch. "Here's the thing. The city is coming back slow from the recession. My guess is that all these beautiful people can't pay for a Spaggia's even once a month. Okay. So maybe once a month, but that's all. In the meantime, they want upscale Italian, but they gotta watch their pennies. So, we give them some unique sweets and really great espresso to tide them over. At top price, because we *are* unique." He socked Alex's shoulder playfully. "And, boom, we're in business. Big-time."

Alex sipped his martini slowly. "I'm beginning to see your vision."

James threw back the remainder of his scotch.

Alex picked up the wine list, scanned it, then closed the leather-bound book. Within seconds, as if he had been summoned by radar, the waiter appeared. "Have you chosen a wine for dinner?"

"James, do you like red or white?"

"Red. No Chianti. I'm not big on Italian

wines. I guess I should bone up, eh? I doubt they'd have a French wine."

"Sure they do," Alex said. "Bring a bottle of Bourquet Gevrey-Chambertin Pinot Noir."

"The 2005, sir?"

"Yes," Alex replied.

Maddie didn't say a word. Because James had come to the meeting with such new ideas, she felt this discussion was out of her league. She didn't want to do anything to destroy Alex's hard work. She guessed Alex and Uncle George were right. She'd done her part. Now all they had to do was see eye to eye.

The appetizers arrived, and while Maddie selected several luscious vegetables from the antipasto plate, she kept her ears finely tuned to the conversation.

"Did you see the year-end reports of the suburban coffeehouses I sent you?" Alex asked.

"Dismal. Just deplorable. Several chains are closing their doors."

Maddie's eyes flew open. "They are?" No one heard her comment.

James pounded the table with his fist. "That's what I'm talking about. You gotta see the future. The future is in the city, at least for this concept. Some soccer mom is not going to spring for a five-dollar cupcake for her kid, except for his birthday. But in the city, it's a different sale. It's for a woman…" He looked around the room. "Like that one over there. She's skinny as a rail. No way is she going to stuff her face with junk food or bake a whole cake. She's going to want something incredible and small. Small indulgences. Oh, yeah. That's another name I came up with."

"Not bad. But sounds like one of those chocolate commercials on television," Alex mused as he finished off his martini and filled his appetizer plate with calamari.

The waiter came with the wine. "May I send your waiter over, sir?"

"Sure. I guess we should order something," Alex said, winking at Maddie.

They all listened to the specials and placed their orders.

"May I ask a question?" Maddie asked once the waiter had left and the conversation had resumed.

Both men stopped talking and looked at her. She saw panic in Alex's eyes and curiosity in James's.

"Sure," Alex replied. "What is it?"

"Did you get a chance to go over the drawings and elevations that we did? Did you like any of our selections?"

James tossed a concerned glance at Alex but plunged forward. "That's what Alex and I are discussing. When I first came on board, I was thinking, yeah, sure. How quaint. Suburbs, little Italian cafés, that kind of thing. But now, I'm thinking city."

Alex rushed in. "Which would be more brass and glass. Granite."

Maddie nodded. "More like mini versions of this place."

"Yeah." James said. "That's what I'm thinking. Same coffee, same recipes. Your made-to-order concept is going to knock 'em dead."

"And you want to build more cafés than you originally intended?" Maddie asked.

"Yeah. We're still doing just the two for now, but I'm thinking in eighteen months, we should be up to six."

Alex placed his hand over Maddie's. "Are you okay with all this so far?"

She looked from Alex's worried face to James's apprehensive expression. "I'm on board. All the way, gentlemen."

CHAPTER SIXTEEN

MADDIE HADN'T KNOWN it was possible to eat and drink and talk that much and still feel completely energized. She couldn't say whether it was the gourmet Italian food, the heady French wine or the realization that her dream, times six, was coming to fruition, but she felt as if she could have stayed awake all night long. Granted, she was having to make a lot of compromises, but in the end, her franchises were actually going to happen.

After dinner, she and Alex bid James goodnight. Alex paid the bill, and she watched as he laid down six one hundred dollar bills as if a dinner such as this was a matter of course. He then walked her down the stairs to the street, where the hired car was waiting.

Alex smiled at her. "I know James can be a handful. He barely lets anyone talk at all, but Maddie, you have to be so…" He grabbed her arms and nearly hopped up and down. "Elated!"

"I'm not sure about everything that happened. But yes. I am. It went well, right?"

Alex frowned. "It was fantastic. I think he'll eventually do all six cafés. I think his idea of going into the city and not the suburbs is brilliant."

"You do? I thought you didn't like it."

"Look. I hired your driver for the whole night. Let's grab a nightcap and then I can explain a few more things. How's that sound?"

"I'd like that," she said.

"Take us to the Drake, Edmond," Alex told the driver as they climbed into the backseat.

They drove up Lake Shore Drive so that Maddie could take in the water and stunning buildings at night. Alex talked about how much he loved the city and pointed out his apartment, which was in a very old complex clustered among several other old and newer buildings, each one more impressive than the last.

"Have you lived here long?" Maddie asked.

"All my life," Alex replied. "I grew up in that very same building. My parents still live there, except for the winters when they go to Florida. They have a condo in Naples."

"What does your father do? And your mother?" she asked.

"Dad is an investment banker. He makes money. Lots of it. Mother is on the board of several charities in town. I swear, she's busier than he is. I always feel I need to make an appointment just to call them." He paused. "Now that I think about it, I do just that." He laughed.

"I think it's wonderful that your mother's so involved. If it weren't for people like her, always giving of themselves, so many services and institutions just wouldn't exist. I hope when I get older and things slow down for me somewhat, I can do more of that kind of thing."

"Is that on your bucket list?" he asked.

"It's certainly on my to-do list. That way I know I'll get it done."

"Ah, here we are," Alex said as the driver pulled up to the Drake Hotel.

They walked into the spacious blue-and-gold reception area. "The bar is this way," Alex said and steered Maddie through an entryway marked Coq d'Or.

The bar was more than half filled with couples and businesspeople, so they were seated at a small table for two. The room was cozy and dark and decorated in wood and red leather captain's chairs. Alex explained that the bar was opened on December 6, 1933, the day Prohibition was repealed, and it had been a real Chicago landmark ever since. He ordered a Courvoisier cognac for himself and Maddie ordered a cup of herbal tea.

"I'm not much of drinker," Maddie said unapologetically.

"It's an acquired taste, the cognac."

She shrugged, admiring the decor. "Guess I've never had the time for this kind of life."

Alex laid his hand over hers. "I think you did just fine working toward your first million. You have all the rest of your life to enjoy the fruits of your labors."

She looked down at his hand and was surprised that it didn't feel inappropriate. It probably should have. This was a business dinner, after all.

Wasn't it?

Alex removed his hand slowly, as if it was the last thing he wanted to do. Or was it that he hadn't realized he'd put it there? Hadn't he meant to touch her? Was it just a natural gesture for him, something he'd done with dozens of clients, consoling and assuring them? The gesture was certainly part of his charm, which was considerable.

He's so different from Nate, and yet he's not....

Nate held people's physical lives in his hands. Alex was responsible for their financial well-being. Both men were earnest, intelligent, committed and handsome.

And suddenly I have two potential romances in my life. Or do I?

As far as Maddie could tell, Nate only intended to stick around for the year of his contract. Then he would leave.

Just like before.

"So, tell me, Maddie, what do you want to do with your life?"

"As in…"

His smile was impish and his eyes gleamed as if he'd just discovered a marvelous secret. "I have this theory that we all come to this earth with an agenda. A list of hopes and wishes and dreams, if you will. Some of us tromp right out there and start accomplishing things practically in grade school. Those people become gymnastics stars and cut records before they're through puberty. Others work their butts off all their lives and don't get a shot at their golden rings until they reach retirement. Or older," he said, arching a brow. "Like Colonel Sanders. Then there are wunderkinds like you. This new breed of young geniuses who transform the internet while they're in college—they boggle the mind. Or these kids who invent some new electronic game at the age of fourteen."

He leaned closer, so that his eyes delved right into hers, capturing her attention and making her believe that for him, in this moment, she was the only woman in the world.

"That's what I admire in you, Maddie. You were able to take a common ordinary thing like a cupcake and see it in a whole new way. You expanded its dimension and possibilities. You took it to a whole new level, which no one had done in a retail situation."

"You," she said, swallowing carefully, "admire me?"

"Yes, I do."

He peered into her eyes, holding her captive, allowing her entry to his thoughts, even his heart. Maddie was stunned.

And pleased.

She felt her smile growing until her face beamed with a radiance that warmed her cheeks. "You know, I love my little town, and my dear friends are irreplaceable. But there's a flip side that a lot of people don't see or want to acknowledge."

"Which is…"

"Jealousy. If someone is different, or odd, or eccentric—and believe me, that's almost a requisite in my town—too many times they are ostracized and no one will befriend them or help them. So many people are afraid of not being 'normal,' when the truth is there is no such thing as 'normal.' When I was young and being raised by a single mother, most of the kids in school treated me like a pariah. Except for Sarah, Liz, Isabelle and a few others. They were different then, and they still are. They weren't afraid to be seen with me. Now I can see that we're all creative and energetic. Or maybe it's just that we're not afraid to try new things."

"I believe that's called courage."

"Possibly," she said, lowering her gaze to her tea. "We support each other a great deal. As I told you, one of my best friends is eighty years old."

"Yes, you did," he said.

"Well, now that I think about what you said, about respecting me and all, I realize my friends respect me, too."

"I should think so. You're so warm and approachable. I mean, I've never met a woman like you."

"How's that?"

Alex sniggered to himself, looked at her askance and said, "Maddie, you're so bright, and though you have your own ideas, you aren't put off by other peoples' opinions. You handled James remarkably well, and that takes understanding, patience and genuine concern for other people. Likeable. That's what you are. When I see you I just want to…hug you!"

She glanced down shyly at her tea, then her eyes flew to his face. "Would that be a quick hug or a really good long hug?"

His jocular expression melted off his face and was replaced with a solemn gaze. "A long hug. A really long hug. One that would last about, uh, I dunno, between an hour and all night long."

"All night long?" She toyed with him. She didn't care if he knew she was playing with him. She was having fun. And it felt really good. "That's sounds serious."

"Not as serious as it could get," he said, leaning across the table, his expensive silk tie ends brushing across the wood, and he moved toward her.

Maddie met him more than halfway and pressed her lips next to his. His lips were soft and strong all at the same time. He tasted like burned sugar and she could only guess that was the cognac that still ringed his lips. And like the brandy, his kiss was intoxicating. She felt as if her mind had been vacuumed out of her skull and in this void were only lightning synapses that exploded like fireworks igniting her responses, both voluntary and involuntary. She'd been gripping the arms of her chair, digging her fingernails into the leather, but after several thunder bursts in her head, her hands reached for his nape as if they had a mind of their own.

His neck was warm, even hot to the touch, and she wondered if she had created this in him. Or was it just his normal reaction whenever he kissed anyone?

And who knew how many women a man like Alex had kissed in his lifetime? She'd seen the smorgasbord of gorgeous women at the restaurant that night and as far as she was concerned, she hadn't the slightest idea why Alex would want to be kissing her and not one of those tall, fashionably dressed dreamgirls instead.

When Alex pulled away from the kiss, Maddie's eyes were still closed. She was still trapped in the magical moment and hadn't come back down to earth yet.

"Maddie."

She thought she heard Alex say her name but wasn't sure.

"I'm sorry, Maddie," he clearly said.

She opened her eyes. She was back. She removed her hands. She scooted back in her chair and smiled at him.

"I take back what I said about the hugging thing," Alex said, clearing his throat.

Feeling as if she'd been doused with a glass of ice water, she looked around the bar to see if anyone had witnessed them kissing. You couldn't be too careful these days. People took pictures on their iPhones all the time. The night truly had a thousand eyes. Now the nights had video as well.

"Take it back?" she questioned.

"Yeah. I think the kissing thing is much better." He smiled and moved his chair closer to hers. Then he put his hand on her neck. He pulled her face next to his. "Now the problem is that once I've tasted nirvana, I'm hooked," he whispered.

He kissed her again. "Maddie. You are so sweet."

"No," she breathed. "It's your cognac."

"Trust me, it's definitely you."

Alex had just pulled away from Maddie when the waiter appeared and deposited their bill.

"We take all major credit cards as well as cash, sir," the slender man said. Then he coughed. Loudly.

Alex grinned at Maddie. "I think he wants us to leave."

Alex took out some bills and tossed them on the tray and they rose.

They walked out of the bar arm in arm.

The Lincoln Town Car pulled up to the curb and the doorman went to the car and opened the backdoor.

Maddie regarded Alex thoughtfully before getting in the car. "You live in the world I always wanted for myself. You live the life I want. Honestly. But this dream of mine is coming at me so fast, and until just a few minutes ago, I thought we were just doing a business deal. I wasn't ready for…this."

"Well, I've been hoping. You're the reason I've worked so hard on this deal, Maddie. You wanted this and I wanted it for you. I am so happy it's come together so well. Believe me, it's not done yet and there is still a great deal left up to fate. If those first two cafés don't make it, we're back to square one. It's not over, by any means. I won't let your ship sink," Alex said earnestly.

"I believe you, Alex," she replied. "I believe *in* you."

"That's all I wanted to hear," he said quietly. "Still, I don't know what got into me, kissing you like that. If I offended you, I'm sorry."

"You didn't."

"Good. Because I'm not sorry. It was pretty incredible. But I have to confess that from the second I saw you in my office, I did have an overwhelming desire. No, sorry, a craving to just hug you. Really tight. Yeah. Squeeze you tight. That's what I wanted. I admit it."

She laughed. "You're funny."

He touched her face with his forefinger, "And you are unforgettable."

He kissed her good-night and stood aside while she climbed into the car. Alex looked at the driver. "Be careful on the Toll Road. She's precious cargo."

"Yes, sir."

Alex leaned down and waved at Maddie through the glass. "I'll call you tomorrow."

"Okay," she said. "Thanks for the wonderful dinner. And tonight. I'll never forget it."

"I hope you don't," he said as the driver started the engine and pulled into the lane.

Maddie turned around to watch out of the rear window.

Alex remained on the curb waving to her until she was out of sight.

CHAPTER SEVENTEEN

THE MORNING AFTER Maddie's heady evening in Chicago, she opened the café, her head still in a dizzying fog as she remembered Alex's kisses. She hadn't slept well at all, which added to the hazy feeling. Or perhaps it was the fact that in a matter of weeks, her life had been turned upside down and she hadn't a clue how to right it.

Alex was clearly attracted to her. A fact that was firmly established last night. Meanwhile, Nate had set fire to the embers of their long-ago love. Except Nate was leaving. Was he implying that he couldn't commit to anything? Was he trying to tell her not count on him? That he was just passing through her life?

At the precise moment Maddie thought she was about to realize her dreams, she was more confused than she'd ever been.

Her stomach was a jumble of nervous knots

and trying to concentrate on her business and daily routines had become a real chore.

Maddie felt an allegiance to Nate, but that wasn't love. That was obligation to their shared past. On the other hand, she couldn't get him out of her mind day or night. She was concerned that she hadn't told him about her business deal and the franchise. She hadn't invited him to her party. What kind of subliminal message was her psyche trying to tell her about that?

She certainly wanted him to share in her joy over her accomplishment, and she didn't want him to hear a misconstrued version through the town gossip mill.

Maddie called Nate on his cell phone and left a voice mail, assuming he was in surgery. She explained that she shut the café down at five, and if he was free, she wanted to meet with him.

The day at the café was busy and bustling with lots of customers, and Chloe, as always, was a great help up front.

Maddie had just put together the batter for her new pineapple cupcakes, when her cell phone rang in her pocket. She looked at the caller ID and saw that it was Nate.

She was amazed that her heart skipped a beat, possibly a beat and a half, just seeing his name. The phone rang a second time. She was so dazed, she'd forgotten to answer the call.

"Hello, Nate?"

"Hi, Maddie. I just finished up for the day and heard your message. I'd love to see you. When are you free?"

"I just have to put this batter away, is all."

"So, how about I pick you up in fifteen minutes? I know just where we should go."

"You do?"

"Uh-huh," he said. "But it's a surprise."

"Okay," she replied. "Can I bring anything?"

"A jacket," he said, and hung up.

Maddie took the batter out from under the stainless-steel beater, put plastic wrap over the top and placed the bowl in her commercial refrigerator.

She rushed into her office, checked her makeup and frowned. Going into the employee bathroom, she applied fresh mascara, a bit of blush and some lipstick. She combed her hair and spritzed herself with Chanel No. 5.

She took off her apron and checked her sweater and jeans for food stains. Thankfully, there were none. She grabbed a pink wind-breaker from the hook on the back of her office door.

Maddie had just turned out the café lights when she saw Nate's Hummer drive up. He hopped out of the truck and came around to open the door for her. He was wearing jeans, a sweatshirt and running shoes. "My lady," he said with a courtly bow.

"Thanks," she said as she climbed in.

Nate shut the door and jogged around to the driver's side. "You're beautiful," he said, grabbing his seat belt. He studied her with that straight, hard expression he often had when he was making judgments. She remembered that look. He wasn't just complimenting her to be courteous or nice. He meant it.

And that meant a lot to her.

"You look…tired," she replied and instinctively put her hand on his cheek. It was amazing, she thought, how easily she fell back to the emotional place they'd been in eleven years ago. She cared about how he felt, both physically and mentally. It felt so natural to pick up where they'd left off. "Are you okay?"

"Just getting used to my new routine at the hospital." He put his own hand over hers and caressed it. "I guess I haven't had much sleep lately."

"I have the same problem," she commiserated. "Tonight will be no exception."

The night before had been filled with remembering Alex and his kisses. When Maddie was with Nate, she felt guilty thinking about another man. It was almost like being unfaithful. But she wasn't, was she?

Nate looked deeply into Maddie's eyes, not understanding her implication. "Tonight?"

"I have to bake about three hundred cupcakes," she said truthfully. *Then after that I'll probably get a text from Alex. Possibly even one from you.*

"Is that all?"

"Give or take," she said, realizing she still had her hand on his cheek. She lowered both their hands together but did not retract hers yet. She liked the way her hand felt in his. She liked it a lot. And that was another surprise to her. She was so unsure of the reactions Nate elicited in her it felt as if her mind had gone away on vacation.

Nate was the guy of her past. Not her present. And who could ever guess about the future? All she wanted to do was tell him the truth about what was happening in her life.

Then he could move on and so could she. It was simple.

But if it was so simple, how come she was tied up in knots worrying about his every grimace and gesture? Why should she worry about Nate Barzonni one more day in her life? *I've spent too many days thinking about him; being terrified that he was in danger; too many sleepless nights and empty days without him when I wanted him.*

"So, where are we going?" she asked, finally able to push aside the barrage of thoughts about Nate.

"Picnic." He turned on the engine. "I've reserved the perfect spot for us."

"Then drive on, sir," she joked.

Cove Beach was covered in so many white pear blossoms it looked as if it had snowed on the sands. The sun was deep in the west, but not yet setting. The trees around the lake were working diligently to push forth their spring leaves. That light green tinge to the winter-bark limbs gave an ethereal, iridescent glow to the landscape. A soft breeze fluttered through blooming forsythia and rustled the white and purple lilacs, filtering the air with the floral essence only nature could create.

Nate pulled the Hummer into the gravel

driveway and then up to a parking place that was designated by creosote-covered railroad ties. Across from them, up a slight incline, was a picnic area with tables, grills and roofed areas with open sides and concrete flooring, to accommodate large reunions or gatherings.

"That's our table right over there." Nate pointed to the lone picnic table closest to the beach. It was only twenty feet to the water. He reached into the backseat and pulled out a bag, a blanket and two bottles of soda. He handed the soda to Maddie. "Our picnic food. Such as it is," he said gleefully. "Come on."

Maddie hopped out of the Hummer and followed Nate to the table. He put their food down and sat facing the water, then patted the spot next him.

Maddie joined him.

"Closer," he ordered, holding up the blanket. "I want to wrap this around us. When the sun goes down, it'll get cold."

"You're right," she said and inched closer until they were hip to hip.

Nate wrapped his blanket around their shoulders and handed Maddie an edge to hold. "There. That's better, don't you think?"

"Yeah," she said, looking first at the tranquil crystal lake and then back at Nate.

He had a thick five-o'clock shadow and his eyes were slightly droopy. His skin was pale, though she remembered how berry brown he could get in the summers working on the farm.

His blue eyes scanned the lake, drinking in all its beauty. It was almost as if she could see the tension in him easing as he stared across the water.

"Tough day?"

"Just the usual," he said.

"Yeah? I don't buy that. I'm watching you. You're wound up tighter than a drum. What's up?"

"I'm learning, is all. A new job, new co-workers and a new hospital to navigate…. It takes time to fit in. It's normal adjustment for anyone. I just want to do a good job for them."

"I'm sure you'll be great for them," she said supportively. "I'm curious about your work on the reservation. It must have impacted you enormously to want to go back. What was it like?"

He looked out across the water.

"We had a clinic, but everything was government-run, government-controlled. I did fairly ordinary heart procedures—bypasses, stuff like that."

"Open-heart surgery is ordinary to you?" Maddie shook her head. "Whoa."

"Well, I mean, it's within my skill set. But now I'm working with incredible equipment, and it's very exciting. It's what I came here for. Last week, I started cold beam laser operations. You see, Maddie, I'd never get this kind of responsibility in a large hospital. These operations would go to surgeons who are ten, twenty years my senior. Here, they don't have enough doctors. And certainly not enough with even my limited experience, which I got during my residency."

"So why the Indian reservation? Why not come here first?"

"I wanted to pay back my loans as quickly as possible. The government has a program that not only pays a salary, but also gives grants to pay off student loan debt in exchange for working in underprivileged areas. I still have almost half yet to pay, but that time on the reservation really helped me financially. Once I go back to Arizona, I'll get the rest paid off. I'm not worried."

"Do you miss it? The reservation, I mean."

"I do. There was so much I could do there

because most heart surgeons don't dedicate their lives to such low income areas. Most of the cutting edge technology and research is based in prominent, well-endowed hospitals in big cities. And many surgeons want the big bucks and fancy lifestyle. Frankly, I was like that until I went to Arizona. With what I'm learning here, I could go anywhere in the country. I could travel from reservation to reservation as the need dictated."

Maddie swallowed hard. "You mean, you wouldn't settle in just one place?"

"No. I've looked into it extensively. I'd be on the government payroll, as a general rule. It would be really exciting. Helping all those people who couldn't afford ablations and other types of heart surgery."

There was a fire in Nate's eyes as he spoke.

"Exciting," Maddie repeated in a low whisper. She'd thought her own dream of moving to Chicago was expansive thinking, but what Nate envisioned for himself sounded like wanderlust. A real adventure.

She marveled at him and felt deep admiration for anyone whose life was driven by humanitarianism. She was in awe. "Nate, I know you'll do well here. I think you could handle just about anything anyone threw your way."

He turned his face to hers. "You believe that? That I'm Mr. Capable?"

"Yeah. I do. I always did."

"Back then doesn't count."

"Sure it does."

"Then I want to say again that I'm so very, very sorry for what I did to you. I wasn't Mr. Capable then. I was a coward. I should have talked to you."

"Maybe," she mused. "Maybe not."

"What?" His expression was puzzled.

"I've thought about this a lot. If you hadn't left, I would have kept you here. I would have enticed you, used every trick in the book to keep you as my own. You wouldn't have gone to the navy or into medicine. You would have had to marry me sooner or later. Your mother would have hated me. You would probably be working on the farm for your father. Eventually, you would have hated me and I would have tossed you out. We would have bickered like cats and dogs."

"You think all that?"

"I do."

"So, I did the right thing. But I still should have told you where I was."

"Yes, Nate. You should have. I won't deny how mad I was. Especially back then..." Maddie felt a catch in her throat as long-ago sorrows rose up like dark ghosts. Tears sprang to her eyes, unwanted and unexpected. She scrubbed them away with the balls of her palms. She turned to him, her eyes swimming in a sea of stinging memories. "You broke my heart, Nate. I swore I would never forgive you." She tried to punch his arm, but her fist fell open like a needy child begging for food. She splayed her fingers across his heart and hung her head. Her tears fell into her lap. "You crushed me."

"Oh, Maddie," he moaned. "I did this to you, and I'm so sorry. So sorry." He folded her into his arms and pulled her to his broad chest. "Can you ever forgive me?"

"I swore I wouldn't..." she said through her sobs. Maddie felt as if she was seventeen all over again. She felt crumpled and discarded. She wasn't good enough for a Barzonni. She was convinced Nate didn't love her enough. Not then and not now.

The fact that she had accomplished so much and was living through the excitement of seeing her dream unfold had no power at this moment. She was without strength and she was astounded that within a few seconds her heart could betray her so completely.

Maddie snuggled inside the blanket and circled her arms around Nate's back. He felt so strong, so warm…and sincere about his apology. His sincerity had always comforted her when they were young.

It was that honesty that she had instinctively trusted when they were young. She had felt safe with Nate.

Because she had trusted him utterly and without condition, his departure had deeply, cruelly affected her.

Nate kissed the top of her head. "I don't deserve one minute of your time, and certainly not an ounce of the love you gave me, Maddie. You were right to hate me. What I did to you was despicable." He rubbed her back and kissed her forehead. "You were everything to me then as well, you know. There was never any doubt in my mind you were the girl for me."

"Really?" Maddie sniffed as she pulled out of his embrace. She wiped her nose on her sleeve. She gazed into his blazing blue eyes, which even as the daylight waned, still bore that inner light that drew her in. It was the light of promise. Of ambition and purpose.

"You are the only girl I've ever loved, Maddie. I know that now."

"Nate, you were right to stay away and get your medical degree. You have so much more to give to the world. I can see that in you. Maybe I saw it in you even back then."

"I think you did," he replied, brushing a strand of hair off her forehead. "In a way, I have you to thank for everything that has happened to me. If you hadn't been so strong…"

"Me? Strong? Look at me. I'm a mess!"

A wistful smile bloomed across Nate's lips. "Maddie, you're still the most incredible girl I've ever met. You always had your head on straight and you understood me better than I did myself at times. You're beautiful—inside and out. You really don't know that, do you?"

"Guess not," she said. She still had too many tapes from a bitter and jealous mother in her head that hadn't fully been erased.

Nate reached into the brown bag that held their sandwiches and handed Maddie a paper napkin. She blew her nose.

"You know, Nate, I would have liked to have been there for your graduation." She smiled to herself. "I would have been so proud of you. Proud to see you in that uniform, all white and dashing." She looked back at him, her mind spinning a fast scenario of what could have been. "But honestly, knowing us back then? We would have rushed to a preacher or priest or whatever, and in two seconds I would have gotten pregnant. Both your parents would have gone bonkers if we'd run away." She smiled impishly.

"Maddie...." Nate wove his fingers into her hair and held her face close to his. "No wonder I was crazy about you back then."

"And now?" she asked with trepidation.

"Now it's worse," he said, and then he kissed her. He wrapped his arms around her and covered them in the blanket again like a cocoon.

"Maddie, you have to tell me that you forgive me," he said, kissing her lips then her cheeks. He moved his mouth close to her ear. "Please."

"I do, Nate. I forgive you," she said. "I forgive both of us." She pulled her head back so she could look at him.

"Thank you, Maddie. That means the world to me. I just don't want my mistakes to count against me. This time we have now is too important."

She smiled but couldn't break free from the mesmerizing hold he had on her. That was the thing about Nate. He could look at her from across a room and she would melt into those blue eyes every time. She had been putty for him back then. Apparently, she still was.

Being this close to him, in his arms, felt right. Or was it just nostalgia?

Maddie had to be sure she was making all the right choices for the right reasons. She'd come so far with the choices she'd made in her life, but that was business. This was her heart. It was one thing to be in love at seventeen. It was another to risk the rest of one's life. The choices she made now were pivotal. Life-changing. And overwhelmingly frightening.

She had always loved Nate, but this was the new Nate. The Nate she didn't know yet. She wanted to know him better so she could make the right decision. She had a lot of right decisions she had to make and they were all coming too fast.

"I'm different now. That's what I wanted to talk to you about," she said.

Nate kissed her eyelids and then her lips again. "I'm listening."

"No, you're not." She giggled.

He loosened the blanket so that Maddie

could sit back, while still keeping her close to him. "Okay, shoot."

"I've been working on a business deal for a couple years now, and well, things have finally started to take off."

"This business deal—is this why you went to Chicago yesterday?"

"How did you know about that?"

"I went to the café for lunch and you weren't there," he said, choosing his words carefully. He'd just won her back and he knew he needed to tread lightly. Maddie was only a hairsbreadth closer to trusting him.

She peered at him suspiciously. "What else did you hear?"

"Chloe said you were going to be like a Starbucks."

"Chloe is young with a big mouth and a much-exaggerated imagination. I didn't say anything to you because—"

"I haven't earned the right," Nate interjected. "It's okay, Maddie. I get that. You have nothing to apologize to me for."

Surprise registered on Maddie's face. "I wanted to be the one to tell you. The fact is that when I left for Chicago, there was only the hope of a deal. Now that I've met with my investor, you truly are the first to know that he's definitely going to buy my franchise."

Nate broke into a wide grin. "Maddie! This is fantastic. How great for you. To see all your hard work and super ideas be accepted by someone else. Wow." He slapped his forehead with his palm. "Man. A franchise. That is really big. Isn't it?" he asked.

"It can be. It's not done yet. Alex convinced him to change the name to Cupcakes and Cappuccino Café, but it'll be my concept. My recipes. My designs. This was just the beginning of the actual negotiations, but it took me two years to come up with the business plan, and then Sarah and Charmaine…"

"Charmaine?" he asked.

"Charmaine Chalmers. She's Sarah's boss. She did the elevations and some of the blueprint drawings."

"Architectural drawings?" he asked.

"Yes. Then Sarah and I worked on the interior designs, fabrics and flooring. I was specific about everything looking Italian, certainly more Italian than what I have here, which is a cottagey, homey look—"

"Which I love to death," he said.

As Maddie continued explaining the ideas and the dreams she had for Cupcakes and

Cappuccino Café, her face lit with an inner fire. Her enthusiasm was electric. She had thought through every conceivable detail. She had done all this work, and he'd been far away. He hadn't been there for her. He hadn't stuck around to offer the support she might have needed from him. Nate had jilted Maddie and himself out of years of friendship and partnership. Suddenly, he suddenly felt as if she was moving away from him, as though some cosmic force was deliberately putting Maddie out of his reach. He didn't know how he could be losing her—he'd just found her again. And she was right here in his arms. Wasn't she?

Something made him increase the pressure of his grip.

"Alex is very connected in Chicago, and he's the one who found my investor…"

"Who's Alex?" Nate asked. The hairs on the back of his neck stood at attention. It was an instinct he had always possessed, but it became pronounced when he was in the navy. Danger had just approached.

"He's a partner at Ashton and Marsh," Maddie continued. "They're the mergers and acquisitions firm that Uncle George found for me."

"Does George know this guy? Personally, I mean?" Nate asked a bit too forcefully.

I'm jealous! Nate realized. Another guy had been Maddie's partner. Another guy had watched her dream grow, and he'd probably steered her in the right direction. Which would make her grateful to him. It was as if Nate could see his own future, and Maddie wasn't in it.

Nate's return to Indian Lake had everything to do with his career and his plan to return to Arizona.

Nate was aware that moving from state to state was how he could best dedicate his life to others. But what would that mean for him and Maddie? Where would that leave Maddie and her dreams? She had to supervise her franchises. Plus, she still had the café here in Indian Lake. She'd told him that her goal was to live in Chicago.

Yet he realized now that he wanted Maddie in his life—always. Suddenly, he felt oddly possessive. He clasped both his hands around hers.

She shook her head. "No, Uncle George hasn't met Alex yet. But he will. Nate? Are you okay? You're holding my hands awfully tight." She shrugged out of his grip.

"Sorry." He rubbed her upper arms. "I just got caught up in your story. It's pretty exciting."

"It is," she went on. "I mean, I always dreamed of doing something big with my life—I suppose everybody does. I just thought you had to do that kind of thing when you were young. You know, like you did, Nate."

"Me?"

"You knew what you wanted, and you left town and took charge of your life. You made things happen for yourself. Well, now it's my turn. I'm going to make things happen for myself, too. This is my dream-come-true time."

"And this is what you want, Maddie?" he asked, peering deeply into her eyes.

"Yes. It is. If I can make the franchise a success, I'll have the money to do all the other things I've dreamed about."

"And what dreams are those?"

"Buy a house. My own house. Later, a condo in the city. Work fewer hours instead of the fourteen to sixteen I work each day with no break till Sunday. I'd like to take culinary classes. I want to go to Italy for a month or longer. Maybe go to culinary school there. I could spend years studying under some of the best pastry chefs in the country. I could study anything I wanted."

"Sounds like you've thought about your dream quite a bit, haven't you?" He lowered the arm he had around her. "I know what that's like, to want something so badly you'd give up anything, everything, to make it happen."

They sat in silence as they gazed out at the lake. The sun was hovering just above the horizon. There were huge purple clouds in the west, an indicator of the rainstorm they were supposed to get that night. Crimson rays fanned across the western expanse of sky and fused with fiery orange, golden and lavender fingers of light. The sunset was magnificent and spellbinding.

Neither of them said a word but kept their own counsel and their own thoughts as they watched the sun drift below the horizon.

"You deserve this time," Nate said, not taking his eyes off the sky. "It's important for you to know how high in the stars your arrows will fly."

She watched his profile and saw the committed set to his jaw. *Military set,* she thought. *This was the kind of focus and concentration he must have had when he joined the navy.* He looked so sure of himself and so confident, he reminded her of the kind of man people elected as a statesman. And it was her bet that Nate would be the best at whatever he set his mind to be. He had the education.

She stopped herself. She was doing it again. She was berating herself for not having a college degree. If she sold enough of her franchises, she could go to college. There was no law that said a person had to be straight out of high school to attend college classes. So, she was a little slow at the starting gate. The point was that she was there now. And she sure felt like a thoroughbred wanting to break out for a run.

Maddie inhaled deeply as her revelation took hold deep within her heart. She kissed his cheek excitedly, and he turned his face toward hers.

"What?"

She smiled happily and kissed him very soundly on the mouth. "Thank you, Nate. Thank you for everything."

"I didn't do anything."

"Yes, you did. You just helped me make my decision."

He swallowed hard. He could tell from her delight, the energy and adrenaline that seemed to radiate from her skin, that Maddie had indeed figured it all out. And he knew that when she'd spun these wondrous things she saw herself accomplishing, she hadn't included him. He'd disappeared from her life.

"I'm glad for you, Maddie," he said, lowering his head.

"Hey, you don't look happy." She tilted his face back to hers with her fingers. "You look sad."

His blue eyes bore into hers. This time the adrenaline he felt was his own. He knew he was capable of picking her up and carrying her off to the South Seas, if he thought it would do him any good. "This is going to be a very exciting trip for you. I can see that. Things are going to change like lightning for you."

"They already are," she said.

"Then I'd like to ask a favor."

"Sure."

"I'd like to be a part of all of it with you. I'd like to be on that speed dial of yours when something really great happens for you. I want to be the first person you think about in the morning and the last person you talk to at night. I'd like to be your friend again. Really."

"Is that all?" she probed.

"Oh, God. No." He gathered her in his arms and held her close. He gazed into her sparking green eyes until he swore he could see her soul. "Maddie. My Maddie. Don't you get it?"

"Get what?"

"Deep down, I really came back to Indian Lake for you."

CHAPTER EIGHTEEN

MADDIE SAT IN bed propped against two pillows, arms folded across her chest, and stared at the wall. She'd been staring at the same wall for three hours and fourteen minutes. There were voice mails on her cell phone from Alex when she'd gotten home from the cove. Nate had left another voice mail at ten-twenty. She hadn't returned that call, either.

Her mind was a jumble of thrilling flashes of riding in a chauffeured car with Alex, sitting in the Drake bar and being kissed by the one man on the planet who held the key to her innermost dreams. It was so easy to imagine a life with Alex. A life in the city. The same city where her cafés would be taking off.

She imagined watching the construction. Being with Alex as the project came to fruition. Going to the theater with him. Eating in glittering restaurants and meeting all the interesting entrepreneurs he must surely know and hang out with. She remembered him showing her his apartment building and talking about his parents. She wondered what his place looked like. Was it all steel and chrome or leather and old books? What would it be like to visit his parents in Naples, Florida? She'd never been to Florida. She'd never been anywhere, and she craved travel.

Alex traveled everywhere, it seemed. London. Paris. Dubai. If she pursued a romance with Alex, there was a good chance he would take her along with him. Was he the kind of man who wanted a companion with him on his travels? Or did he consider the company a burden?

Was he a nervous traveler who double-checked every item in his bags or was he a procrastinator who forgot his passport in his rush to the airport?

She and Nate had often gone to Chicago on the weekends when they were in high school. They never argued about the traffic or the cost of parking or what to do when they were playing tourist. They'd chugged down the Chicago River in a sight-seeing boat and walked every inch of North Michigan Avenue window shopping. Nate's arm was always around her waist as they talked about the play they'd just seen or a Cub's game they'd missed.

They had been so easy with each other. Always courteous and caring. Always tender and attentive.

When she thought about life with Nate, that's what she imagined for them. Except for the fact that his future involved a great deal of moving. And none of it would be near a city. If she went with him, she would have to give up her franchise dreams. She would have to leave her Indian Lake friends, and who knew how long it would be until she could return to see them? What if she only saw them on holidays?

Then there was the disquieting question that had lurked in the back of Maddie's mind since the night Alex kissed her. What if she turned him down, romantically? Would he dump her and her franchises? Would he refuse to represent her if she decided she didn't want a relationship with him?

The truth was that Maddie didn't know Alex all that well. She didn't understand his motivations. She sensed he was sincere in his feelings for her, but he was a salesman, after all. He sold people, especially investors, on his clients. Alex's charms had to be well-practiced, otherwise he wouldn't be as successful as he was.

Just thinking about the cost of her involvement with Alex made her nervous. Maybe she should consider Alex off limits.

But if she acted too quickly, she would squelch her own deal.

And that was definitely not the right move for her to make. Maddie shot to her feet and arched her back. "Ugh! This is driving me crazy."

She went to the window and pulled open the navy blue cotton drapes she'd bought at a garage sale for two dollars. She looked out onto Lily Avenue, where only the streetlights burned this late at night. There were no cars, no people about. No one coming home from an after-theater party or midnight supper after the ballet. It was two o'clock, and in a small town the only activity the night would see was the shift changes at the factories around three in the morning. The blossoming trees blocked what little view she sometimes had in the winter of the lighted clock tower on the courthouse, which was still one of her favorite sights. But even that reminded her of Nate.

Many were the nights during the past eleven years when she'd gazed at the clock tower, wondering if, when she woke up, Nate would have come home. Would he try to see her? Would he even remember her?

For years, she'd thought of no one else. There had been no one else. The tiny labyrinths in her ears still echoed with the sound of his voice. "You're my girl, Maddie." And she had believed him.

Nate. She whisked her arm down, closing the drapes. *Why did you have to come back here and complicate things?*

Maddie flopped back on the bed, focusing on the ceiling and the cracked light fixture. *I was almost over you*.

Almost.

Every aspect of Maddie's well-planned career track was moving in the right direction. She had the best contractual attorney, George Regeski, an enthusiastic investor and Alex. Even if she chose love, she could choose Alex. He was definitely interested. She could have it all.

Oddly, she didn't want love with Alex. At least she hadn't thought so when he'd first expressed his romantic interest. She'd only been interested in her deal.

Then he'd kissed her. And something had changed.

Maddie had harbored a fear of relationships since the day Nate left. Understandable. Even expected. No one would fault her for that one.

But something in Alex's kiss had opened her mind to the possibility....

Illumination struck her and she jumped.

I didn't kiss Alex first. I kissed Nate in the café that morning. Alex's kiss was days later.

Now she was more confused than ever. She groaned, shoving her fingers into her short hair.

This was not the time for consternation over men and romance. She'd told Nate this was *her* time. It was her chance to shine. She'd worked too hard and too long not to experience it. With her emotions running wild over Nate and Alex, she couldn't think about business longer than a few minutes.

"Nate. Alex. I should just flip a coin and be done with it."

Exasperated with herself, Maddie then remembered the day she'd seen Nate at Bride's Corner. His appearance in town had felt like a ghost or someone rising from the dead. And tonight he'd claimed that he wanted her. He wasn't an apparition. He was real.

Maddie, this is not the time to fall crazy

mad in love with Nate Barzonni again. He's like opium to you.

She sat bolt upright and her eyes flew open. *That's it! I'm not in love with Nate at all. I'm just addicted to the memory of him.* All those years, she'd used his rejection to gain sympathy. That was wrong and very immature. *Not a good move, Maddie.*

Still, their breakup had motivated her to get on with her life.

Maddie crawled under the covers and pulled the comforter up to her chin. *I can't fall for Nate. I shouldn't fall for Nate. I haven't even found out who I am yet.*

CHAPTER NINETEEN

THE GOSSIP ABOUT MADDIE Strong spread around Indian Lake faster than a late-autumn forest fire. Cupcakes and Coffee had always been a rendezvous spot for Helen Knowland and her band of eavesdropping, busybody friends, but these stories did not start inside the café. Instead, Helen and her ilk met at the Book Shop and Java Stop, the public library, the Indian Lake Deli and the garden patio at the Pine Tree Lodges. The most active center of conversation was the Louise House, since Louise Railton had opened her ice-cream and candy shop on the first of May for the summer tourist season.

Since there wasn't much demand for her homemade frozen treats in the bitter winter months, she shut her doors and used the time to visit family in Florida. Louise had returned in April, tanned and taut from long, barefoot walks on the beach, and she was filled with inspiration for new tropical ice-cream flavors to develop over the summer months.

Louise was waiting on Sophie Mattuchi at Louise House on Friday afternoon. Sophie had put in a very long day and a half at the hospital, and had assisted with an emergency surgery the night before. She had a sweet tooth, and when she was depressed, she often ordered a cone with two scoops and bought a couple pints of various flavors to take home.

Today, however, Sophie ordered only a single scoop. Black walnut.

"That all you want, Sophie?" Louise asked, taking two dollars from the pretty girl.

Sophie smiled as if she was trying to suppress a secret. "That's all," she answered, sitting down at a round table. "You put new fabric on the chairs." She smoothed her palm over the aqua-and-white cabana-striped cotton that now covered all the seats in the little shop. "I like it."

"I'm going tropical this year," Louise announced with a firm nod. "There's going to be some changes in the menu. Maybe put some tropical plants in here. Ferns. Banana trees."

"Wow. Sounds great," Sophie said.

"You gotta have change all the time. Keeps the mind going and the body young."

"Well, I'd say there are quite a few in this town who would agree with that."

"Not really. Nothing ever changes much in Indian Lake." Louise continued polishing her retro milk shake mixer.

"I wouldn't say that. Look at Maddie Strong."

Louise stopped polishing. "Maddie? What's changed about her? If you'd said Sarah Jensen, yeah, I get that. She's getting married. Becoming a mother to those two kids. Cute kids. Polite, too. Not like most of the kids who come in here." Louise held a stained white kitchen towel in her hand as she clamped her fist onto her hip. "So, tell me about Maddie."

Sophie took a long lick of her ice cream, then obliged. "Seems the word is out that some hoity-toity Chicago businessman is going to invest in Maddie's café."

"She's expanding?"

"Franchising. But that's not all. Maddie had to go to Chicago to meet with all these people. Big shots. And they're so rich, they sent a limousine for her. All the way to Indian Lake. The word is that they're going to make Maddie rich."

Louise walked over to Sophie's table and sat down. She folded her hands in her lap and waited eagerly for Sophie to continue.

"But that's not the biggest part of the story," Sophie said in a conspiratorial tone.

"That's pretty big," Louise said.

"One of the rich guys, he sends Maddie expensive flowers nearly every week. He sends them to the café, so you can go over and see them if you don't believe me."

"He's courting her?" Louise asked. Sophie's smile was twisted with a bit too much self-satisfaction for Louise's taste, so she kept her poker face on and played her cards close to her chest.

"Apparently. Looks like Nate Barzonni is going to have a run for his money."

"Nate Barzonni? What's he got to do with anything? He's old news. Besides, no one has heard from him in over a decade."

Sophie shook her head and snickered. "You shouldn't stay away from Indian Lake so long, Louise. Otherwise, you're going to miss a lot of drama around here. Nate not only came back to town, but he signed on at the hospital's new cardiac center. He's my boss. Well, one of them." Sophie grinned satisfactorily. "Now that this new, rich guy is in the picture for Maddie, my bet is that Nate doesn't have a whit of a chance with her. I've even heard some of Maddie's friends joking about whose wedding will be first, Sarah's or Maddie's."

Louise waved her hand in front of her face, brushing off the comment. "That's crazy. She just met the guy."

"I know. But he sent a limousine and all those flowers. It must be serious," Sophie countered.

Louise's eyes narrowed. "You need to get out more, Sophie. City guys are different than hometown boys. City guys do all kinds of outrageous, romantic and flamboyant things for a woman, and it doesn't mean squat."

"I've never met a guy who's acted like that."

"I have."

"Really? How?"

"I've been to Florida."

Now that Louise's ears had been pricked, it seemed they were homing devices for every tidbit of information about Maddie Strong. When she went to the post office, Louise heard two people who were in line waiting for service whispering about the "fancy car" that had come all the way from Chicago to give

Maddie Strong a ride when she was perfectly capable of driving into the city by herself.

By the time Louise had overheard another man at the grocery store and one at the hardware store, she could discern one common tone in their voices: jealousy.

And she didn't like it one bit.

Once jealousy set in, the truth was always twisted and tortured until the person being discussed was hurt, or their reputation ruined. Louise hated that. She'd heard a lot of gossip since the day she'd bought the Rose Street Grocery from Raymond Beabots and turned it into the Louise House. Most of it meant no more to her than the buzzing of summer flies dodging the slow-moving blades of the ceiling fans. However, when the stories involved one of Louise's friends, turning a deaf ear to the gossip was not the right thing to do.

Getting to the truth of the matter required one course of action. Louise had to visit Mrs. Beabots.

Louise twisted the antique doorbell that was mounted in the middle of Mrs. Beabots's front door. The first promise of summer was moving across Indian Lake in the form of a warm breeze that swept through the Boston ferns Mrs. Beabots had placed around her front porch. Louise noticed that dozens of daffodils were in full bloom in the garden, along with forsythia and French lilacs.

The door opened with an impressive *whoosh*. Louise knew Mrs. Beabots was in her early eighties, but for her money, the woman didn't look or act a day over sixty-eight.

"How are you, Louise?" Mrs. Beabots asked brightly.

Louise scrutinized her friend. She wore her blue-rinsed white hair in a shorter-than-normal bob. "You have a new hairdresser. Or that's a wig."

Mrs. Beabots smiled. "Observant as always, Louise. I have a new girl, and she's just the ticket." Mrs. Beabots cupped her hand beneath the exact curve of the hair close to her ear. She tilted her head. "What do you think? Too young?"

"Lord, no. It's great. I wish I had thick hair like yours, instead of these feathers." Louise rolled her eyes. "I'd kill to have that style. It's very becoming."

Mrs. Beabots stood back and allowed Louise to enter the foyer. She closed the door behind them. "I'm glad you approve. I thought we'd go into the parlor."

"Excellent." Louise followed her into the room, which was filled with spring sunshine. Nearly every cachepot, bowl and container was filled with blooming plants. "Good heavens, it looks like a greenhouse in here."

Mrs. Beabots sat down and motioned for Louise to take a chair. "It is. These are my forced bulbs and some seedlings I've been playing with. Keeps me busy till it's planting time. Thank God that time has arrived. Winter just seemed so long this year."

"I've only been back a few weeks."

"How was Florida?"

Louise knew if she answered completely, they would spend all day talking about her, and that wasn't the purpose of the mission. "It was fine. Listen, I know you're always busy and I've got a million things going on, but quite honestly, I had to speak with you about…"

"Maddie?"

Louise was taken aback. "Well, that's getting right down to it. Yes, as a matter of fact. Seems I can't go anywhere that she isn't the topic of conversation."

"I'm not surprised," Mrs. Beabots replied with a slight purse to her lips.

"It's true then? She's franchising her café and she's going to be a millionaire?"

"That's quite exaggerated, but if it all goes through and it's handled correctly, I'd say that in a few years, Maddie won't have to scrimp anymore."

"There's another matter I wanted to discuss."

"Since we've already covered the money part, that only leaves romance." Mrs. Beabots leaned forward. "I don't like people talking about someone I love, and I know you don't spread gossip...."

"I don't," Louise assured her.

Mrs. Beabots nodded again. "So are they talking about Maddie and, well, anyone in particular?"

"Two men. Nate Barzonni—I just found out he's back in town—and then some rich Chicago person. Is that true?"

"Yes."

"And he sent a limousine?"

Mrs. Beabots swatted the air with her hand. "Don't be ridiculous. People don't do that anymore. It was a Lincoln Town Car."

"But hired. I get it. And he's sending flowers?"

Mrs. Beabots nodded.

"Maddie has always been close to you and Sarah. I figured you, of all people, should know what's going on," Louise said.

Mrs. Beabots looked down at her hands and then out her beveled-glass windows to the blooming flowers along Maple Avenue Boulevard. "Honestly, Louise, I don't think that girl has the first clue what's going on at all."

CHAPTER TWENTY

NATE PEELED AROUND Maple Avenue in his Hummer and barreled to an abrupt stop in front of Cupcakes and Coffee. Still wearing his scrubs, he jumped out of his SUV and slammed the door. He bounded up the steps to the café and went inside.

Nate was surprised not to see any patrons inside, but then he remembered Maddie telling him that past three o'clock in the afternoon, she usually didn't have much business.

"Nate!" Maddie said with a bright smile as she came out of the backroom. Her face fell as she glanced at the clock. "What are you doing here? Don't you have a surgery?"

"Canceled," he said. He spotted a silver vase filled with at least four dozen red roses. His eyes tracked around the room until they fell on a second crystal vase with drooping white tulips.

Maddie watched him as he walked slowly toward her. "You've heard."

"The gossip? Yeah. Couldn't avoid it. Seems the nurses in my unit talk about nothing else."

"Really?" Maddie settled a hand on her hip. "I wonder who instigated the topic."

"Does it matter?" he asked, moving to the counter. He pointed at the roses. "Alex, huh?"

"Yes." She raised her chin haughtily and pierced him with her eyes. "He likes to send flowers. He's been doing it since Valentine's Day."

"Seriously?"

"Yep. I usually give them to Sarah or Mrs. Beabots. Hazel likes the tulips, and sometimes Chloe takes them home."

Chloe came out from the backroom. "I go for the daisies. He sends those on Fridays," she said without missing a beat.

Nate rolled his eyes. "I can only guess what Alex wants."

Chloe tried to stifle a laugh. Maddie glared at her. "I'll take out the garbage," Chloe said as she hustled away.

Maddie turned back to Nate. "Alex wants to come to Indian Lake and take me out to dinner. I told him I've been too busy. I'll see him in a few weeks for our next meeting with the investor," she said flatly, still staring at Nate with an uncompromising expression.

"He doesn't just want dinner, Maddie."

"I know that."

"Has he put the moves on you yet?"

"That's none of your business," she replied.

"It's not. But I'd like to know," Nate said sincerely.

"Okay. So, I kissed him."

Nate swallowed hard. He didn't know why he hadn't been prepared for her answer. Or maybe the truth hit him harder than he'd imagined it would. "Must have been some kiss." He exhaled, casting a glance at the roses.

Nate felt like the earth had just dropped away from under his feet. The last time he'd felt this devastated was the night she'd refused his proposal. He'd recognized, then, that her refusal would change his life. But this time he would do something differently. This time he would fight for her.

"Nate, when you came here that morning and I kissed you, it was for revenge."

He sucked in his breath and held it. "Revenge? Well, I guess I deserved that one. Great. That's great. And what about the kisses at the beach? Were those for revenge, too?" He spun around and headed for the door.

"I hated you so much, Nate!" Maddie shouted after him. "My emotions were on fire. I thought if I kissed you I would get you out of my system for good. Expunged. Exorcised. Whatever. I wanted you gone. Until I kissed you."

"And then?" He turned back to her.

"Frankly, I'm off my fulcrum here. Out of whack. Out of balance. You make me nuts, you know that? I don't know what to think. I had everything all planned out. My life, I mean."

"And Alex was a part of it?"

"Not in that way, no."

"Not then, you mean. Not before you kissed."

She pursed her lips. "And not now, either, Nate. No man is."

Nate was silent. He nodded. "Thanks for being honest. I appreciate it."

Nate walked out the door feeling as if he were going to explode. Anger at Maddie wasn't going to get him anywhere. Cursing at fate hadn't helped in the past either.

Maddie wanted a life of her own. Without him.

His head told him that giving Maddie time and space was his best option, but right now, his heart was fearful that he would lose her.

When he'd lost her before, he'd been young and filled with the need to escape from his father's grip and make his own way in the world. Losing Maddie then was a thousand times less painful than this.

This time he knew he wouldn't recover.

This time he felt a cold chill of deep loss and sorrow crackle through his body like life-sapping frost.

Nate knew what it was like to feel dead inside.

CHAPTER TWENTY-ONE

IN INDIAN LAKE, the second Sunday in May was undoubtedly like most towns and cities across America. Churches were filled with mothers and grandmothers dressed in their finery, gathered together to be with their families for the holiday. Every restaurant in and around Indian Lake served its own version of a special champagne brunch. Live bands, trios and string quartets played at private homes, hotels and beach cafés.

What made Mother's Day in Indian Lake unique was the riotous affair that took place up and down Maple Avenue in the gardens of the majestic Victorian mansions. From the moment Pastor Joe Blake from Bethany Lutheran and Father Michael from St. Mark's Episcopal Church released their congregations, the rush to the town nurseries was on.

In a matter of hours, salmon, pink, white and lavender impatiens; petunias of every color and ruffle; geraniums from scarlet red to bubblegum pink; begonias; black-eyed Susans; hydrangeas; marigolds; vincas; salvia; firecrackers; hibiscus; climbing roses; knockout roses; cane roses; and stunning rose trees would be whisked off the nursery shelves and the planting wars would begin.

By early evening, Maple Avenue would be transformed from natural spring gardens to haute couture spring and summer gardens. Not a brown leaf would be seen anywhere. Fresh mulch would cover and outline the flower beds so they looked as if they'd been scissored in by seamstresses. Hundreds of Boston ferns would be hung before sundown from the posts of expansive front porches. Wooden rocking chairs appeared from basements and cellars. Palmetto blades were attached to porch ceiling fans and yellow bug lightbulbs were screwed into garage and backdoor light fixtures.

Huge clay pots were filled with red geraniums, blue ageratum and spikes.

The fact that Ann Marie Jensen was almost singularly to blame for the current flower addiction along Maple Avenue had not escaped Sarah one bit.

As much as she loved her fellow townsfolk,

this was one time when they really were com-
paring her to her talented mother.

Sarah had worked out a detailed planting diagram for her garden, just the way her
mother had instructed. She ordered the flats
of color-coordinated annuals, bags of potting
soil and red bark mulch from the Indian Lake
Nursery well in advance of the rush. She had
been as organized and prepared for this day
as she was about her work and her wedding.
Everything was in place.

But this year was different. Very different.

Maddie stood in Sarah's kitchen after Sunday services at St. Mark's making a pot of
espresso for Sarah and Luke. She had just re-
trieved a pitcher of heavy cream from the refrigerator, when Sarah hit her with her news.

Maddie whirled to face her best friend.
"What do you mean Luke's parents are coming today?"

"Just what I said," Sarah replied, brandish-
ing a knife over the head of a fresh pineapple.

"But you've never met them."

"Obviously," she growled.

"Did you know this was happening? Or
did Luke just spring it on you? Which, by the
way, doesn't sound like him at all."

"No, we talked about it. But last week we

said we'd go see them up in Oak Park. Then Timmy got the flu. It was just a twenty-four-hour thing, but we canceled the trip. That was the second time we had to cancel, so finally we told them to come here. It's also Mother's Day. Luke wanted to do something for his mom, and we were dying to meet each other."

Maddie put her hand on her hip. "So here we are. With a meal to prepare. A yard of the century to plant. The Indian Lake Garden Club breathing down our necks. Oh, the pressure!" Maddie threw the back of her hand against her forehead.

"Shut up," Sarah retorted.

"Okay. I get it. You're nervous," Maddie said nonchalantly, and then she turned to Sarah. "Oh my gosh. You *are* nervous."

"What if…" Sarah began.

"Don't…" Maddie shook her finger at her. "Don't! It's not possible."

"They're the kids' grandparents. And I've only been a career woman. Not a mother." Sarah stared at Maddie with doubt in her eyes.

"Listen, those kids adore you. And if you need any help being a mother to them, they're the kind of kids who will tell you you're messing up, so you can fix it right away. Besides, no parent actually knows what they're doing. They just do it."

Sarah stayed silent.

Maddie took a deep breath. "Okay. Look at it this way. No matter what you do, you always know you'll do a better job than Babs did."

Sarah nodded slowly. "I'll take that one. Let's fix the sausage-and-cheese soufflé. While it's in the oven, we can get an hour of work done on the yard."

"Fine with me. I brought my gardening dungarees. Put me to work."

"Don't laugh. I will," Sarah replied.

Just then Miss Milse tromped into the kitchen. She wore a pale blue cotton uniform dress that Maddie remembered the woman wearing at least fifteen years ago. Maddie was amazed that the dress looked brand-new. Miss Milse's steely-gray hair was tied up, as usual, in the tightest bun any human could possibly twist on top of her head without drawing blood.

"I set the table in the dining room. It's done. I fix the fruit. And the sausage." She shoved Sarah away from the sink.

"I was going to make the soufflé," Sarah retorted.

"Your mother's recipe?" she asked.

"Yes. It's tradition."

"It's good. I make." She picked up the paring knife and pointed to the garden. "You go to work. In the garden. You make it nice, like your mother."

Sarah nodded and turned to Maddie. "Come on, we have about an hour or so before Luke and the kids get here with his parents."

"Can I change in your room?"

"Sure. Meet you outside. I have some gardening gloves for you."

"Peachy."

MRS. BEABOTS wore her wide-brimmed straw gardening hat, new pink gardening gloves and a long apron over a buttercup-yellow dress. In the pockets of the apron, she carried all manner of tools. She'd had the Indian Lake Nursery deliver her flats of annuals the day before, and this year she'd told the nursery to put her pots of geraniums, spikes and blue forget-me-nots together for her. Lifting the bags of potting soil was getting to be more of a bother to her with each passing year. There were just some things she'd decided to ask others to do for her. Each year she'd planted more and more perennials and bulbs and fewer annuals. By this point in her life, she'd participated in the grab for the Indian Lake Yard of the Year Award often enough. And besides, if she put her full court press effort into what she knew she could do well, she might steal the prize from Sarah. This year, she truly did think Sarah should win.

Sarah had worked very hard last fall to put in new beds and to plant her bulbs early-flowering forsythia and French lilacs. Mrs. Beabots had seen Sarah's diagram for this year's garden. The stunning design included two weeping cherry trees, which were among Mrs. Beabots's favorite plants. Yes, it was time for Mrs. Beabots to take the downshift. She'd save up for next year. Or perhaps the next.

Mrs. Beabots heard the chatter coming from Sarah's yard. Although she was invited for Mother's Day dinner at Sarah's later that evening, she knew her neighbor wouldn't mind an early visit. Putting her gloves in her apron pocket, she walked down her driveway-and onto the sidewalk, nearly bumping into Father Michael and three of his feisty house-keeper's children.

"Happy Mother's Day, Father Michael," Mrs. Beabots greeted him with a sly smile while staring at Colleen Kelly's brood. The girl and two boys were dressed in their Sunday clothes.

"I'm taking them for a walk. It's my Mother's Day present for Colleen," he explained. "It seemed the least I could do, considering she has three more at home besides these to deal with."

"Children are a blessing, Father," Mrs. Beabots reminded him.

"Yes, but not in groups," he grumbled.

"Still, it's a kindness you're doing her."

"I told her to take the day off, it being Mother's Day, and all, and she's over at the rectory making me a chicken salad."

"She wants you to be healthy."

"I'd rather have her potpies and she knows it."

Mrs. Beabots smiled. "Well, I have a recipe that is lower in fat and cholesterol and just delicious."

"How can you do that? Potpies are butter, cream and piecrust. Colleen says they're the worst thing for me."

Mrs. Beabots winked. "I use olive oil and triple the sherry. I'll whip one up for you sometime."

"That's delightful, Mrs. Beabots. Just delightful." Father Michael beamed at her. Then he looked down at the children, who were staring up at him patiently. "Okay, I think I hear your mother calling you," he joked.

"Good day, Father," Mrs. Beabots said.

"Good planting," he replied, and shuffled off with the youngest Kelly toddler hanging on to his pants' bottoms, still sucking his thumb.

Mrs. Beabots walked around the hedges that separated her yard from Sarah's. "Yoohoo! Sarah," Mrs. Beabots called.

Maddie was planting salmon-colored impatiens and blue salvia under one of the weeping cherry trees. Sarah had just finished piling peat moss around the sides of a new Princess Diana rosebush. "Mrs. Beabots, hi!" Sarah yelled back.

Maddie smiled. "Thank heaven. The cavalry." She rose from her knees and dusted off her gloves. "Please tell me you made lemonade."

"Goodness, no, dearie. I don't even have the begonias in yet." She leaned over to Sarah and whispered, "Lester is coming over to help me."

"That's great to hear, Mrs. Beabots. I should invite him for dinner tonight."

Mrs. Beabots shook her head. "He won't come. Not with Luke's family here and all. But we should make him a plate."

"Good idea," Maddie said, bounding up and placing her hand on Mrs. Beabots's shoulder and planting an impromptu kiss on her cheek. "After I help Sarah, I'll be over to plant your marigolds and black-eyed Susans in the backyard."

"No rush, dear," Mrs. Beabots said.

Maddie's mouth fell open. "Are you kidding? The garden police will be roaming the boulevard by six this evening. We're on a tight schedule here."

"It's just fine," Mrs. Beabots assured her.

Maddie eyed the elderly woman suspiciously. "What's gotten in to you? This is opening Sunday of the garden wars. Half this town is checking your progress. Okay," she acquiesced. "Yours and Sarah's."

Sarah checked her watch. "I better get back to it. Luke will be here before I know it and I'll need to shower before I meet his parents. I wonder if I should wash my hair again?" Sarah looked at Maddie for reassurance.

Mrs. Beabots narrowed her eyes. "Are you all right?"

"She's fine," Maddie said before Sarah

could get in a word. "Just nervous about meeting the parents."

"Oh, good Lord. I thought it was something important. Like forgetting another flat of impatiens, which is what that bed is going to need to win the trophy," she said, pointing at Maddie's handiwork.

Sarah and Maddie surveyed the flower bed.

Mrs. Beabots started walking back to her own yard.

"Do you think so? Is that what it really needs?" Sarah asked, digging her cell phone out of her jeans pocket and dialing the nursery. "I hope they have some left," she said to Maddie.

Maddie swatted the air between them dismissively as she returned to her flower bed.

Just then, she heard the roar of a very familiar car engine.

Maddie whirled. "It can't be…"

Nate parked his Hummer close to the curb and got out. "Maddie, can I talk to you?"

He was wearing a dark blue sport jacket, white shirt and navy slacks. His stride was confident as he approached her.

"Sure, Nate," Maddie said, projecting an ease she didn't feel. The truth was, her heart was in her throat and her knees were definitely on the wobbly side.

She hadn't heard from him since their encounter two days ago at the café. She hadn't called him because she didn't know what to say. She didn't want to lose him, but at the same time, she couldn't make any promises. And he hadn't told her that he loved her. He'd implied a great deal, but he hadn't come right out and said it.

Maddie's guess was that they both needed time to get to know each other all over again.

"How did you know I would be here?" she asked.

"When we were in high school, you always spent Mother's Day here with Sarah and Mrs. Jensen. You said you liked planting the flowers, and because your mother beat it out of town to some bar in Michigan, this was your home for the day."

"You remember that?"

"I remember a lot of things, Maddie," he said, brushing a lock of hair off her forehead.

Impossible as it was, Maddie couldn't tear her eyes from his. A long time ago, she'd told him she could spend her life just gazing into his eyes. She'd been young and naive. But now she had no excuse, and she still felt the same way.

"I remember that your mother has a huge family dinner on Mother's Day, and if I'm not mistaken, you'll get a tongue-lashing if you aren't there."

"That's why I need your help, Maddie. It's for my mom."

"What is it?"

He looked over her shoulder at Sarah. "Can I steal you for about an hour? I need you to help me pick out flowers for my mother's gift."

She stared at him for a long moment. "You don't need my help for that."

"I don't," he confessed. "I just wanted to see you."

A soft smile creased her mouth. "I thought so. I wanted to see you, too. But I can't leave. I promised Sarah I'd help her with the planting. Once I've got these flats in the ground, I can break away for a bit, if you really want me to."

He grinned. "I do. Tell you what. I'll help you out here. We can finish up twice as fast."

She beamed at him. "Thanks, Nate."

"I'm glad you're not mad at me. For the other day, I mean," he said.

"If I was really mad at you, Nate, you'd know it. Besides, I missed you."

Relief flooded Nate's face. "I missed you so much. I—" Without another word, he pulled her into his arms and kissed her.

Sarah caught them out of the corner of her eye and instantly finished her call. She shoved the cell phone in her jeans pocket. "Guys?"

Maddie and Nate didn't pay attention. They were oblivious to everything except each other.

Suddenly, Maddie heard Beau barking and Miss Milse shouting commands in German. Then Beau came bounding around from the back of the house. He raced across the wide lawn toward Maddie and Nate, gold fur flying.

Beau jumped up on Nate. Maddie jumped aside, realizing Beau thought Nate was an attacker. An intruder. The enemy.

"No! Beau! No!" Sarah yelled, lunging forward.

Beau had grabbed Nate's lapel between his teeth and was trying to pull him down. Nate lost his balance and stumbled backward. "Whoa. Whoa!" he yelled.

He crashed to the ground, bringing Maddie down on top of him.

Sarah rushed toward Beau, trying to grab his collar before he did any more damage, but she tripped over an open bag of potting soil. When she raised herself up on her palms, her entire front was covered in dirt. She spit out a mouthful. "Beau. Stop. Now!"

Maddie was laughing so hard, her voice rang across the street. "Oh, my gosh! Just look at us. Dirt, grass stains and doggie slobber!"

"I love it," Nate said, joining in the laughter.

Maddie squeezed her eyes shut and pursed her lips to avoid Beau's tongue.

"Beauregard Jensen. You leave them alone this instant and come over here," Sarah commanded, anger rising in her voice.

Beau lifted his head, and with a huge doggie smile on his face, bounded across the small distance and jumped on Sarah.

Sarah tried to push him away. "Oh, Beau. For goodness' sake, stop!"

At this precise moment, with the three of them on the ground, Beau now trying to lick Sarah, and Maddie laughing her head off, Luke pulled into the driveway in his pickup truck with Annie, Timmy and his parents.

Maddie watched Luke take in the scene,

and stared from his parents' shocked faces
to the devilish delight in his children's eyes.

Luke tore his eyes from the scene and
turned to his family. "It's not what it looks
like."

CHAPTER TWENTY-TWO

IN THE Barzonni house, the family tradition for Mother's Day had nothing to do with planting gardens and everything to do with honoring Gina Barzonni. As with most holidays in the Barzonni household, the boys' attendance on this day was mandatory if they wanted to maintain the peace within the family. The only time there had been a vacancy at the large, formal dining room table had occurred when Nate was in the navy.

Fortunately, Nate was home again.

This Mother's Day, Gina had two pots of tomato sauce cooking on her six-burner gas range. In a third pot were Italian sausages and peppers. Painted Italian casserole dishes containing cheese ravioli with pesto sauce and penne with vodka sauce and mushrooms filled the oven. The distressed black-walnut kitchen island was crowded with freshly washed salad greens and all the makings for an enormous Caesar salad.

Earlier, Gina had pulled three loaves of Italian bread from the oven and put them aside.

In the middle of the kitchen was a huge trestle table made of olive wood that had been in her family since the early 1920s. She had the table and several other old pieces of furniture that she had always loved shipped from Italy. A second large dark wood table stood in the dining room, beneath a Venetian-crystal chandelier that had belonged to Gina's grandmother.

Gina was proud of her family heritage, and she pulled out all the stops for Mother's Day.

Today she had a surprise for Nate. While shopping at Judee's dress shop earlier in the week, she'd run into Sophie, Nate's scrub nurse. Her conversation with Sophie was friendly and comfortable as they exchanged stories about Italian family traditions, and Gina was so taken with the pretty woman that she asked Sophie to join them today. Sophie was just the type of Italian girl she would like as a daughter-in-law. The fact that Sophie and Nate shared a love for medicine was the icing on the cake.

Gina just knew Nate would be pleased.

Gina could hear the male laughter of her

husband and sons as they worked together to fill the swimming pool, backwash the sand filter and test the water. Gabe was checking the pumps and equipment. Mica was planting the Italian pots with red geraniums that marched around the edges of the flagstone patio and pool deck. Rafe was dragging bags of potting soil for his brother, and Angelo had just finished setting up the new fake-wicker chaise longues with flamboyant yellow-and-white-striped cushions that Gina had ordered over the winter.

Gina had made a large pitcher of sangria and had chilled a bottle of Soave, which was from the Veneto region in Italy. It was Mother's Day after all.

She walked out to the patio and placed the drinks on a table nearest the longues. "So, what do you think, Angelo?"

Angelo put his hands on his hips and smiled at her. "It looks like Napoli."

"Excellent," she said. "Then I have succeeded. Come and have some wine with me."

She poured a glass of the Soave for herself and a glass of sangria for Angelo.

They sat on their new chaises, and Gina gazed lovingly at her sons. Then she sat upright. "Where's Nate?"

Angelo took a gulp of his sangria. "I don't know. He said he had something to get in town."

"In town? There's nothing open on Mother's Day."

Angelo avoided her icy expression. "I doubt that."

"What could be open on Mother's Day?" she demanded.

Gabe and Rafe wiped off their hands and bounded across the flagstones toward her.

Gabe flopped down on a chaise next to Gina. He reached out his hand, grabbed hers and kissed it. "Happy Mother's Day, Mom."

"Thank you, sweetheart."

Rafe sat on the end of Gina's chaise. "I love you, Mom. You sure look beautiful today."

Mica walked up and peeled off his garden gloves. "I think you look great, too."

She looked from one face to the other. They were good boys. Honest. Trustworthy. Loyal and dependable. And they were all lying to her about something. "What's going on?"

"Nothing," Gabe said, just as they heard Nate's Hummer coming up the driveway.

Nearly in unison, the boys sighed in relief, jumped from their seats and took off.

"Nate's here!" Mica said, pushing Gabe out of the way.

Gina caught Angelo's eye. "What's going on?"

"They're boys. How should I know?"

NATE STEPPED OUT of his Hummer and saw his brothers racing toward him.

"You're late!" Rafe growled. "Do you have any idea how close you came this time?"

"Did you see her?" Mica asked.

"Yes." Nate punched Mica's shoulder. "And it was good. She was happy to see me."

"Well, that's a win, isn't it?" Gabe asked.

"I'll take it," Nate replied.

"That's right," Rafe chimed in. "No city-slicker moneybags is going to take my brother's girl from him! We're in this together, man." Rafe slapped Nate's back. "You gotta fight back, I always say."

Mica peered inside the Hummer. "So did you get it?"

"When I got to the nursery, they had two rose trees set aside for me to decide. I couldn't choose. So I bought both. Then I got four yellow hibiscus because I knew Mom just got those new chairs for the pool. These will match."

Gabe grabbed Nate's shoulder. "Good thinking. Bribery works with this woman. That's been established."

"I don't know, guys. I owe Mom and Dad for leaving the way I did. You guys, too."

Gabe frowned. "Listen. What happened back in high school is ancient history. Nobody holds a grudge forever. The Maddie issue is another story."

"You're telling me. I want her to figure out what she wants and experience some of the successes I've had already, but honestly, this thing with Alex makes me very nervous."

"You love her, don't you?" Mica asked.

Nate stared at his brother. In that millisecond, he realized he'd never stopped loving Maddie. He loved her as the young girl he'd known in high school and he loved her as the accomplished beautiful woman she'd grown into. "I do."

"Well, then I say go for it. Ask Maddie to marry you."

"What if she says no?"

Mica rubbed his chin. "She wouldn't do that, would she?"

"Sure she would," Nate said. "She turned me down once…"

"That wasn't a real proposal, man!" Rafe

guffawed. "That was so lame anybody would have turned you down."

"I was sincere," he said defensively.

"Of course," Gabe said, "Maddie's really smart. And she knows all of us."

"You're right, Gabe. What woman in their right mind would want this family?" Rafe laughed again and the other brothers joined in.

Nate opened the Hummer's backdoor. "Come on, let's get this stuff unloaded."

The four brothers tromped around to the pool.

"Happy Mother's Day!" they shouted.

"What's all this?" Gina sat up and put her wineglass aside. "How beautiful! And it's just what the patio needed. So elegant!"

Gina rose and kissed each of her sons and thanked them.

"I almost have dinner ready," she said. "Do you boys want to help me bring it to the table?"

Nate swallowed hard, trying to find courage. "We could have a glass of wine first," he offered.

"Certainly," Angelo said, and happily poured the sangria for his sons.

They toasted their mother and drank.

"Lovely," Gina said, rising from the chaise. "Now I need to get to my dinner. I really could use some help. We have a guest coming today."

"Guest?" Angelo asked. "Anyone we know?"

"Yes. It's Nate's friend from the hospital. She's been here before. When you boys were in high school, I think she said. She's such a special girl." Gina leaned close to Nate. "I like her a great deal, Nate." She winked at her son.

"Who?" Nate asked, wondering if Maddie and Gina had planned a surprise for him.

"Sophie Mattuchi. Such a lovely girl." Gina swished into the house.

CHAPTER TWENTY-THREE

MADDIE OPENED THE café at six o'clock on Monday morning as always and greeted Chloe, who was standing under the new awning over the front door.

"Mornin', Maddie. I like the new awning. When do the ones for over the front windows get installed?"

"Today. Along with the window boxes. And the new chairs will be here in a few weeks."

"Gosh. It's going to look so…Italian," Chloe gushed. She stopped as she reached the counter.

Next to the register was a ruby crystal vase filled with multicolored roses and white orchids. Chloe pointed to the vase, whirled and shot an accusatory look at Maddie. "Alex sent more flowers."

"I see that," Maddie said, coming over to join Chloe. "But look over there." She pointed to the corner by the windows.

Sitting on top of one of the tables was a two-foot-tall cylinder that held purple orchids and purple roses clustered in a tight nosegay at the top. "Those are from him as well," Maddie said. "He's in London on business, so he can't call or text like he usually does. I think he sends the flowers so I won't forget him."

"I like this guy," Chloe said.

"So do I," Maddie replied with a pensive smile.

Chloe went around to the sink and filled a pitcher with water to start the coffee machines. "Let's see. Last week he sent you three bouquets when he was in Santa Barbara."

"Those flowers I gave to Mrs. Beabots and to Sarah."

"Hmm." Chloe rolled her eyes, but Maddie could see her braiding motives, actions and intentions like colorful ribbons in her mind as she assessed Alex more critically. She shot Maddie a suspicious look. "I thought you had to go to Chicago soon for some kind of final deal or something. You'd be seeing him then. He's moving in for the kill, if you ask me."

Maddie tilted her chin up as she polished the copper-and-brass espresso machine. "Alex wants a date. But not in Chicago. He wants to come here."

"And the problem is?"

Maddie walked behind the counter and busied herself filling a pastry bag with a new batch of Italian crème icing. Her fingers fumbled with the tip and the bag. The icing fell off the spatula into a big plop on the counter. Maddie's mind was a battlefield of confusion, indecision and fear. For most of her adult life, she'd avoided relationships, buried herself in her work and kept her fear of rejection caged and padlocked.

Now she felt as if all her demons had been released. Alex was pushing her toward… something, but she didn't know what. Nate claimed he wanted her, but hadn't committed to anything. Both men were intelligent, handsome, ambitious and just as career oriented and goal-driven as she was. Maddie could count on one hand the nights she'd actually slept peacefully in the past two months. She noticed that her catering orders were not as organized as they had been last month. She wasn't just preoccupied, she was distraught and confused to the point of paralysis.

"I don't know what to do."

Chloe walked over, picked up Maddie's

left hand and looked at it. "Nope. No rock there. No gold band, no commitments. So, why would there be a problem?"

Maddie looked down at her hand. She felt like crying. She'd seen Nate just yesterday, and last night he'd called to say good-night. He told her that his mother liked the flowers they'd picked out for her at the Indian Lake Nursery, but he said their dinner had been a quiet affair. He said he would call her this morning after his first surgery. Maddie had the nagging feeling that there was something he wasn't telling her, adding a new worry to her insurmountable pile of anxiety.

She had to admit that the more she talked to Nate, and spent time with him, the closer she felt to him. But Chloe was right. There was no commitment between them. She had told him she needed time to sort out her feelings. She was getting precisely what she wanted. But if that was true, why were her animal instincts on high alert?

"I don't know, Chloe. I just don't know."

Just then, Sophie Mattuchi walked in the door. "Hi, Maddie! How are you? Am I too early for a double espresso?"

"Not at all. Chloe can do the honors." Maddie took in the startling change in Sophie's appearance. Gone were her long dark tresses. "You cut your hair."

Sophie grinned with delight. "And highlighted it. I've got four different colors of browns and golds. I thought it was time to go lighter. Summer and all. It's really a change, isn't it?"

"Just like one of those television makeovers," Maddie said with a forced smile. "I've always liked short hair myself."

"I know," Sophie said, touching her bare nape. "It's going to take some getting used to. But what the heck. It's easier, that's for sure." Sophie giggled.

"Would you like a cupcake or pastry with your coffee?" Maddie asked.

"No, thanks. I've been watching my calories and I've lost a dress size already. So, I'm going to keep at it. I will take one of those apples though."

"I've got some homemade granola I'm testing. You want to try some? It's low-fat and has no sugar, but there's honey in it. All natural. No charge."

"I'll try a sample. Sure. Thanks, Maddie." Sophie dug in her purse for her wallet. When she looked up, Maddie saw her eyes fall on the roses and orchids in the ruby vase. "Oh, my gosh! Those are incredible. Where did you get them?"

"Secret admirer," Chloe piped in as she put a cardboard sleeve on the steaming cup of espresso.

"Wow. He's got great taste," Sophie remarked as she paid Chloe.

"They are something to behold," Maddie agreed, admiring the arrangement.

"I gotta run. Early surgery this morning. Can't keep the doctor waiting," Sophie said. "Good luck with your secret admirer."

They watched Sophie walk out the door and get into her car.

"You know her pretty well?" Chloe asked.

"Since high school. She's two years older than I am. She used to row with Sarah, Isabelle and the rest of us. She's kind of part of our crowd, but because of her nursing schedule, she's always bailing on us when we row or throw parties and dinners."

"You work a lot, and you don't bail."

"She also dates around a lot."

Chloe chewed her bottom lip thoughtfully. "Yeah? How so?"

"She usually only dates a guy once or twice. She says they always bore her. I think she's scared of commitment."

"She doesn't look scared to me now."

"No?" Maddie asked, and finally turned to Chloe. "What does she look like?"

"Like she's trying too hard. Like she works for Nate Barzonni and she just got her hair chopped off so she looks more like you. She goes from brunette to almost blond overnight and you don't think something's up?"

Maddie froze. "But she's one of my girlfriends. She wouldn't go after Nate when she knows—"

Chloe shrugged. "What does she know?"

Chloe was only twenty-one, and yet she was already more astute than Maddie, who had always liked to believe she was wise. Clearly, Maddie had been living in a bubble for too long. "Don't tell me you can see this and I can't."

"You have five hundred bucks' of flower arrangements in here. And those are just the new installments. Look around. Do you see Dr. Nate parkin' his toothbrush anywhere? Uh-uh."

Maddie grabbed her apron and tied it around her waist. "I have to think about this."

"That would be good. And make it snappy. Sophie is in a big rush, even if you aren't."

CHAPTER TWENTY-FOUR

ALEX PERKINS DROVE through the i-Zoom lane on the Chicago Skyway in his two-year-old Lexus convertible listening to Rachmaninoff's Prelude Opus 32, No. 2 in B-flat Minor. His mind was not on the music. His mind was on Maddie Strong.

Alex had closed his casino-and-theme-park deal with the investors from Dubai and put together another merger involving a London bank and a new film division of a major studio in Los Angeles. He was feeling mighty fine. According to his calculations, he should be offered a partnership in his firm before the end of the year. The accumulation of overtime hours, his family connections and networking with university roommates and friends from his postgrad at NYU were finally paying off. Over the past three years, he'd brought more money into the firm than the two owners put together. His bosses had patted his back so much lately that his shoulders were sore. He felt invincible.

Alex, however, was smarter than those of the previous generation. He squirreled away his assets and kept his spending, except for business purposes, on the lean side. His condo and car had been paid for in cash. His only extravagance had been the flowers he sent to Maddie.

"Maddie..." He sang her name along with his favorite strain of the music.

If things went exceptionally well, he might actually be able to take a four-day vacation in the middle of the blasted winter. It would be his first vacation in six years.

His goal was to have Maddie at his side on that trip. He was thinking Cap Juluca in Anguilla. St. Bart's would be nice, but not as remote. The blindingly white sands and turquoise water in Anguilla were definitely the best for long sunset walks. Unless, of course, he considered Marbella. That was an option.

As always, Alex felt the best decision was to keep his options open.

Zooming down I-94, Alex took the turn-off to the Indiana toll road, which took him straight to Indian Lake.

Driving past the lake, Alex called Maddie's cell.

"Hey. I'm almost here," he said. "So give me directions."

IT WAS NEARLY four o'clock, and the café was closed for business. Maddie wore a white linen sheath dress, espadrilles, aquamarine earrings and a matching bracelet that she'd borrowed from Mrs. Beabots.

Maddie walked out of the office and glanced apprehensively at Chloe, who had just finished cleaning the sinks and was folding her apron and towel.

"You look good, okay?" Chloe said. "He'll drop. Promise." She giggled and raced out the door.

Chloe had just disappeared around the corner when Alex drove up. He got out of the car, straightened, buttoned his pearl-gray suit coat and waved as Maddie unlocked the door.

Spreading his arms wide, he appraised the building from the curb. "So, this is it? This is the inspiration?"

She nodded proudly. "This is it. I'm just starting my renovations to evolve it into the Italian café I've always envisioned, but this is the seed of the dream I planted."

He breezed up to her and kissed her cheek. "It's marvelous. Smaller than I'd imagined. But that's a good thing."

"Good?"

"For the PR campaign," he said. "Can I come in?"

"Sure. Sorry," she said, stepping aside.

Alex placed his hands on his hips and assessed the interior. "When does the painting start?"

"Tomorrow. Chairs arrive next week. And I just put the awnings up outside."

"I saw." He continued to scrutinize the space, then turned to her with a grin. "So, you got the new flowers."

"Alex." She shook her head slowly. "I asked you to stop sending them. And I told you I give them to my friends. Their houses are filled with flowers."

"So donate them to the local nursing home," he said, moving closer and putting his hands on her waist. "I don't care." He kissed her cheek again. "Boy, you smell great. Chanel, right?"

"Yes. I love it."

"Me, too. On you, of course."

"Would you like a cappuccino? A sandwich?" she asked.

"I was thinking of champagne and escargots," he replied. "Where can we rustle some up?"

She laughed. "In Indian Lake? Not hardly."

"You're kidding."

"No, I'm not."

"Then I'll drive us back to Chicago. I know this place off Rush Street—"

"Alex," she interrupted, feeling a tingle of nervousness. "Why exactly are you here?"

"It thought it was obvious. I wanted to see you. Since you're always too busy to come see me… Well, ta da." He extended his arms again, like an opera singer ready to release the last high note of an aria.

"Hey," she cut him off, jabbing an accusatory finger at him. "You're the one who goes to Dubai and London and Hollywood. You haven't been in the office for three straight days since we met with James."

"Guilty as charged," he said. "But I thought about you all the time I was gone."

"Did you?" she asked, keenly aware of the twinkle in his eyes and the soft smile on his lips. "All good, I hope."

"I thought that what I have to say to you should be said in person. Because, Maddie, you're right. I *have* been away a great deal.

We've talked on the phone. We've emailed and texted. We even used FaceTime when I was in London. Remember that?"

"You looked so funny."

"I was trying to be funny. It was a funny day." He chuckled. "Anyway, I believe we've come to know each other fairly well over the past months, wouldn't you say?"

"I would say that," she replied, wondering how well they actually could get to know each other over the phone and via email. Was the true self revealed more in writing than in speaking, as some psychologists believed? She knew that oftentimes, what people said wasn't what they meant. There was no end to the miscommunication that could arise once two people opened their mouths. It amazed her that anyone ever bonded with another person at all.

"And we get along pretty well," Alex continued. "Not to mention that I think I have a solid understanding of what you want out of your career. I believe I've managed to pair you with the best investor for your needs."

"You've done a wonderful job, Alex."

He took her hands in his. Although Alex impressed her as a man who was always in control, she noticed that his hands trembled slightly as he reached for her. He was nervous, and that surprised her.

"Maddie, I have a confession to make."

"My investor wants out, doesn't he?" Maddie said, her imagination running wild. Her mouth went dry and she felt suddenly weak, as if her body had been sapped of energy. She was a puppet to her own goals and she realized, quite sadly, that she'd put too much value on achieving them. Her business wasn't who she was. It was an outlet for her creativity, but it wasn't her essence. She hadn't known, until right now, that she was more than her café. If James backed out, she still had her café, some of the best friends anyone could wish for, and a very full life in Indian Lake. She was healthy and young. She wasn't a quitter. She had proven to herself that she was persistent, determined and smart. It took courage to stand up to rejection. She wondered if Alex knew these things about her.

"No, nothing like that," Alex assured her. "James is on board. All the way. I was just going to say that when I told you that my partners were behind your idea and concept, that wasn't *exactly* true."

"It wasn't?"

"Actually, they thought I was nuts. They

said it couldn't be done and that there wasn't anything extraordinary or special about some cupcakes. I fed them the same Becky Fields line I gave you. I believed in you, Maddie. And after we started working together, I was determined to make your dream a reality. I wanted to be your knight in shining armor. I wanted to give you what no other man had given you."

Maddie felt her throat tighten. Another close call. She had come close to losing it all and she hadn't even known it. Alex was her hero even more than she'd known.

She owed him a great deal.

"Alex, I don't know what to say—just that I'm so grateful."

He lifted her chin with his fingertips. "Maddie, I don't just want gratitude. I want you." He kissed her sweetly and lightly. "Maddie, I want to know if you would consider moving to Chicago."

"You know I've dreamed about living there someday, Alex. I told you that."

"I meant with me, Maddie. With me."

CHAPTER TWENTY-FIVE

MADDIE SAT ON a Victorian chair in Mrs. Beabot's front parlor. She kicked off her espadrilles and accepted a small glass of sherry from her friend.

"So, you're still trying to figure out who the new Maddie is? And who the old one used to be?"

"I am, and it's so hard."

"I've always found that if I give things enough time, they generally work themselves out."

Maddie let out a sigh of frustration. "I was afraid you'd say that. The thing is, I feel like I've given it time. Eleven years. This is when things are supposed to work out."

"Many people believe that young love doesn't count. That it's some kind of throwaway phase that we learn from, or that shapes our opinions of ourselves. But I've never seen it that way. I think it's the time when the heart is free and unfettered. I met Raymond when I was very young. Even younger than you and Nate were. I knew he was the one for me. It took several years for us to work out the details—I had college and he wanted to be an entrepreneur."

"Really?" Mrs. Beabots rarely spoke about her husband or their past together.

"That story is for another day," Mrs. Beabots said. "The point is, there's nothing wrong with exploring yourself and your feelings for Alex."

"Yes."

"But I will say, that from what I saw between you and Nate the other day at Sarah's, I think you have your answer."

Maddie wiped her face with her hands and clamped them on her knees. "That's the thing. Nate came back to town to boost his career. Then he realized he might still have feelings for me. I told him I wanted to find out who I am, now that I have some success. When he left, I felt so alone and guilty because I'd hurt my friend. I felt like my heart was breaking when he walked away, even though I also knew I needed time to understand myself better. Nate was my best friend when we were young, and in some ways it still feels like that when I'm with him. But he hasn't told me that he loves me. Maybe he's not sure how he feels. To make the situation even worse, tonight, Alex asked me to move to Chicago to be with him. That was exhilarating, like I'd won the top prize. If I chose Alex, I would realize nearly every aspect of the dream I've had since Nate left town. I feel respected and special when I'm with Alex, but I'm not sure if he loves me, either. On top of all that, I found out that Sophie Mattuchi is after Nate."

"Sophie? Your friend?"

"Yes."

Mrs. Beabots shook her head. The frown on her forehead was deep with concern. "That is a new development. And I don't like it."

"She works with Nate every day. He has great respect for her, since she's his surgical nurse and all."

Wagging her finger, Mrs. Beabots said, "Don't say things like that. He has respect for you as well. And Nate knows about Alex?"

"Yes, but not about what Alex said tonight."

"I was wondering if you've seen any signs of jealousy on Nate's part?"

"Yes, now that you mention it…."

"Hmm…" Mrs. Beabots tapped her cheek with her forefinger thoughtfully. "And you've displayed some jealousy of your own over Sophie's interest in Nate."

"I have?"

"Decidedly so."

"I feel more scared than jealous."

"That's even better," Mrs. Beabots replied. "What you're really saying to me, Maddie, is that you love Nate but he won't commit. Or hasn't. In the meantime, you see Alex as a second option if Nate doesn't pull through for you."

"Am I really doing that? It doesn't feel like I'm using anybody. It feels like I just can't decide."

"Alex is part of the dream you created for yourself when you were a little girl. Nate left you, so you started thinking of running away yourself. Running away to Oz, to a land of golden streets and beautiful people. And now Alex has shown that the world you conjured up in your head is a real place. People live like that every day. They work very hard and they have problems of their own, but they don't live in Indian Lake. Their priorities truly are finding the best gelato and the best cappuccino in town. They do all the things you wanted to do all your life."

"Like go to college," Maddie interjected.

"That's right. But you can do all those things on your own terms. You can take time off and go to school and study what you want. You take this franchise business by the tail if you want, and work it night and day until you become even wealthier. You can travel and meet all sorts of people. You can have this romance with Alex, or not. You can see where things lead with Nate and make a decision later."

Maddie pressed her palms to her temples and cheeks. "See? This is what is driving me mad! I want it all!"

"No, you don't."

Maddie gaped at her friend. "I don't?"

"I think you want almost all of it. And you're young. You have enough years to do all these things. Just make sure you do them with someone you truly love and want to spend time with, someone who feels the same about you."

"So, you think it's Nate?" Maddie asked, her mouth dry.

Just then Maddie's cell phone rang.

She swallowed the lump in her throat and answered the phone on the second ring. "Hi, Nate," she said, and she smiled with enough energy to light fireworks.

CHAPTER TWENTY-SIX

THE DELIVERY truck in front of Cupcakes and Coffee took up four parking spaces, including the room necessary for the long metal unloading ramp that the driver would need to haul out Maddie's new chairs.

Maddie walked up to the beefy man dressed in baggy jeans and a faded plaid shirt. He carried a clipboard with a pen dangling from a shoelace. He took off a pair of cheap sunglasses before he spoke. "You Maddie Strong?"

"I am."

He made a check mark on his clipboard, then showed her where to sign.

"Sorry about this bein' after hours and all, but I had a delivery in Indianapolis that took a lot longer than I'd planned."

"That's fine. I didn't think they'd be here for days, so this is a nice surprise."

The man walked up to the cab and tossed

his clipboard on the seat. "If you'll just show me where…"

"Right through the front door," she said. "Do you need help?"

"No, ma'am." He pulled on a pair of work gloves. "I got my dolly. I'm all set."

When the driver had finished unloading the chairs, Maddie said goodbye and went back inside. Minutes later, Nate's Hummer pulled up. She went to the door and unlocked it. She watched him check his hair and she smiled to herself. She was amazed how much that tiny gesture meant to her. He wanted to look nice for her and that knowledge made her glow.

Maybe I'm more in love with Nate than I realized.

The evening sun was behind his back and outlined his physique as he stepped out of the car. He was wearing a pair of camel slacks and a black short-sleeved shirt that showed off his well-defined biceps. He paused when he caught sight of her, his expression serious.

"What's wrong?" she asked.

"Nothing at all. You came outside to greet me," he said, closing the distance between them in three eager steps. "That means a lot to me." He kissed her nose.

"I was excited to see you," she said, surprising herself with her answer. Her own smile warmed her, and she liked the way that felt.

"Thank God," he breathed.

"Come on in. You may be sorry you volunteered to help me tonight."

"Why's that?" he asked.

"Because my new chairs came, and now I have to move the old ones down to the basement. Then we have to unwrap the new ones and get the place set up for business in the morning."

"What about the cake batter? You said we were going to bake." He forced a pout. "I was looking forward to licking the beaters. Or whatever it is you use. I'm only here for the batter and icing."

"Oh, really," she said, moving closer, peering into his blazing blue eyes. She put her hand on his chest, right next to his heart. "So, am I to understand that you just want the sugar?"

She leaned into him, her hand still on his hammering heart. He put his arms around her and pulled her closer. Cradling her, protecting her, loving her.

Maddie remembered their innocent sweetness and naive trust. She wanted to be that young girl again, trusting Nate. Trusting herself to love Nate fully and totally, the way she once had.

Gazing into his eyes, she searched for answers to questions that were still forming in her head. But as much as she wanted clarification and understanding, she was afraid of it. In some ways it was easiest to just leave everything as it was. But that wasn't fair.

Not to her and not to Nate.

He kissed her, but she pulled back.

"What is it?" he asked. "Talk to me."

Nodding, she said, "I guess that's what we should be doing more of—talking. And not kissing."

"I wouldn't go that far," he joked.

"In high school, that's all we did. We kissed. But we didn't talk enough."

Nate released her and led her to one of the tables. "I remember it differently."

"You do?"

"You were my best friend," he said, holding her hands. "I could tell you everything. And I did. Don't you remember that?"

"Yes, I guess so. I always felt like we were hiding in the shadows, kissing behind the gym doors or in the back of your car so no one would see us. But what I've really been afraid of lately is if any of it was real between you and me. I was afraid that maybe back then I was using you to negate all my insecurities. That maybe you weren't a real person to me and that was all it was."

Nate was silent.

Maddie saw true deep pain in his eyes. If she'd sliced him open with one of his scalpels, she couldn't have cut any deeper. And her heart broke for him.

He shook his head slowly, his eyes glistening with the smallest prick of tears that he battled to discourage.

Suddenly, she had her answer.

"Nate," she pleaded, touching his cheek. "I'm so sorry. So very sorry, but I had to say it."

"Jeez. I'd rather have the punch in the gut," he quipped morosely. Then his eyes bore into hers. Probing. Demanding answers. "You didn't finish, did you? What about now?"

"I was wrong," she admitted. "I do believe like you do that what we had was very real. I feel we are in a very good place right now. And very honestly, I feel we've talked more and shared more about who we are and what we want out of life since you've been back than we ever did."

"But it's not enough?" he asked readily.

"It's not. We see each other in snippets. Our phone calls at night are short. And I know how tired you are. Your work is grueling. I'm tired by the end of the day, too, and then I have to bake cupcakes all night long. We just don't have enough time together."

Nate nodded his head and said, "I totally agree with you on all counts. Frankly, we have to make some changes."

"What kind of changes?" she asked.

"First of all, you need to hire someone to do the baking at night. Together we can find someone trustworthy. I know we can."

"Fine," she said, noticing that Nate still seemed a bit anxious about something, rather than being relieved. He kept rubbing his thumb against her fingers and looking down at their hands. "What is it, Nate? Is there something wrong?"

He took a deep breath and raised his head. Twice since walking in the door he'd thought he should propose to Maddie. Twice he'd chickened out. He thought he should have bought a ring first. Then he'd thought better of it. What if Maddie wanted to choose her own setting? What if she wanted something very specific? It had to be the perfect ring for her. It couldn't be just any ring, either. He should have gone to Chicago and hit up Tiffany or C.D. Peacock and gotten something last weekend, but he'd been on call and had that emergency surgery.

Then again, what if she turned him down?

She'd already told him that this was her turn in life to discover all kinds of things about herself that she'd never had the time or money to pursue. Things were different for her now. She had the satisfaction of a major accomplishment in the business world. It wouldn't surprise him if she wound up on the cover of an investment magazine. She was a hive of new ideas that buzzed around her just waiting to pollinate. She was so full of life, it made him feel even more alive just to be near her.

Nate was all too aware that he could really blow it if he pushed her too fast when so much was changing for her.

When he first walked in the door, he'd scoped out the café for signs of the expensive flowers his competition was sending to Maddie, but there was nothing like what he'd overheard Sophie talking about. In fact, there were no flowers in the café at all.

Nate knew he had to win Maddie from Alex Perkins.

Nate wanted a huge family wedding. He wanted lots of family holidays, with his mother and Maddie chatting in the kitchen, along with his grandmother and aunts, while they made Thanksgiving turkey. And when the time came, he wanted both his parents to be happy when their children were born. He wanted to give Maddie the kind of real love and affection that his family was capable of providing. She'd never had a family and he wanted to give her that.

Nate knew he had to play every one of his cards the smart way and with extreme care. He had to take his time and not be impatient with her or himself. He didn't mind the gamble. Maddie was worth risking his heart. But there was no way he was going to blow his chances with Maddie a second time.

No way.

"There's nothing wrong, Maddie. Except that I think we should get these chairs set up for you. The sooner your work is done, the sooner you can go for a moonlight drive with me to the beach."

"Ah, so you do have ulterior motives," she joked.

He exhaled deeply and kissed her. "Where you're concerned, I have all kinds of ulterior motives."

"Okay, then. Let's get to it."

It didn't take long for them to move the old chairs to the basement and stack them against the brick wall. Maddie got out a couple box cutters so they could cut away the shrink-wrap and brown paper covering the new chairs.

"I'm really excited about this," Maddie said, slitting the plastic. "I should show you the drawings, Nate. Sarah and Charmaine made them. They're incredible. Just gorgeous interiors. My franchises will all have Italian decor."

"Italian," he repeated. He straightened and balled a roll of shrink-wrap in his hands. "My mother would love it." Nate conjured more visions of what marriage to Maddie could be like and the notion fit quite well with him. He liked the way she was lit like fire when she talked about her café and the changes she wanted to make. He was impressed and proud of her. It took a lot of persistence and determination to come as far as she had. She was a great deal like him in that regard. They were a perfect match in so many ways. His problem was going to be trying to keep up with her. He wished he could promise her the moon, but the reality was that he was offering a life on or near an Indian reservation—maybe several. Maddie dreamed of moving to Chicago. She would have to give up an awful lot just to be with him.

Nate's nerve dwindled like a lost helium balloon in the sky.

"The Italian theme is one of the requisites. I've been a stickler about it. But yeah, I spent months working with Sarah and Charmaine on the colors and the theme. The logo. Everything is geared to the cappuccino theme. All the cafés have to have a brass-and-copper cappuccino machine similar to mine." She stripped away the last of the paper from one of the chairs. "Don't you love it?" she asked.

"Don't you love the yellow-and-white stripes?" Maddie asked, sitting on her new chair and beaming happily up at Nate.

Nate stared at Maddie. The chair was covered in upholstery that was a dead ringer for the fabric his mother had just chosen for her new chaise longues around their pool.

He thought about his mother inviting Sophie Mattuchi to Mother's Day at their house. Nate had realized his mother was trying to play matchmaker, but because he wasn't sure about his future with Maddie, he hadn't said a word to his mother about his intentions. After dinner, however, he'd made it clear to Gina that he wasn't romantically interested in Sophie.

"Do you like it?" Maddie asked again.

"Love it," he said with a wistful whisper, moving closer to her. Nate didn't believe in divine signs, but there was no other explanation for this coincidence. He felt the urge to take action.

Be bold. Be bolder.

Carpe diem.

Suddenly, all his fears vanished. His path opened up to him, and at the end of it was Maddie.

"Nate," Maddie said. "Are you all right?"

He dropped to his knee, took her hands in his and kissed her palms. He gazed up into her eyes and felt the love in his heart explode throughout him. "I know I've asked you this before, but Maddie, will you marry me?"

Maddie was speechless. She wasn't any more prepared for this proposal than she had been for the first one. How had they gotten here so fast? Or maybe this was eleven years overdue. She felt an overpowering eruption of emotion.

"Marry me, Maddie," he said pleadingly, but his tone was firm, as if there was no other alternative.

Slowly, his words broke through. It was as if she'd been walking through a storm and suddenly the clouds parted and sunbeams shot through, illuminating everything around and inside her. "Right now? Tonight? I mean, are you asking me to elope again?"

He chuckled and kissed her hands again, then squeezed them. "No, my darling. I want everything to be perfect for us. I guess this isn't the perfect proposal. I had a dozen different ways I was going to ask you, and this wasn't one of them. I don't have a ring for you. I wanted to get you one, but then I thought maybe you could pick out the ring yourself."

Maddie smiled, then she started crying and she couldn't stop. "Oh, Nate. I would love any ring you chose."

"Okay. So we'll get one tomorrow. Or tonight. Can you buy that kind of thing online?"

"I don't know." She laughed. "Probably."

He leaned up and kissed her with a passion so sweet, so endearing, Maddie knew she wanted to remember this moment all her life. Then she broke away.

"What's wrong?" she asked. "Oh, my God. Did I even answer you?"

He shook his head.

"Yes," she said, laughing again. She kissed him and he kissed her back.

"I promise you, Maddie, that whatever you want to do in your life, I want you to do it. Whether you want to go to school and study or run the café or build more franchises, I don't want to stand in the way of any of your explorations. I want to be there for the ride. I've missed so much of what we could have done together all these years, I don't want to miss another nanosecond."

"Are you sure, Nate? Because I'm beginning to realize that I want to do a lot with my life. More than I'd ever thought I wanted to do."

He threw his head back and laughed. "This is just what I love about you! Don't you see? You're never satisfied. You're always looking for ways to make things better."

"I do that, it's true," she said, peering at him for a long moment. "You know, when we were in high school, we always dreamed of living on the shores of Indian Lake. You said the serenity of the water helped you think. And I've been wanting a condo in Chicago all these years. But now, your dream has changed, too. You want to work in Arizona."

Nate's smile dropped instantly. "I do."

"So I would have to come with you," she mused, staring at her hands as she pondered the immensity of the situation. "Where is this reservation, exactly?"

"There are clinics all over northern Arizona. Tuba City, Fort Defiance, to name a couple."

"And where did you live?"

Nate rubbed his chin. "In the doctors' lounges mostly. And I had an apartment in Tuba City."

"And that's where we would live?"

"We'll find something much better. Arizona is God's country, Maddie. The vistas make you think you're in heaven. Up north, there's a change of seasons and all kinds of lakes around. We could get a house on a lake up there. And wait till you see the incredible blooming cactus flowers that are just everywhere," he said excitedly. "I'll find a great place for us to live."

"I know you will. But Nate, I have to think

about how I'm going to do this. My franchises haven't even gotten off the ground, and I refuse to abandon them now."

"I don't want you to," he said letting his troubled eyes fall to the floor. Then he brightened and looked at her with renewed enthusiasm. "You could open your cafés in Arizona."

"But how long will you be in each place?"

"A year…or less."

She glanced around the little café she'd nurtured for a decade. She was so proud of all the changes she was making and the plans she had. She'd spun a tapestry of dreams within these walls. Would she ever see it again? Would she have to sell it? And what about Chloe? Where would she get another job like this one, where Maddie let her take time off whenever she went chasing another acting class with Deb DuPont?

Each time Maddie thought of one change she would have to make, a dozen others sprung to life like Hydra heads, bent on defeating her and destroying her bliss.

Nate saw doubt and fear cloud Maddie's green eyes, and he knew he had to banish them before they took a foothold. Otherwise, he would lose her for good. "It's not going to be easy for us, Maddie. But together we'll take each of these challenges and fight them head on, okay? We'll work it out. The important thing is that we'll be together. All the rest, we can discuss and we'll find a way. I believe in us, Maddie."

Maddie felt her heart swell. He made it all sound so simple. It had been a long, long time since Maddie had trusted anyone with her life. And that someone had been Nate. Maybe he was right. They would be together. Love would always find a way.

She kissed him and smiled.

"Maddie, girl," Nate said nearly in a whisper.

Maddie could still hear trepidation in his voice.

"There's something else, isn't there? I can feel it. It's not about the ring, is it? The ring isn't important, Nate—"

He cut her off. "It's not the ring."

"Then what is it?"

"Could you do me a very big favor?"

She put her arms around his neck. "I thought I just did."

"I was thinking of something else."

"What's that?"

"Could you tell the other guy to take a hike?"

CHAPTER TWENTY-SEVEN

MADDIE HAD THOUGHT that once her decision was finalized, all the pressure and anxiety she'd been experiencing would be relieved. She'd believed that once she had Nate's ring on her finger, the conflict she felt about Alex and the possibility of a life in Chicago would vanish.

It did not.

When Nate proposed, Alex had been in London for three weeks of business meetings. He had texted her that he'd be flying back to Chicago right after Memorial Day, and he wanted to see her then. Maddie made arrangements through Alex's assistant and confirmed a lunch.

Maddie was shocked to realize she was looking forward to seeing Alex again, even if it was to officially inform him about her engagement to Nate.

She picked out a black-and-shocking-pink summer dress at Judee's Dress Shop to wear, and this time she chose the location—the Atwood Café in the historic Hotel Burnham in downtown Chicago. Maddie loved the theater district and had bought herself a ticket to a matinee. She figured it was a good way to cover her bases because she had no idea how Alex would react to her news. She might end up spending more time with him and not make it to the play. Or he could have the opposite reaction, which would result in a very, very short lunch.

Maddie knew she would have to be extremely diplomatic because she was bound to Alex and his company for years to come. Each time one of her franchises sold, Alex would handle the negotiations. There was the chance that he would turn her business over to someone else in his office, but her suspicions were that Alex was not leaving her life.

Maddie arrived at the Atwood Café at ten minutes to noon and asked the hostess to seat her. The table looked out onto Washington Street, where she could watch the shoppers and the theater crowd.

She had just ordered a glass of iced tea when Alex arrived. He was blindingly handsome, dressed in a pearl-grey suit, white shirt and a grey-and-black-striped tie. He thanked the hostess and sat in the chair opposite her.

"You look beautiful," he said, taking the napkin from the table and spreading it in his lap.

A waitress came up and asked for his drink order. "Perrier and lime, please," he said, barely taking his eyes off Maddie.

The waitress left and he folded his hands on the table, leaning toward Maddie. "Don't you love this place?"

"I do. I picked it because it's so historic. It used to be a hangout for Al Capone," she said. "Isn't that interesting?"

"I know. This is one of my favorite areas of town."

"What's your very favorite?"

He thought for a minute. "The lake. I love all the beaches. When I need to come up with a really great idea or solve a problem, I can go to the lake and look out over that water and it's like all the pieces of my problems fall into place. And *boom!*" He snapped his fingers. "I get my answer. Yeah. Definitely the lake."

Maddie smiled. "That's so funny. It's the same for me. Only my lake is Indian Lake. I take a notebook and pen and I come up with all kinds of ideas watching the sunset. Or the sunrise. My girlfriends and I sometimes row on Saturday mornings at dawn. It's just gorgeous. Serene."

"See? There's another thing."

"Thing?"

"We're so much alike, you and I."

Maddie was incredibly nervous and didn't quite know how to bring up the subject of her engagement. Should she just blurt it out? Or slowly lead into it? It seemed unkind to just hit him over the head with it the second they sat down together. "How was London?" she asked.

He didn't miss a beat. Once the subject was changed to his interests, he transitioned over like a bullet train switching tracks. "Super. Fantastic. Now, *there*'s a town. I can sense the money being made in that place. I would wager there are more billionaire Arabs in London than there are in Riyadh. Anyway, my meetings went well. I closed one and put together two more. One died quickly, but I knew it going in. It was a long shot." He shrugged his shoulders. "It's all just a numbers game anyway."

"Numbers game?"

"Yeah. I work about a dozen clients on my

front burners. Then another two dozen on the back burners."

The waitress came to take their order.

Alex hadn't even looked at the menu but said, "I'll have a baby-beet salad and the smoked trout with the hazelnut sauce."

"And you, miss?"

"I haven't looked—" Maddie began when Alex interrupted.

"Do you like fish? Their halibut with coriander beurre blanc is great."

"Great. I'll have that and I'll try the beet salad as well."

The waitress left and Maddie leaned slightly forward. "You come here so much you know the menu?"

"No. I looked it up online. I do it all the time."

"Online?"

"On their website," he said, hearing his cell phone buzz in his pocket. "Excuse me. I have to take this. London."

"Sure, go ahead."

Maddie made a mental note to talk to Charmaine or Sarah about a website. She hadn't thought about posting daily choices on a website. But that was the future. It was more work for her—unless she could train Chloe to post the daily changes. Maddie was so involved in her own thoughts she hadn't realized that Alex had finished his call.

"Maddie?" he asked. "Is there something you want to tell me?"

She was playing with her hair, which she did sometimes when she was creating or planning. With her left hand. The one with Nate's ring on her finger. They'd picked it out at the Indian Lake Jewelry the day after he proposed. She looked at Alex, who didn't take his eyes off the ring.

"I do," she said, feeling her mouth go suddenly dry and all the nerve endings in her skin suddenly misfire and make her feel very anxious. There was one way and only one way to handle the situation now. "I'm engaged," she said. "Before I announce it formally, I wanted to tell you in person."

Alex folded his arms on the table, and peered into her eyes. He took a deep breath as if he had four sets of lungs to fill. He didn't expel. "So, you're not moving to Chicago."

"Not." She continued gazing into his eyes. She couldn't tell if his apparent calm was born of shock or apathy.

Then he swallowed hard and cleared his throat. "Do you…love him?"

It struck her that Alex had never told her that he loved her. He had not mentioned the M word. There were a lot of things Alex had not said. All he had asked was that she move in with him. It wasn't much of an offer, now that she thought about it.

"Yes. Very much," she replied.

"For how long?"

"Twelve years."

Alex's head jerked back as if someone had slapped him. "Well, don't I feel like an idiot. You've been dating someone for twelve years?"

She took a deep breath. "Not exactly. This," she said, pointing to the ring, "is a new development."

"So, when we kissed?"

"No, I wasn't with him then. Not really."

"But you said twelve years. I'm confused."

"We were boyfriend and girlfriend in high school. We were crazy, young and in love. And then, he left. I didn't hear from him for eleven years. He just recently returned to Indian Lake."

Alex whistled. "I've got to give this guy credit. He moves fast."

"You think so?" She remembered far too vividly all the years of pain and worry. She

also knew that if she hadn't truly been in love
with Nate all that time, she would have forgotten him and the memory of her heartbreak
would have faded. But it never had."

"It would seem that way to me, yes," he replied, sitting back and casting stern eyes on
her. He forced a smile. "Here I was being all
gallant and romantic and doing my thing in
London and this guy moves in for the kill."
He was trying to be flippant, but Maddie
didn't miss the catch in his throat.

He reached across the table and held her
hand, the one with the ring on it. He looked
at the ring. "Not bad, but I would have done
better."

"I'm sure of that," she said.

When he looked at her, his eyes were filled
with sincerity. "I was falling in love with you,
you know."

"I felt that, yes."

"I really think I would have been over the
moon for you, given more time. The right
thing to do is let you go, but I don't like losing, either. Not that you are the prize in a
game—" He stopped himself midthought and
Maddie could clearly see he was fighting his
emotions. "Answer me this. Is he what you
really want?"

Maddie paused for a long moment. Then she nodded. "Yes."

"You hesitated. That's a sign. A sign that there still may be a chance for me."

"I hesitated because there are a lot of things about you that appeal to me, Alex. I like you a lot. And you're right, there are many things about us that seem very much the same. You almost feel like family."

"Don't say like brother and sister. I couldn't take that one."

She chuckled and squeezed his hand. "I won't. But you represent or are part of a dream I dreamed of all those years when Nate was gone and I didn't know where he was or why he left me. When I truly hated him. I wanted, and I may still want, to have a life in Chicago. I'm still working on that one—how I'll incorporate that into my new life because Nate wants to live on an Indian reservation, possibly in Arizona."

"You really do love this guy," Alex said with a deep exhale. "What about James?"

"It's important to me that my franchises do very well for James. I hope he wants to set up more cafés, or that someone else wants a franchise. I've even thought of a travelling café of sorts that I could take to Arizona. Maybe buy an RV that I could fix up and sell cupcakes and cappuccino from wherever we live." She rolled her eyes. "I don't know, Alex. I've got a dozen ideas floating around in my head. I want my creation to go on forever."

"We can always hope. The public is always looking for something new," he said, flicking away a crumb on the white linen tablecloth.

"I'm sorry, Alex."

"So am I, Maddie."

"It's also important to me that we still be able to work together. Can we do that?"

His eyes delved into hers as a slow smile crossed his face. "We can do that. That doesn't mean I won't still long for you, but I'll keep a rein on it. Just as long as you remember one thing."

"What's that?"

"I don't give up on something that I think is a winner. You and I together would have been a real win, Maddie. We could have had the ride of a lifetime. So, if this Nate ever screws up, you let me know."

Maddie's eyebrow racheted up with surprise. "Alex, what are you saying? Really."

"This isn't an idle promise, Maddie. I mean it. I was falling for you. I've never done that. It's kind of a big deal to me to finally find someone that I'm simpatico with. You know? So, if this is what you want, I'm happy for you. But I'm not going to go away. I'm going to be here. Chicago is my town. I wouldn't be happy in a place like Indian Lake, I don't think. I like the energy of a big city. I like the noise and the creativity and the diversity of humanity. I like the arts and the pioneer spirit that Chicago has. That's what I felt in you. You like changing things and making them better. A billion guys have come along trying to reinvent Starbucks and failed. But you did it. With sugar. So simple. Why didn't anyone see it? You did. I love your brain," he said, tapping his temple. "And I love your heart, which makes you passionate enough to be persistent. Don't ever lose that, Maddie. I hope this guy is your brass ring. Because I believe if he's not, I am."

The waitress brought their meals, and Alex ordered two glasses of champagne.

Maddie looked at him. "We're toasting?"

"Absolutely. I'm going to drink to your happiness."

"Well, thank you."

He grinned at her mischievously. "I will

not drink to your engagement. I will drink to your happiness because I believe I'm the guy who can make you happy."

CHAPTER TWENTY-EIGHT

THE AIR-CONDITIONING was cranked up to just below freezing in the surgical wing as Nate finished up a particularly difficult ablation. When he exited the OR, Carla, the office receptionist, was standing near the door waiting for him with a note in her hand. "Dr. Caldwell needs to see you. Now," she said with a fluster in her voice and a breathy sigh that signaled trouble.

"Tell him I'll be on my way after I talk to the family," Nate instructed.

After speaking with the patient's wife, Nate headed to the office area and rapped on Roger Caldwell's door before opening it. "You wanted to see me?"

Roger spun around in his chair and hung up his phone. "Sit down. There's been a development."

Nate sat in the chair opposite Roger's desk. "I don't like the sound of that. Are we being sued?"

Roger reached into a folder and pulled out a piece of paper. It was an airline boarding pass. "I'm doing your surgeries for you tomorrow," he said, handing the page to Nate.

"This says Phoenix." He looked up at his boss. "What's going on?"

"Last month, I sent a glowing letter about your accomplishments to the board at Northwestern and to your mentor, Dr. Klein. I told them how quickly you'd come along and that your skills were nearly surpassing mine."

Nate's eyes widened. "That's very kind…."

"It's the truth," Roger continued. "But listen, the head of cardiac surgery at the reservation in Arizona, Charles Jessel, just quit. Lung cancer. He and his wife are going to retire if he makes it through this. This is a request that you return to Arizona."

"Poor Charles," Nate said. "I liked him. When do they need me?"

"Tomorrow. They don't have anyone else who's proficient with cold beam laser."

"That soon?"

Roger bit his lower lip pensively. "The job is yours. Permanently."

Roger stuck out his hand as Nate rose. "I knew you were too good, too skilled to stay around here for long. I just didn't think it would come this fast."

Nate felt a flush of victory surge through his veins. He was on fire as the realization hit him full force. He was going to be top heart surgeon at the reservation. He was being given a shot at making a real difference in so many people's lives. This was everything he'd sacrificed for and dreamed of. All those years in the navy. Med school. Internship. Residency. Now Indian Lake. Nate was as ready as he'd ever be. His only dilemma was how he'd break the news to Maddie.

When Nate proposed, they'd spoken briefly about where they'd live, how they'd accommodate each other's dreams. But it had been such a joyous moment that they hadn't wanted—hadn't needed—to hash out any of the details. Nate still had nine months left on his contract, and they'd thought they had plenty of time to plan for the future.

Now, they'd be apart until the wedding, which was certainly not what Nate had in mind when he'd asked Maddie to marry him.

He'd day-dreamed about moonlit summer nights on the beach at Indian Lake and barbeques at his parents' house. Maddie was going to want a very special wedding. But if he took this job, which he intended to, he wouldn't be around for much of the planning at all.

He wondered how Maddie was going to take this news.

"That must have been an incredible letter you sent to the Northwestern board. Thanks to you, I have this opportunity." Nate shook the boarding pass.

"Do me proud, Nate," Roger replied.

MADDIE STOOD WITH Nate in front of the chalkboard of choices at The Louise House later that night.

"I'll have Jamaica fudge," Maddie said. "In a cup."

"Two scoops of coconut almond for me," Nate told Louise.

"Comin' right up," Louise replied, shoving the scoop into a barrel of ice cream.

Nate led Maddie to a tiny round table near the window. A family of four walked in, chatting amongst themselves, as Maddie sat in the chair.

"So, how was Chicago?" Nate asked. Before she could answer, he grabbed her hand and kissed it. "Gosh, you look beautiful."

"Thanks," she replied. "Don't worry, Nate.

Chicago, at least that part of it, is ancient history."

"I wasn't worried," he said. "Much."

Maddie placed her hand gently on his cheek, letting her eyes delve into his. "You have to know there never has been or will be anyone else for me."

Just then, Louise walked up and held out their ice cream.

Beaming and taking the heaping cup of ice cream from Louise she said, "Except for Jamaica fudge, that is."

"Enjoy," Louise said, then went back to her other customers.

"Well, I need to keep hearing that, especially after what I'm about to tell you, Maddie," Nate said, biting off a hunk of ice cream.

"What's that?"

"Roger called me into his office today to tell me that I've just landed a new job."

Maddie put down her spoon. "Job?"

"It's in Arizona. At the reservation clinic where I worked last year." Her eyes widened and she smiled brightly. "That's fantastic for you! It's what you wanted. Isn't it?"

"Actually, I'll be chief of cardiac surgery. Head of the whole shebang."

"Oh, Nate! Your dream. I couldn't be more

excited for you." Then she noticed he wasn't smiling. Something was wrong. He wasn't happy. "But this is a promotion for you, isn't it?"

"Yes. The current head, Charles Jessel, had to quit—health reasons—and they need a replacement immediately. Tomorrow, in fact."

"Tomorrow?" Maddie felt her stomach roil. "That…is soon." She looked around the ice cream shop blankly, desperately trying to keep from welling up. The attempt was futile.

"I'm sorry, Maddie," Nate said. "I'm so sorry."

"You have to go," she said matter-of-factly.

"I'll fly back for Sarah's wedding in two weeks, and then after that, we'll take turns. I can fly back here or you can fly out there. We can make our wedding plans over the phone can't we?"

"Sure. I guess."

"Of course," he mused, chuckling and kissing her hand again. "You could run away with me to Vegas and then there would be no problem at all."

"Except for my café."

"Except for that," he replied regretfully.

She lifted her head. "I'll figure that out. Right now, you have to be so proud. This job is wonderful. I want you to have this, Nate. You deserve this. You've worked for this all these years. I've talked to Uncle George about how I could open a travelling café out in Arizona. I could make my cupcakes and sell them out of the back of an SUV. I could—"

Nate's eyes welled. "Maddie, girl. You love me that much? So much that you would drive your little cakes around to where I'm working?"

"Yes, Nate." Then she looked away with an unexpected burst of tears.

"Maddie, what is it?"

"You know, Nate, I'm trying to be strong and creative and figure this out, but frankly, I'm not really sure where I'll fit into your life and your plans." She rubbed her temples. "I do love you, Nate. I love you like I never thought I could love anybody ever again, but I feel angry and cheated because no matter what idea I come up with, it's not enough to satisfy me and my needs," she said, jabbing her chest with her forefinger. "I just stepped onto the biggest stage of my life and now I feel like it's being yanked out from under me. I feel lost and really scared."

Nate's expression was filled with compassion. "I know. I understand. There just hasn't been time. I have to go so soon. It's nearly like I'm being shipped off to war."

Her eyes locked on his. "That's exactly what it's like."

He leaned over and kissed her cheek. "I can do better by you than this. I'll think of something. I promise. Just don't stop loving me, Maddie."

"I promise, Nate."

MADDIE STOOD NEXT to Nate at the bus stop where he would catch a coach to O'Hare Airport. Though dawn was just breaking over the horizon, a summer wind blew hot, strong and humid from the south. Maddie wore apricot capris, espadrilles and a white short-sleeved blouse.

"Thanks for the ride, Maddie," Nate said, smoothing a lock of hair behind her ear. "You could have slept in."

She shrugged. "You know I'm up before dawn every day. Chloe can handle things till I get back. Besides, this gives us a chance to talk some more."

"Uh-huh," he mumbled, kissing her cheek. "I'll call you when I land. It's about a two and a half hour drive to the reservation from Phoenix. Someone is supposed to meet me at the airport and drive me there. I'll call you again when I'm settled."

"You said it's pretty there."

"Red rock, cactus, brilliant blue sky that almost stings your eyes to look at. I can't wait to show you around. I'll get my surgery schedule as soon as I get there, so I'll let you know when will be good for you to come visit. I'll miss you," he said kissing her.

"Miss you already," she replied kissing him back.

In the distance they heard air brakes screech and gears being downshifted as the whale of a bus lumbered around the corner and up to the stop.

Three people got out of their cars and wheeled their rolling luggage up to the bus.

Nate turned to Maddie. "You take care of yourself."

"I love you, Nate. Have a safe trip."

He stepped aside as the other passengers climbed aboard. Nate hung on to the handle. "I'll see you, Maddie. Love you," he said, and took the steps two at a time onto the bus. His shoulders seemed to fill the narrow entry and she was struck with his enthusiasm. He was that adventurous Nate of their youth again, the Nate who would disappear for more than a decade, risking his love for her, his family, everything—in pursuit of his passion for medicine. It was that reckless, hard-driven side of Nate that terrified her, and yet she understood it profoundly.

I'm his mirror. It just took me longer to get there.

The driver immediately followed Nate onto the bus, shut the doors and pulled away from the curb.

Maddie stood waving as the bus disappeared. A tear ran down her cheek and she wiped it away. Looking down at the tear, she wondered how many times she would be saying goodbye to Nate as he moved from reservation to reservation. Searching for the next life to save.

A TRIPLE-SHOT espresso didn't have the caffeine to equal the nervous high Maddie rode all day waiting for Nate's call.

She knew that he was supposed to land at ten thirty, but he hadn't called or texted. If it took another two and a half hours to drive to the reservation, plus a lunch stop, he should have called her by one o'clock. Still there was nothing.

All afternoon, she paced the café and busied herself cleaning the already sparkling equipment. She baked cupcakes she didn't need and frothed icing she wasn't sure she would sell that day.

By four o'clock, Nate still had not called.

At five, when she shut the café and said good-night to Chloe, she texted Nate, her fears flapping like bats inside her belly. Nate didn't text her back.

By six o'clock, she was too riddled with anxiety to be alone any longer. She called Sarah and asked if she could come over and work on wedding-table decorations alongside her and Mrs. Beabots. Sarah, of course, was happy to have the help.

By ten o'clock, Maddie and Sarah had finished arranging sparklers, silk white roses and ribbons in aqua-colored clay pots. They'd made over two hundred aqua bows to hang in the trees at Cove Beach, and they'd filled mason jars with sand and votive candles, which Sarah's friends would also help hang in the trees.

Mrs. Beabots put her scissors in her white wicker sewing basket and bid them good-night.

Sarah turned to Maddie. "Would you like

a glass of wine? After all this work, you deserve one."

"Sure," she replied, looking at her cell phone.

"Why don't you call him?" Sarah offered as they entered the kitchen. Sarah let Beau into the yard.

"I did. And I left a voice mail. He was supposed to call me when he got to the reservation. I don't know what could have happened."

Sarah took out two wineglasses and put them on the island. "I can tell you what didn't happen. He wasn't in an accident. No plane or car crash. You would have had a phone call from some state trooper or a hospital by now."

"I wasn't thinking that," Maddie said, the dull edge in her tone wavering between conviction and disbelief. "The truth is that Nate has just been handed his long-held dream. And he's not thinking about me."

At all.

"He's probably just busy, is all." Sarah handed Maddie the wine. "Would you like to sit on the porch? I put in the bug lightbulbs, so it should be nice."

"Yeah."

They walked out the front door and sat in

two Adirondack chairs. Maddie noticed Sarah's eyes flit to the third floor of Mrs. Beabots's house where Luke and the kids lived. In a few short weeks, they would all be living here in this house, Sarah's family home.

Family home.

Maddie couldn't help wondering what that was like. Nate had a family home with his parents. He'd been living there these past few months. He'd told Maddie that he'd considered a few places, but that he wanted a house on the lake itself. Nearly impossible to find. Cate Sullivan had told Nate he'd have to wait till someone died, and even then, the house would likely be gone in seconds. Nate was undaunted. He knew the right house would come along.

But now they wouldn't need a quiet retreat by the lake. They'd be living far away among red rocks. What was that like? Would she hate it? Or love it?

And just how exactly was she going to make her own dreams work if she was in Arizona? Or Alaska for that matter? The life of a doctor's wife was a lonely one. She'd heard that a million times, and the saying didn't even account for the frequent moves and isolated conditions life with Nate would entail. So it was imperative she had her own career and her own interests.

Most importantly, if Nate wasn't calling her now, when they'd just gotten engaged, when he should be thinking about her non-stop, what was it going to be like when they'd been married for five years? Fifteen? Would he ever have enough room for her in his thoughts?

"Luke and I were talking about the re-hearsal," Sarah began. "Since Nate has agreed to be the best man, Luke told him he doesn't want any of that bachelor party non-sense. Especially because Luke was married before. Nate offered to take him to dinner at the lodge. Just the two of them. That's was very thoughtful. Don't you think?"

"Thoughtful. Yes." Maddie replied wood-enly.

"He'll call you later tonight and tell you everything that's going on. I know he will," Sarah said. Maddie heard the hollow ring in her friend's voice.

"You're right. He's just busy. Besides, he'll be back next weekend for the wedding. This trip just came up so fast. We didn't get a chance to talk about much."

"No kidding. I know my mind would be

a jumble if I just discovered Luke was moving to Arizona…and that I'd be joining him," Sarah said.

Maddie raked her fingers through her hair. "I know! And each time I think I've figured out a solution to one question, ten more questions pop up. And only Nate can answer them for me. It's so frustrating."

"You should write them all down so you don't forget them," Sarah advised.

"I should," Maddie agreed. "Well, I'd better get going. I have a lot of work to do tomorrow, and I want to get the cupcakes for your wedding made and into the freezer. I'll ice them the night before the wedding, so after the rehearsal I won't be hanging around for long."

"I understand," Sarah said.

Maddie nodded. "Thanks." She hugged her best friend and rushed down the front steps to her SUV. Maddie didn't want Sarah to see her crying.

IT WAS NEARLY eleven o'clock the next morning before Maddie got a text from Nate saying cell service was practically non-existent where he was. He told her he'd landed safely, and once he'd arrived at the clinic, he'd gone straight into surgery. He was seeing patients back-to-back. He said he'd keep trying to call her.

However, by the end of the day, she still had not heard from him.

Maddie believed she knew the truth.

Nate had been swept away from her.

He'd been offered the job of his lifetime and he'd taken it. She was standing on the shore. Left behind. Abandoned. Again.

And that was as it should be.

Nate had made no bones about the fact that he wanted to work with this clinic at the reservation, and to devote his career to helping people in need around the country. His goals were altruistic and compassionate and she loved him all the more for them. He'd been given his shot. She would have been the first one to tell him to go for it.

Maddie never, ever wanted to be the person who held him back. She believed in dreams. Hers and his. If she loved him, she would let him go. Clearly, Nate was so immersed in his world that there just was no place for her in his life. When he was in Indian Lake and he'd seen her nearly every day, he might have believed they could make it work. But what he'd shown her in the past few days gave her a glimpse into the future.

And it was heartbreaking.

Despite not hearing from Nate, Maddie couldn't believe, even now, that she'd ever given Alex a second thought romantically. She was absolutely, totally in love with Nate and always would be.

But being married to Nate would place a difficult burden on her. She would be constantly reaching out to find new friends, trying to set up a new café, finding a new home.... And she might come to resent Nate for leaving her alone a great deal of the time. She would miss Sarah, Mrs. Beabots, Liz, Cate and all her other friends. She would miss Indian Lake. She hadn't factored these things into her equation previously, but now she found they carried a much greater weight than she'd imagined they would.

Even when she dreamed of living in Chicago, she knew she'd only be an hour away from Indian Lake. Her dreams always included her friends.

With Nate's sudden transfer to Arizona, her life had turned upside down. Again.

But above all, she wanted Nate to be happy. He was an extraordinary man and it would be wrong of her to hold him back.

She would have to let him explore every

avenue of success and experience that he craved. Nate deserved it all and more. He was the best of the best and she was proud to have even been a speck in his personal history. She'd been honored to have known him.

Shoving another two trays of cupcakes into her commercial oven, Maddie realized there was only one thing she could do.

Just the thought of it caused a pinching pain around her heart, and her head felt as if it would explode into a torrent of tears. Maddie sucked in a deep and stabilizing breath. She did not drop dead on the spot as she thought she might.

Instead, she reached for the telephone.

CHAPTER TWENTY-NINE

BREAKING UP WITH Nate was even more impossible than Maddie imagined. She called him four times and left messages for him, but she never got a callback. As the hours and days clicked by, Maddie felt her old insecurities crawl out of their hiding place and gnaw at her psyche. She felt insignificant and as small as a human could feel.

For eleven years, Nate had made a life without her. Was he doing that again now? Was he always going to be like this? And would that life—a life revolving around his career and his patients' needs—be enough for her?

Maddie was a person of action, and releasing Nate from their engagement seemed like the right thing to do.

But in the dark of her room at night, when she felt lonely and empty, she contemplated booking a ticket and flying to Arizona to find him. The problem with that scenario was that she didn't know exactly where he was. And she didn't want him to think she was insecure, which she clearly was right now.

Finally, on Thursday, she received her first text from Nate. It had apparently been sent three days prior.

Maddie, just had about the worst day of my life. I nearly lost a patient. Little boy. Electrical storm here. Lines are down. I hope you get this. I love you. Nate.

She texted him back, but didn't receive another message or call. She knew cell reception was bad out there, but Maddie took this as confirmation that Nate's focus was where it should be. He could have called or found another way to contact her if he'd wanted to. His lack of communication told her everything.

Silence was Nate's modus operandi.

After six days of angst, Maddie took off her ring. She told herself that she and Nate had moved too quickly into their engagement. She'd allowed herself to be romanced and hadn't paid enough attention to facts and logistics. If she were honest with herself, she hadn't wanted to face the hard issues that life with Nate posed.

Nate needed a stronger, more flexible woman. Someone educated and…

No, Maddie. Don't do that to yourself again.

Maddie was amazed at how easily she fell prey to her frailties. Beating back negativity for her was a full time job. But being ignored by Nate was more than painful. It was unbalancing.

She put Nate's ring in a heart-shaped ceramic box that Ann Marie had given her as a graduation present from high school. Maddie's eyes were filled with tears as she placed the cover on the box, wishing with all her heart that Ann Marie was alive so she could ask her advice. She wiped her face with her palm. "Oh, Sarah. How do you do it all without your mom?"

Maddie walked out of her office, grabbed an apron and had just tied it around her waist when Sarah rushed into the café.

"Maddie!" Sarah swept up to her friend and grabbed her arms. "Have you heard from Nate?"

"Yes. Finally. He's really swamped with surgeries."

"And he's still planning to be here for my wedding?"

"As far as I know."

"But you're not sure. Has he said he'll be

here? For certain? I mean, the wedding is one week away and I need to know if the best man is going to be MIA," Sarah groaned. "Luke doesn't know what to do. We could have Jerry stand in, I suppose. But should we go ahead and ask him? And it's too late to have him fitted for his blazer and white slacks."

Maddie was thoughtful for a minute. "Asking Jerry would be good so that there are no hiccups for you," she replied.

Sarah touched Maddie's arm. "What's going on? Really?"

Maddie's shoulders slumped. "I've had to do some very hard thinking since Nate left. Maybe we weren't as right for each other as I thought. He has high aspirations, Sarah. Very high. I can't take that away from him. I understand him. Maybe this is all for the best. Maybe this is the universe telling me that what we had as kids was never meant to last into adulthood."

"I can't believe that," Sarah said quietly.

Maddie put her hand on Sarah's shoulder. "You're getting married in seven days. You're all spun up in romance and bliss, and that's the way it should be for you. Nate is a great guy. Perfect for me, really, but this is what he has to do to reach his full potential. If I truly love him, I'll give him that."

FROM THE MINUTE Nate walked off the plane in Phoenix, his heart thrummed with excitement. He was met by his former assistant, Dan Chee, at baggage claim. Nate hugged the tall, broad-shouldered man, who grinned at him in return.

"Are we ever happy to see you again, Doc," Dan said enthusiastically.

"Thanks. Same here," Nate replied, grabbing his duffel bag.

"I've got some patient charts in the Jeep so you can acquaint yourself with some of the cases on the drive up to Tuba City."

"Thanks, Dan. I was really sorry to hear about Dr. Jessel. It must have been sudden, huh?"

"Very. Some of the staff said they'd noticed he was getting tired lately, but that was all."

"Tired? The man was always a whirlwind. How many clinics did he serve again?"

"Four, including Chinle and Fort Defiance."

"I forgot about that," Nate said as they climbed into the Jeep. "He travelled all over the northern part of Arizona, didn't he?"

"Sure did. So will you. We've got patients

scheduled out till the end of next month," Dan told him. "I hope you've been getting caught up on your beauty sleep lately because there won't be much time for that, except when I'm driving you to the next clinic." Dan laughed.

Nate frowned and took out his cell phone. His battery was almost dead. He had enough juice to call Maddie. He tapped out her number but there was no answer. For some reason, her voicemail didn't pick up. "I'll call her later," Nate said aloud.

When they stopped in Flagstaff for gas, Nate rummaged in his briefcase for his phone charger, but couldn't find it. Searching through his duffel bag, he realized he'd forgotten his charger altogether. He sent Maddie a text and then turned off his phone to conserve the battery. Once they were in Tuba City, he'd have to buy a new cord.

Nate and Dan arrived at the clinic in Tuba City only to find a Code Blue underway. Though the nurses had handled the matter competently, clearly, if Nate hadn't arrived at the exact moment he had, scrubbed in and taken over, the seventy-one year old man would have died from his cardiac arrest.

It was nearly midnight when Nate collapsed on a cot in the doctors' lounge.

He was back.

And it felt good.

FIFTY-SEVEN HOURS passed before Nate realized he hadn't eaten anything more than a moon pie, a soda and a bag of Sun Chips from a vending machine, and he'd only caught six hours of sleep—all in small doses. He still hadn't had a chance to buy a phone charger. Each time he'd come out of surgery and tried to call Maddie, a nurse had rushed in with yet another emergency, another task that he needed to perform.

On his first full day at the clinic, Nate realized Dr. Jessel must have been ill for quite some time and had likely been covering up his illness. It was clear to Nate that the doctor had misdiagnosed or failed to diagnose several patients. There was a young boy who needed surgery immediately, yet Dr. Jessel had chosen to observe him and not proceed with the operation.

Nate held a conference with the parents and explained that it was critical their son undergo the procedure. Perhaps because the boy's condition hadn't been treated sooner, the operation nearly resulted in his death, and it took every ounce of Nate's skill and knowledge to save the boy.

On the second day at the clinic, a massive electrical thunderstorm moved across the area causing flash floods, rock slides and power outages. The cell phone tower was down. The internet was out and the clinic operated on a back-up generator for three days.

Nate used the last of his cell battery to send Maddie a text about the boy he'd saved. What he would have given to be able to go home to Maddie at night and tell her everything. He couldn't help but think about her during his surgeries. When his mind would start to wander, he saw her loving face, her sparkling green eyes urging him to continue. Pushing him to do his best. He heard her voice telling him that she loved him. He remembered holding her and drawing strength from her courage and her indomitable spirit. Maddie had no idea how much of an inspiration she was to him. If she could do all that she had done with no formal education, with nothing but spunk and self-pride to bolster her ambition, he could make it through another eight-hour surgery. He could save another life. He could help one more person live a better life.

Scratching the two-day-old stubble on

his cheek, Nate rolled off the cot where he'd zonked out for the past ninety minutes and placed his hands on his knees. "A pace like this could kill me."

Just then, Dan Chee walked into the lounge twirling his car keys around his index finger. "Time to go, Doc."

"Right. The clinic at Chinle. Think it will be any better than here?"

"Worse." Dan smiled wryly.

Nate yawned. "Say, is your cell phone working yet?"

"Yeah," Dan replied. "Why?"

"Can I borrow it to call my fiancée?"

"Sure. But then we have to go," Dan said handing Nate a battered flip phone.

"Thanks."

Nate placed a call to Maddie but it went to voice mail. "Maddie. It's me. I'm so sorry. I hope you got my texts and my other voice-mail. I'm borrowing a phone from a friend. I left my phone charger at home, so my battery is dead. I'm leaving this clinic for another one today. Love you."

Nate and Dan drove to Chinle, where the clinic was just as backed up as the one in Tuba City. From the minute he arrived, Nate went straight to work.

Dan brought meals in from a diner down the street, but Nate was almost too exhausted to eat.

After a five-hour operation, Nate borrowed Dan's phone again to call Maddie. When he realized it was nearly midnight, he sent a text instead. He could only hope it would go through.

Nate performed four bypass surgeries and six angioplasties in the next day-and-a-half. He was sitting on his cot, unshaven and throwing back an energy drink, when Dan walked up with his flip phone. "This call is for you, Doc."

Nate glanced up, feeling as if his eyes were full of gravel. He took the phone. "Hello?"

"Nate."

"Maddie!" he said, brightening immediately. "How are you?"

"Nate, we need to talk," she replied, her voice infused with trepidation and regret.

Nate knew that tone. It was the sound of an ending. He felt his stomach hit the floor. "About what?"

"Us," she said. "I want you to know that I'm really happy for you. I mean, this job is what you wanted. It's all you've talked about since you came back to Indian Lake."

Nate stood and began pacing. "You sound different. What's going on?"

"Your life is there, Nate. In that world where you don't have time to call me very often and where so many people really need you. Their lives depend on you. I want you to have that life, Nate. I do. But I've also re-alized I don't think I can be a part of what you're doing. I would just be an adjunct. A footnote, really. And I need more than that."

"Maddie, it wouldn't always be like this—"

"Honestly, Nate? Be serious. Of course it would be. That's just you. And that's okay. I've had time to think about what it would be like moving around all the time, leaving Indian Lake, not seeing my friends. Giving up my café. The franchises. What about your family? I'm just getting to know your mother and I like her. Really I do. I'm being realis-tic, Nate."

"What are you saying exactly, Maddie?"

"I'm giving you your ring back."

Nate nearly fell onto the cot. "Is this about the other guy?"

"This has nothing to do with Alex."

"Maybe it does, maybe it doesn't," he said. "Look, Maddie, I know I messed up. I had to get out here so fast. I barely packed, much less had time to talk to you about what this move was going to mean to you. To us. It's been a whirlwind. I tried to call you, but I was just so busy. I didn't have time to buy a new charger and..."

"I get it, Nate. You just made my point." Maddie spoke with such finality, Nate felt as if he'd been cut out of her life with a scalpel.

"I guess we don't have anything else to say," Nate replied, feeling his mouth go dry.

"Guess not."

"Bye, Maddie. I...I wish you love."

CHAPTER THIRTY

MADDIE WORE A lime-green linen sheath to the wedding rehearsal and walked down the aisle on Jerry Mason's arm. No one had expected Nate to be Luke's best man after Maddie had broken their engagement. Of all the depressing exercises a person could go through, being the maid of honor in a best friend's wedding only a few days after one's own breakup, had to top the list, Maddie thought.

Though Maddie saw Mrs. Beabots sitting in the front pew smiling at her, she was barely able to crook the ends of her lips upward. Father Michael gave instructions as to who was to stand where and at what point they would walk out of the church, but to Maddie the words were muddled, as if she were swimming under water.

All Maddie thought about was Nate. She remembered him as the young boy she'd loved so desperately, and then her mind was filled with visions of him sitting at Cove Beach watching the blood-red sun sink into the dark horizon. Nate, who helped her move furniture and bake cupcakes when she knew he was exhausted and should have been catching up on his sleep. In her mind, they had fit together like fingers in a glove. Before he left, it was almost as if the decade of emptiness and anger had never happened. She had been filled with only love for him.

How am I ever going to live without him?

Her decision to let him go to pursue his dreams didn't seem so noble anymore. It might have been the right thing to do, but the reality of knowing she'd pushed Nate away for good was killing her.

Maddie wasn't sure if the sharp, stabbing pains in her heart would subside. They hadn't dissipated completely during the first decade of their separation. She'd dealt with the loneliness and emptiness by turning to anger. This time, she knew she could never be angry at Nate again. She loved him too much.

Maddie watched Sarah and Luke as they gazed into each other's eyes, happiness radiating from them. Though she wished Sarah all the best, Maddie was saddened and even a bit jealous that all that love could have been hers.

At that moment, Maddie knew that even at seventeen, her heart had steered her right. She'd been Nate's girl and she always would be.

At the rehearsal dinner at the lodge, Maddie sat at the far end of the table, next to Luke's father, Paul, with Sarah on her right. The table was decorated with an arrangement of white roses, variegated pittosporum and silk aquamarine ribbons that Sarah had made the night before. Maddie had brought red velvet cupcakes for dessert and had helped Sarah wrap her bride's gifts in aqua paper and glittery ribbon. Though the conversations were happy and lively, Maddie felt as if she were standing on a foreign shore, looking at life from a great distance. She was disconnected and adrift and she didn't know how she would find her way back. Common sense told her that eventually she'd find her way again, and she'd build a life without Nate just as she'd done before. Maddie also knew that everything about her was different this time. Although she was grieving the loss of Nate, she'd learned that she didn't need to a wear a mask of anger and hate any longer. She wasn't interested in revenge. She'd learned exactly how much she'd contributed to her first breakup, and that a great deal of the heartbreak and pain she'd suffered had been self-inflicted. Yes, she'd used those negative emotions to spur her desire for achievement in her career, but now that she was reaching her dream and experiencing the inner fulfillment of her successes, she found that none of it equaled being with Nate. Sharing with Nate. Planning a future with Nate.

She was astounded at how much she loved him. It seemed impossible that her love could run so deep. Deep enough to let him go forever.

LUKE SAW HIM first and placed his hand on Sarah's arm to still her conversation. Mrs. Beabots held her breath and slowly turned her head.

"Maddie?" Nate said, approaching the table without a word of apology to anyone else. "Maddie, I need to talk to you."

Maddie's heart stood still. She felt wonder and surprise flood her body and no matter what her intentions had been a second ago, she was overjoyed to see him.

"What's going on? You're supposed to be in Arizona," she said, rising quickly and moving toward him.

He reached out his hand. "Let's go down to the shore."

"Okay…" Maddie glanced at Sarah, who was smiling at her. "Sarah, will you excuse me?"

Sarah shooed her with a wave of her hand. "Go!"

Maddie gladly put her hand in Nate's, feeling his gentle but strong hold. Suddenly, she knew. She was no longer drifting. She had found her mooring. She smiled up at him and he smiled back as they headed down to the beach.

The sun had barely set and the moon was full in the east, casting silver-and-gold rays across the water.

Nate stopped by a huge maple tree and pulled Maddie close. "I want you to know that I understand what you did."

"Which was?"

"Breaking up with me. You thought you were doing me a favor, but it was the worst thing that could have happened to me."

"But your career…"

"Is just that. My work. It's not my life. When I first came back here, I admit I thought of it only as a means to an end. A stepping stone to running the clinics out in

Arizona. And then I saw you in that wedding gown, and I swear, Maddie…" He wrapped his arms around her. "I thought I would go insane. I felt I lost you. And I can't take that."

"Really?" she asked, feeling there was more to the story but knowing he wanted to do the talking right now. She'd made enough mistakes where they were concerned. She was glad he was taking the lead.

"Yeah," he said, kissing her cheek and then nuzzling into the crook of her neck. "Maddie, you have to know I wanted to stay here for you. You're all I've ever really wanted."

"Nate, I love you so much. I'll always want what's best for you. You sacrificed so much for this opportunity in Arizona."

"No, Maddie. Don't you see? It's not enough. I want *you*. And I've thought about this ever since your phone call. I don't have to move to Arizona at all. There are reservations all around Lake Michigan, not far from here. I've already checked into a couple of the hospitals that serve those reservations. Their need is tremendous. We don't have to move away from your friends or my family at all. We can build a lake house together. Some day, we can get a condo in Chicago, if you want it. We can take trips to Italy for you to study or just drink in the experience. I want to be there. I don't want to miss a day of exploring all of life with you." He hugged her excitedly and then released her. "It's going to be hard work sometimes for both of us, but I think we can make it happen. Neither of us has ever shied from a challenge. And I'm willing if you are."

"More than willing, Nate," she replied, touching his cheek.

"When I think of all the fun we'll have, just the two of us, it fills me with more desire than I've ever known. I swear, I'll jump out of my skin, I'm so on fire with it all."

"Nate. I haven't seen you like this since..."

"We were kids?"

"Yeah. And I like it." She grinned.

"Me, too. So, now will you put my ring back on?"

"Yes. I love you, Nate," she said as he tightened his embrace.

"I love you, Maddie. Forever and always."

SARAH'S WEDDING DRESS finally found her. It was a strapless, full A-line gown in gossamer-thin organza with a white taffeta underskirt, aqua sash at the waist and a cascade of silk white-and-aqua roses down the back train. Sarah believed the gown had been made for her.

Maddie's gown was a simple aqua organza over an aqua linen sleeveless sheath. She wore gold, low-heeled sandals and carried a nosegay of white roses with aqua streamers.

Maddie was proud to walk down the aisle on Nate's arm, and she thought that he and the groom looked especially handsome in their navy blazers, sand-colored slacks, white shirts and aqua-and-white-striped ties. Maddie thought that hers and Nate's happiness at being together again was equaled only by the joy of the bride and groom.

The ceremony at St. Mark's was heartfelt and moving as Sarah and Luke spoke their own vows to each other. Mrs. Beabots cried, and Annie and Timmy were filled with so much joy, they could barely stand still.

Cove Beach glittered under the setting sun, and all of Sarah's well-planned and exquisitely executed decorations added sparkle and festivity to the ambience. The flickering mason jars looked like fat fireflies in the tree limbs. Huge baskets of summer flowers hung from the tent poles and the hundreds of aqua bows and crystal Italian lights streamed throughout the tent's interior, creating a summer night's dreamland effect.

The round tables were covered in white linens, as was the buffet table. Sarah's simple menu of cold salmon, ham, Caesar salad and Italian breads was enjoyed by all their guests.

The steel-drum player added just the right tropical touch to the occasion, and even those who didn't normally dance got up to twirl around on the sandy beach or on the portable wooden dance floor.

Mrs. Beabots toasted the bride with champagne after Maddie and Nate offered their toasts. Timmy recited a poem and Annie sang a heartfelt rendition of "Unforgettable" that brought everyone to their feet in applause. Charmaine Chalmers accepted an invitation to dance from Edgar Clayton, while Isabelle and Scott Abbott held each other and barely moved to the music.

Nate had just pulled Maddie onto the small dance floor when they heard a woman scream.

Nate was instantly on alert. "What the…"

Nate and Luke shot to the edge of the tent and looked toward the poorly lit parking area. A man was outlined by a street lamp.

"Maddie!" the man yelled.

Maddie's breath froze in her chest and her heart skipped a beat. "Alex."

Luke ground his jaw. "What's going on?"

Nate pulled Luke back. "It's Alex. Let me handle this."

"I'm here to back you up, bro," Luke assured him.

Maddie rushed up to Nate. "What's he doing here?"

Nate shook his head. "Go back with Sarah, Maddie."

Alex stopped on the shells and gravel ten feet from Nate. "I came for Maddie," Alex said, slurring his words. "It's okay, Maddie. You can come with me."

Maddie was aghast. She boldly took a step toward him.

Nate grabbed her arm, but she shook her head. She kept her eyes locked on Alex. "You've been drinking."

"I came to my senses, is all. I know that a girl like you wouldn't be happy just living with a guy. I was stupid to offer you so little. You want it all. So, I'm here to give it to you. Your entire dream. The franchises. The city life. Me. Marry me, Maddie."

A gasp raced through the wedding guests. No one moved.

Maddie was undaunted. "Alex. I thought we had this all out this morning when you called me. I told you that I'm marrying Nate," Maddie replied, feeling sympathy for Alex.

"Maddie," Alex said. "Be reasonable."

She stepped away from Nate and started to move closer to Alex, but Nate held her back. "No, Maddie."

Nate put Maddie behind him and took two very long strides toward the distraught man. "You need to sober up and go home, Alex."

Alex clenched his fists, swaying a little. "I wanna talk to Maddie."

"Okay, let's go to that picnic table," Maddie urged. "We'll talk there."

Nate cast Maddie a pleading look. "Are you sure?"

"Yes. I'll be fine," she said, taking Alex's arm to steady him as they walked over to the table.

Luke put his hand on Nate's shoulder. "Don't give him more than five minutes."

"Maddie's my girl. She could go off with him for two days and I'd trust her."

"Good for you, man." Luke slapped his back and then returned to Sarah.

Once they reached the picnic table, Maddie faced Alex angrily. "What in the world were you thinking? You could have killed yourself or someone else driving in a condition like this!"

"Sorry," he said morosely.

"Alex. For goodness' sake. You didn't honestly think I would go away with you, did you?"

"I was hoping you'd see that I was serious."

"Desperate, you mean."

"Okay. That. But we're such a good team, Maddie," Alex said more soberly. "I think we can do great things together."

"I know we will. And I'll always want you for a friend. That's important to me. Can we do that, Alex? Be friends and business associates?"

He looked up at the stars and paused for a long moment. "Yeah. Yeah, I don't like it, but maybe that's the best for us after all."

"You take care, Alex," she said and kissed his cheek.

He smiled lovingly and touched her nose. "You, too."

"If I get one of the guys to drive you over to the motel, will you book a room and sleep this off? I don't want you driving anywhere right now."

"Fine. I'll go wait in my car."

"In the backseat," she warned.

"Okay." Alex rose and walked slowly toward his car. Maddie turned around and found Nate standing with arms crossed over his chest next to the tie-down ropes on the tent.

He smiled as she walked up. "Everything okay?" he asked.

"Could Mica drive him to the Cove Inn and get him a room? He needs to sleep this off."

"Sure," Nate said looking over Maddie's head as Alex flopped into the back seat of his car.

Maddie beamed up at Nate, curled her arms around his neck and kissed him. "Everything is right in the world," she said. "Especially in my world because I have you."

Nate folded his arms around her. "Yes, you do, Maddie. You have me always."

* * * * *

Reader Service.com

Manage your account online!

- Review your order history
- Manage your payments
- Update your address

**We've designed
the Harlequin® Reader Service
website just for you.**

Enjoy all the features!

- Reader excerpts from any series
- Respond to mailings and
  special monthly offers
- Discover new series available to you
- Browse the Bonus Bucks catalog
- Share your feedback

Visit us at:
ReaderService.com